FINDING MAISY

A love story forged by heartaches and destiny

K.D. Elledge

Emerald Moon Publishing

ISBN: 979-8-218-42440-4

Published by Emerald Moon Publishing

For my husband Mitchell, who listened, without complaint, to countless hours of my ideas and epiphanies. You are my heart, soul, and inspiration. You are the wolf to my phoenix.

Note to Reader!

This book contains references to sex, violence, sexual assault, physical abuse, mental abuse, drug usage, alcohol consumption, and sex trafficking.

This book is intended for a mature audience.

A Playlist for Lost Souls Waiting to be Found

Available to download on Apple Music

https://music.apple.com/us/playlist/book-draft/pl.u-aZb0gGDTPJx91ZZ

LINKIN PARK – Crawling

Danger Mouse and Karen O – Drown

Billie Eilish – Ocean Eyes

Metallica – Fade to Black

David Kushner – Skin and Bones

Metallica – The Day that Never Comes

Coldplay – The Scientist

Goo Goo Dolls – Iris

Matchbox Twenty – If You're Gone

Kesha – Praying

Daniel Seavey – Can We Pretend That We're Good

The Pogues – Love You 'til the End

Gary Allen – Best I Ever Had

Mazzy Star – Fade into You

Neko Case – I Wish I Was the Moon

Hozier – Work Song

Florence and the Machine – Never Let Me Go

Dave Mathews Band – Crash into Me

Metallica – Hero of the Day

For *Finding Maisy* aesthetics, check out my Pinterest board in the link below.

https://pin.it/6TsRdeaDT

PROLOGUE

Present Day...

"Do you know what Stockholm Syndrome is?"

My mind has drifted elsewhere while staring at the pealing antique wallpaper that covers Mrs. Everly's office when it registers that a question has been asked.

"Ms. Murray, do you know…"

"Yes…of course I know what Stockholm Syndrome is." I bristle at her implication as I cut her off. I am picking incessantly at my nails. What is wrong with me? I agreed to come here—to do this. So, why does she make my skin crawl?

For the last hour, she has grilled me for information with the pretense of helping me move past what has happened. However, it feels like an invasion of my privacy. Even the detective hasn't pressed me this much.

Looking out the window, I catch a glimpse of my reflection in the glass and can't take my eyes away for a moment. A woman stares back at me, not the naive girl I was before. There's the same long dark mop of wavey hair now braided down my back, the same wide green eyes. I touch the scar on my head out of habit and the strange comfort it brings me.

"Stockholm Syndrome is when you trust or have affection toward the one who kidnapped you. Is that what you think I have?" I ask, still not able to say his name out loud to anyone. No one can know about him. "Because I assure you that is not the case," I continue. She must assume the same thing that the news has reported. She has no clue how wrong she is.

Mrs. Everly stares at me with narrowed eyes and says, "Improbable, but never impossible. You seem defensive. Are you protecting someone? Or…are you *scared* of someone? You were missing for over a year and presumably held captive. You seem to be withholding something. I need you to let it all out, and this is the safest place for you to do that…when you are ready, of course." She smiles, but it doesn't quite reach her eyes.

When I am ready…and what does she mean about 'presumably held captive.'

This seems wrong, and I can't figure out why I feel on edge. I fiddle with the phoenix pendant on my necklace. If only I could let it all out, then maybe they would understand. I feel myself tensing up. Just the thought of reliving everything that happened over the last eighteen months is paralyzing. First, my spirit was broken, then my body, then my heart. I know this is supposed to be the place to release pent-up emotions and reveal all your sad stories, but I have lost all trust in people…well, all except one. It is hard to give *even a smidgen* of trust to Mrs. Everly, considering the way she makes me feel.

She dresses like she's from the 1950s and puts off the aura of wholesome Southern Belle, but underneath those black-rimmed glasses and coiffed blonde hair, something is off. She is *no* sweet Southern Belle. I just cannot quite put my finger on it, and she looks very familiar. I even asked if we had met before, but she said she didn't think so, and I let it drop…even though I'm positive we've met before. I'm good with faces. Some will, most likely, haunt me forever.

She stares at me with what seems to be exasperation. Surely, I must be mistaken. "Are you ready to talk about your time in captivity today?" she blatantly asks.

"No, I'm sorry." Only one person knows everything that happened, and it will stay that way if I have anything to do with it.

Silently, her eyes bore into mine as if she is trying to figure me out. "Have you told anyone about your whereabouts or who you were with?"

Well, that was perceptive of her. Her questions confuse me. It doesn't come across as helpful and therapeutic. Again, I feel like I'm in an interrogation—like she is digging for information and not assessing my feelings or state of mind. "No," I say bluntly.

She huffs lightly, pursing her lips. "What about Detective Sawyer? Have you told him what happened to you?"

My brows scrunch together. What is her agenda here? "No," I say again, more forcefully this time.

She smiles then and motions to the refreshment bar in the corner, "Well, let us take five, shall we? I have some tea, coffee, and a few pastries. Help yourself. I have a call to make. Be back shortly, dear."

And with that, she leaves me in the office more bewildered than ever with her strange behavior. I grab a scone and a cup of coffee as I walk around the room to stretch my legs. I'm still contemplating her direct questioning and how unsettled she makes me. This has me remembering one of my conversations with *him*. He told me to pay attention to my surroundings, and if something doesn't feel right, it probably isn't right.

I sip my coffee and then set the cup down and try to look more closely around the room—pay attention to detail. It was already unusual to me that this location was secluded and run down. I vaguely recall that this building used to be for insurance sales. I am almost certain that I was here as a child. It just doesn't make sense. This odd location; her demeanor. I hear a voice in my head telling me to look harder. I am about to shrug off that voice and ignore it when something catches my eye. There is a large painting of a rural southern landscape just above Mrs. Everly's desk. I've looked at it a few times this evening, but never paid much attention to it. There…in one of the bushes seems to be something shiny. It's odd and out of place in the landscape. Scrunching up my face, I ease around her desk and then touch the painting lightly.

Once I am directly in front of it, it no longer looks like a shiny speck in the painting…it's an actual light that is *definitely* not part of the painting. I gingerly take the edge of the painting and move the thick, heavy frame out from the wall.

I jump back, startled, letting the painting flop back. It looks to be some sort of camera positioned toward my chair. I'm not sure if it is legal to hide a camera unbeknownst to a patient, but either way, it rubs me the wrong way, giving me full-body chills.

Just then, the door swings open, and a more anxious Mrs. Everly hustles in. *"Is everything okay, dear? We heard a clatter."*

Fumbling for words, I clear my throat and sheepishly reply, "I am so sorry, I ugh…tripped…and bumped into the wall." I've always been a terrible liar.

She looks between where I am standing and the painting. Inquisitively and slowly, she says, "Well, if everything is good and you feel up to it, I think we should get back to our discussion."

My hackles are rising along with my nerves. I can't deny my instincts any longer. Something is not right here. "I don't think so. I think I am done for today," I say as I grab the coffee abruptly and take a step toward the door.

Suddenly, I feel a little woozy. I place my hands on the desk to steady myself as the coffee smacks the floor. I shake my head but become more disoriented. Then it hits me…she had said, *"We* heard a clatter." My gaze then catches the bush in the painting and then back to her smiling face, and then ever so slowly…my eyes drop down to the coffee…

CHAPTER 1

Seven Months Earlier...

My heart pounds in my chest like a drum as I run through the forest. I suddenly feel grateful for those morning jogs I used to enjoy even though I'm not in the shape I once was. It gives me a slim, teeny spark of hope that I will get away. Blood is trickling down various parts of my body, and some streams from my head, clumping areas of my long dark hair.

The sun has just set and with the darkness settling in, I'm hitting every rock and limb along my way. My bare feet should be killing me, but adrenaline pushes me to keep going and ignore the pain. I am barely aware of the fact that I have very little clothing on. I can deal with finding shelter and clothes if I can just push a little farther. My mind is still hazy, but not enough today to slow me down. My lungs are just beginning to burn when I hear a man's voice growling with anger through the trees.

"When I catch you, little bird…you are mine! GET BACK HERE NOW YOU LITTLE BITCH!"

Tears stream down my cheeks mixing with the dirt and blood. I can feel him gaining on me. I cannot go back. *I WON'T* go back! I would rather die. My body tries to betray me as my breathing gets more and more labored. I was told from a young age to remember mind over matter. My father always said you can make it through anything with a strong enough mind and will. He was a Naval Officer and knew a thing or two about surviving hardships, but I'm not sure if he could have ever imagined what was in store for his daughter. He's probably rolling over in his grave right now.

Shaking my head to clear the unwelcome thoughts, I plead for my mind to stay in fight or flight and not give up. It would be so much easier to just stop running. Nausea is swelling in me. I swallow hard and keep pushing as his cursing grows louder and closer. I know for certain that I am done for if he catches me. The tears have now become a constant flow, and the realization sets in that the odds are not in my favor. It's very likely that I will not escape. All this time, feeling hopeless, and finally, an opportunity for escape presented itself tonight. This can't be the end.

I'm getting slower. I can feel it.

Suddenly, something slams into me, knocking what breath I have out. I am pinned to the ground under something or *someone* heavy. I try to scream but feel a cloth go over my mouth muffling the sound before it can be heard. I fight back with what scarce strength I have left and finally suck in a deep breath. That is when I realize what is on the cloth one second before it's too late. The world begins to fade into darkness.

I feel trapped in the strangest dream. I'm being carried through the forest, and the scent of sandalwood and mint surrounds me. The next time I open my eyes, someone is leaning over me, dabbing at my face as I struggle. I fade in and out of the dream. Ocean-like blue eyes seem to be watching me. I feel a piercing pain lance my head but can't move. My body trembles and aches and I feel sweat trickle down my temples. Where am I, and what is happening? Those eyes are there. Who are you?

The fog starts to lift from my brain, and I instantly remember I am fleeing for my life…only I am no longer outdoors, and I can't seem to move anything.

Wiggling a bit, I get the sensation of being in quicksand. What is going on? The pain hits me as I try to move. Every cell in my body aches and stings. My head pounds like I've been struck with a sledgehammer. I crack open my eyes a sliver and see a ceiling of rough-cut lumber, cabin style maybe. Attempting to rub my eyes, I pull my hand toward my face, but nothing happens. Looking down, I can see why. My arms and legs are bound to bedposts with rope.

"No, no, no…," I chant. This can't be happening again! A crackling noise leaves my dry throat when I try to scream. My mouth feels like sandpaper.

These are not my usual surroundings. This looks and smells like a cabin. The bedroom I'm in is bare and normal. If you forget that a whole person is tied to the bed. There is a nightstand to my right with nothing on it save for a lamp and spider carcass. I shiver and continue surveying my surroundings.

Everything is basic. There are two doors; one looks to go out of the room and one to a bathroom possibly. No pictures, no windows. *Just nothing.*

I tip my chin back to see the bed I am strapped to has a wrought iron head and footboard. I huff. "No chance of breaking off a rail to get loose," I whisper. I squirm some more and clench my teeth through the pain to try to loosen my bonds but to no avail. They only get tighter. I try to understand the situation, but nothing in this room makes sense. I squeeze my eyes closed and replay my last memory.

I was running through the woods in the dark after escaping. The man chasing me was Tony. That much I know for sure. His voice is one I will never forget, having listened to it for so long now. Tony was my handler that took me from point A to point B. He always followed the rules and the explicit instructions given to him. He would *never* undermine his boss and take me somewhere else.

I had been with them for a while now, not exactly sure how long. I tried keeping track in the beginning but gave up along the way. Seems likely that it was around six months or more. Tony was highly paid to keep me untouched and my skin unblemished until the day his boss, 'my owner,' would find the perfect buyer. Tony would have taken me back to him. So where am I?

I was so close to being free of the monsters I have lived with and now I'm in a new and strange purgatory.

I stare at the ceiling trying to recall what a normal life would feel like. I had normal once. Everything was simple and full of possibilities. My biggest concern was date nights and browsing colleges. I was looking at an application in the back seat of my parents' 1970 Mustang the day everything changed. The day I was kidnapped. Even thinking the word now seems ridiculous. I was almost twenty at the time. I was *not* a kid by no stretch of the imagination, but young, and sheltered all the same.

That was the day I learned how cruel the world could be. The day I lost everything.

I attempt to move my leg but try as I might, I'm going nowhere. I contemplate yelling. Whether that turns out good or bad it would give me an idea of where I am and maybe what is happening.

My body trembles with fear. What is waiting on the other side of that door?

Good idea or not, I finally decided to call out. "*Hello…is anyone here?*" My voice creaks out of me. Clearing my throat, I try again, "Hello! Is anyone here?" Just as I am about to yell a third time, the door to the bedroom opens. My body shakes uncontrollably.

In walks a man I've never seen before. Slim and tall with a strong build, wearing hunting clothes. He has stubble on his face and dark hair, a little on the longer side. His eyes are a piercing blue that seem to cut right through me. He has a menacing look about him. His shirt sleeves are pushed up enough to see tattoos covering one arm.

I try to memorize every person I meet in the hopes that one day, I'll be free and be able to give a composite sketch. I used to be such a crime junkie, but now I seem to be living in a Dateline episode.

I'm shaking like a leaf by the time he is by the bed looming over me. He begins looking me over, his brow creasing slightly. His strong jaw clenches. "Have you been pulling at these?" he asks, fingering the tie at my wrist. His voice is low and guttural.

I stay silent.

"Humm," he mutters, "these are Miller's Knots and will continue to get tighter the more you pull against them." He looks at my face, then quickly looks away, with visible anger radiating from his scowl. He turns to leave.

"*WAIT, please!*" I plead. "*Where am I? Who are you? Why am I here?*" I throw questions at him in the hopes that he doesn't intend to leave me like this.

He stops briefly without turning around as if he is about to say something. I can see the tension in his stance. Then he just walks out.

I am left with no answers and more questions than ever. I go over basic facts in my mind to attempt to find anything I may be missing. I was in the captivity of Jacob Rainer before I got away. He is a well-known political figure. He rubs elbows with presidents—the type of person the media has portrayed as perfection. The only reason I know anything about Rainer is because my father insisted that I go with him to every event while he was running for the senate. Dad made sure I was aware and a part of what was happening in the country. He wanted me to know that one person can make a difference. They just have to be brave enough to try.

Tony Rousy is Jacob's trusted assistant of sorts. With them, I was kept in one main location, a house Jacob had put in someone else's name. I never knew where it was, only that no one would ever find me based on how far out in the mountains we were and the security. I was kept in a small basement bedroom. The perfect Jacob Rainer was one of the leaders in the underground trafficking of humans. Something I never even knew existed—a world so hidden and dark that, in my mind, it must have been fictional.

One thing is for certain, I was never held in a cabin and have never seen this man before. Whoever this guy is, he must not be associated with them, or I would already be turned over. So just who is he? Is it possible to be taken twice in a short span of time? If it weren't absolutely horrifying, I would be laughing at the irony.

Tears begin to fall freely leaving trails down my cheeks into my hair. Tremors rack my body, making the aches worsen. How is it humanly possible to have such bad luck? I think back to the day my life was turned upside down.

After a time, my eyes grow heavy, and against my will, my body begins crashing. I try my best to stay alert, but with my injuries, malnourishment, and wicked fatigue, I eventually close my eyes, drifting away.

CHAPTER 2

I bolt upright in the bed, screaming. The vivid nightmare still replaying as I frantically take in my surroundings. Immediately I rub my wrist and heave a sigh of relief when I realize the bonds are gone. I don't have time to ponder this before the door slams open, and the mystery man from before comes rushing to the bed. I flinch and scurry backwards, but he grasps my shoulders holding me in place.

"What the hell happened?" He looks murderous and concerned all at the same time, which is very confusing. His eyes trail over my face. "Answer me, Maisy!"

I gape at him when it registers that he said my name. *My real name.* I haven't heard it in so long. I try to pull away from his grasp, but he doesn't budge.

"*How do you know my name? Please…*tell me where I am and what is going on…*please,*" I beg.

He lets go but keeps his eyes on mine as if daring me to move. "What happened?"

Maybe it's my last few months' experiences nudging me to behave, but my self-preservation kicks in, and I look down and nod. "I…I had a dream, that's all—a nightmare."

A pained look crosses his face briefly.

I bite my lip and close my eyes, thinking of the sun and wind on my face from the back seat of my parents' car. The dream was so real. It was like being back there on that day again. I recall the fear in my dad's eyes and shudder.

He moves toward the door that I assumed was the bathroom and opens it, flipping on the light. Then looks at me like he is contemplating something. He stalks over to the bed and holds out his hand. When I only stare at his outstretched hand without moving, he swears under his breath and swoops me into his arms.

I squeal and struggle until he looks at me and there's a clear warning in his eyes. He carries my shaking body into the bathroom, places me on the toilet. New fear starts to rack my body as some morbid memories come to mind. I stare at him, waiting for whatever he has planned.

His eyes trail over me—analyzing. Silently, he pulls out bandages and ointment from his pockets, along with some alcohol. He then turns on the shower behind me.

"You've been out of it…off and on for two days, but now that you are up, I need to tend to those wounds." He gestures to all of me. "I have soup going. It's not much, but it'll do for tonight, but you need to shower first."

My mouth drops open with clear confusion. A few days…what does he mean I've been here a few days?

I look down at my body in horror, never realizing the extent of the bruises and other injuries. I try not to think about the fact that I am in nothing more than a tattered tank top and underwear. The horror of getting undressed in front of strangers has not abated. I take the edge of my filthy top and begin to pull it when he places his large hand over mine, halting me.

"*When* I shut the door, you can undress. *Not* before that." He looks me up and down, and his jaw ticks. Anger is written all over his face, but something more.

"I'm sorry," I whisper, "I thought…," my face burns with humiliation, and I can't muster the courage to say what exactly I thought.

"Just get cleaned up," he says sternly. He backs away, shutting the door, and I hear him leave the bedroom. Carefully, I peek out and make sure he's gone. I see no inside locks on the doors. Looking around the bathroom gives me no inclination about this man or where I am. Plain as the bedroom with nothing but a few toiletries and a towel.

I glance at myself in the mirror, and my mouth drops open. My eyes are dark purple underneath, my face has cuts and bruising everywhere. That, however, is not the shocking part. I have sutures from my hairline down a few inches on the right side of my forehead. Did he stitch me while I was sleeping? I recall blood streaming into my face as I ran through the woods. Just more questions without answers.

I strip quickly and step into the shower, moaning when the warm water caresses my body. It stings in many places, but it feels heavenly. Dirt, grime, blood, and tears wash down the drain, along with some of my tension. I notice the toiletries are distinctly manly. No women's toiletries, but beggars can't be choosers. I scrub every inch of myself as if I could wash away the past. As I am lathering up my hair and body, it gives me time to think about this mystery mountain man.

He could be working alone or with someone, but how is he connected to the others? Maybe he isn't connected at all and just happened to be a hunter who stumbled onto a girl half naked and took the opportunity to be a creep. However, that doesn't explain why he had chloroform on his person. I was tied to the bed when I awoke, yet he did not want me to get naked in front of him. So, who is he, and why does he know my name? What is his motive?

After the shower, I found a pair of men's sleep pants and a white T-shirt on the freshly made bed—a bowl of soup on the nightstand, and thankfully, the spider carcass is nowhere to be seen. I plop down on the bed and greedily grab the soup. The aroma is amazing, and my tummy takes that moment to growl loudly. I suck down the entire bowl as if I have never eaten in my life. Which, it kind of feels that way lately. There is a mystery meat in the soup, but I don't even care.

The door opens suddenly, and *he* walks with more first aid supplies. He is wearing dark jeans and a fitted black t-shirt that shoes off the contours of his body. It is clear how much stronger he is than me and it makes me immediately pull away when he nears the bed. I set the bowl down and keep my eyes on him as he lays everything out.

"You don't have to do that." I motion to the bandages. "I can do it myself." My voice comes out stronger than before after the moisture of the shower and soup.

He lifts one eyebrow as if I am incapable of caring for myself. "You have a nasty cut on your forehead that I cleaned and stitched while you slept. I need to look at it and clean around it." Without another word, he begins dumping alcohol on a cloth.

I reach my hand up to feel the stitches on the right side of my forehead going into my hairline. "Why did you do that?"

His blue eyes shift to mine as he pours more alcohol. "Because it needed stitches. Look, this *is* going to hurt, but if these cuts get infected, it will hurt a lot worse. Now hold still," he commands with his low, gravelly voice.

I nod and look away, bracing myself so I don't flinch from his touch again. He dabs and presses into each cut, then he meticulously moves from my face down to the ones along my arms and legs. Next, he applies some ointment to each.

For a gruff guy, he is slow and gentle when it comes to my injuries. It makes me question, even more, his motives. Leaning in, he hovers right over my face as he places a gauzed bandage over my stitches. He's so close. His scent envelopes me. It's a manly and clean smell, like sandalwood and mint.

His voice shocks me out of my headspace.

"You should always know your surroundings. It should be common knowledge, but most people take safety for granted. You never saw me coming. You never saw a lot of things coming." He stops briefly as if deciding what to say and then continues. "If you want to survive this world, know your surroundings. Pay attention to people, their actions, or mannerisms. Look at the details…they matter. If something doesn't look right…it's probably not right." He moves away from me, gathering the materials off the bed.

Why is he giving me survival advice? My brows crease together.

"Why am I here?" I take my shot. Hoping he will tell me something, anything.

He ignores me completely and heads for the door. "Do not try to leave," he says as he exits the room. I hear it when the door closes, a clink on the other side. *A lock.* I know that sound all too well. So, this answers one lingering question…am I a prisoner again?

Yes, apparently, I am.

CHAPTER 3

I awake to a smell that has not graced my nose in a long time…coffee. After my wounds were taken care of and my belly was sated, I must have passed out. I groan loudly as I sit up and see a mug by the bed. When I reach for it, I hesitate. My mind wanders back to Rainer's basement. I remember the morning they brought me coffee and told me it was time to prepare for the show.

"Drink up, little bird," Tony says while he looked me up and down slowly and vulgarly. His horrendous cologne burns my nostrils as usual. His top three buttons are undone on his white dress shirt showing off his meaty hairy chest.

I keep my sneer to myself, knowing it will only end up getting me punished.

Having no idea what was in the coffee, or when I will get some again, I down it…moments later, I feel lightheaded. Tony grabs my arm as I start to stagger.

"Easy does it, little bird…follow me and don't give me any shit today!"

I follow him, as instructed, and in a daze as he leads me through the mansion. Ceiling chandeliers leave streaks of light trailing with me. I move my free hand watching the light dance across it.

The room we enter is a circular room with a dome ceiling. More chandeliers gleam above me. It looks like a ballroom. Who has a ballroom in their house? How ridiculous.

I giggle out loud, and Tony squeezes my arm and gives me the stink eye.

It is getting harder to concentrate.

In the center of the round room is a raised area resembling a stage, and all along the walls are projector screens. My vision blurs in and out. Even in my groggy state, I can sense the wrongness there.

I attempt to back away only to be shoved hard right to the center of that stage. Inside, my body begins screaming. Something is very wrong. My eyes widened when I see chains hooked into the floor. I try to scream, but it comes out as a whimper. I'm pushed to the ground and feel metal squeezing into my wrists and ankles. I gag as a cloth is tied around my head into my mouth.

Tony violently strips me of my clothing. Trembling and crying, I try to get free to no avail. I feel hands grip me and they force me to stand upright; that is when I hear people talking.

I look around me, and to my absolute horror, the screens are on, and men are leering at me from all directions. I move to cover myself, however the chains are placed just enough apart to make it impossible.

From a distant doorway, I see a man leaning against the door frame. He wears an immaculate three-piece suit and is holding a pistol. His eyes are throwing daggers into mine. Once he has my attention, he smirks and winks, then holds up the gun and begins tapping his head. It is a clear warning even my fuzzy mind can comprehend. I straighten up and keep my eyes on the ground. My heart is racing in my chest. Tears drip onto the floor as he proceeds to introduce me to the men using a false name and begins to enlighten them about why they should consider me as their future purchase.

The door clinks from the other side, bringing me back to the now, and I clasp my hands together, refraining from reaching for the cup. In walks my nameless new captor. Today, he's wearing bootcut jeans and a flannel with the sleeves rolled up part way, showing that sleeve of tattoos that flow all the way to end on top of his hand.

Looking from me to the cup, he raises an eyebrow. "Is the coffee not to your liking?"

My brain can't help but remember the helpless feeling of being drugged over and over again.

"I am not sure; I haven't tried it yet." I keep looking down so as not to make direct eye contact. My memories have left me shaken.

Grunting, he walks over and takes the cup, lifting it to his lips and to my surprise, he takes a sip while keeping his eyes on me. "It tastes fine to me. Drink up. Breakfast will be ready soon." He waits, and I can't help but feel the urge to bolt. "Drink up" is exactly what they always say right before you are drugged.

However, I watched him drink it. Not to mention, I ate his soup last night. With a sigh, I take the cup, press it to my lips, and sip it slowly. The aroma is *wonderful,* and the taste…even better. I taste cream and sugar, but not too much. I look up, and he is still staring me down with what looks like amusement on his face. That look is quickly replaced with his normal serious and "to the point" scowl.

"I put a toothbrush and some toothpaste in the bathroom. There are some towels and fresh clothes." He hesitates momentarily and rubs his stubbled chin. "When you are ready…come to the kitchen." With that, he walks out.

Interestingly, the door does not clink on the other side. Am I being tested?

Growing up, I was told never to look a gift horse in the mouth, and so I made a beeline for the bathroom. It's the most "freedom" I've had in a long time. Freedom to dress and bathe with no one around. Sweet privacy that I never knew I could miss so much.

Once cleaned up, I found a black Metallica shirt on the counter and some women's jeans. In the floor sits a pair of black combat boots, size 8.5. I'm an 8, but this will do.

As I shake out the shirt, a pair of panties and socks fall out. I don't want to *even* know where this stuff came from because it's most definitely used clothes, but at least they are clean. It all fits a little big on me, but I am content to be in normal clothing again. I go check myself in the bathroom mirror. I am short so I can't see all of me, just my upper half. I am skin and bones. My face used to be fuller, and I had hips. I used to be strong… nothing like the gaunt woman before me. My green eyes and dark wavy hair haunt me sometimes reminding me of the features I carry from my parents. I brush out my hair quickly and French braid it down my back.

Walking to the bedroom door, I hesitate with my hand near the knob, not knowing what to expect next is unnerving. I take a long, deep breath and open the door. On the other side is a small hall lined with pictures of wildlife and deer heads mounted. Their creepy soulless gazes follow me as I move ever so slowly. There is another bathroom at the end right before an arched open doorway that leads into a small kitchen. The dreamy smells are already hitting my nose and making my stomach come alive.

As I round the corner into the kitchen, I slam right into the mysterious mountain man, mid-pancake flip. He steadies me, stopping my fall as the pancake flops on the floor. Immediately I turn red and begin backing away and apologizing profusely, "I am so, so sorry. I didn't mean to."

He holds up his hand as if calming a wild animal. "It's okay, it's just a pancake." His lip pulls up into a slight grin that's gone as quickly as I notice it.

"I made plenty." He looks down at my trembling hands and back into my eyes. Then he says something that shakes me to my core. "Let me clear something up for you, I will *never* hurt you…do you understand me? I don't know what all you have been through, but rest assured you will be safe here."

My eyes drift all around the room, anywhere but his. I wrap my arms around my waist to attempt to hold myself together. I can feel my eyes becoming watery as his words really hit me.

To say I am confused is an understatement. How do you trust someone who used chloroform on you and tied you down? I must admit to myself that if he wanted to rape or kill me, he would have surely done it by now.

He sets everything down, turns off the stove and motions me to sit. He takes one look at my tears about to fall and hands me a napkin but averts his gaze. He doesn't speak anymore for a bit, and I am good with that. After he cleans up the floor pancake, he begins making plates and setting the table.

We eat in silence, and I savor the pancakes. They taste like heaven. Light and fluffy and *real* butter! I am stuffing my face for several minutes when I finally raise my eyes to see him looking at me with clear amusement. My face burns and I attempt to slow my enthusiasm for the pancakes.

I use this time eating to survey my surroundings. After all, that is what he said, know your surroundings.

The cabin is small with the front door entering into a quaint living room that connects to the kitchen. All open, nothing separating them other than one set of stairs to the right of the front door. I realize there must be a loft up top. Which has me wondering, is he sleeping in the loft? There doesn't seem to be another bedroom down here other than the one I'm in.

I tuck that information away just in case it may come in handy one day. The only windows are boarded up, and the door has several locks on it, which makes me shift uncomfortably in my seat. There is a large gun safe in the corner beside a small green sofa. Everything is manly. No signs of a feminine touch anywhere. As I am taking in my surroundings, I see it…a calendar. It's stuck to the refrigerator with a deer head magnet that says Grady's Taxidermy below it.

I swallow a huge bite of pancake and throw back some more coffee, almost choking out the words, "*What day is it!?*"

He stops eating and looks at me hard, "It's Saturday."

"*No, what is the full date!*" I plead.

He glances at the calendar and, with some concern, looks back at me. "It's Saturday, June 3, 1999."

My head spins, and I think I might be sick. I thought I was keeping up with the date or at least close to it. I figured it up to be roughly six or eight months since I was taken. I have been gone for a year! How is this possible? I was drugged often, to the point that I had withdrawals from whatever they gave me, but I could never have imagined it was this amount of time. I feel lightheaded and begin to see stars. I hear him saying something, but it all just becomes background noise, I feel my head smack into something and then I see black.

CHAPTER 4

"Wake up…Maisy, wake up. Come on, that's it. Open your eyes!" I crack my eyelids apart as I feel someone shaking me.

"Ughhh," I groan. "I'm okay just leave me be." Then I get the sensation of floating…not floating but being carried.

His deep voice is low and not surprisingly still stern as he says, "You are not *okay*. Keep your eyes open and look at me." I do as he says and look at him. Why is there worry on his face?

Up close his eyes are not *just* blue as I originally thought. They have a ring of deep navy around the edge, and the center is as bright as tropical waters. Ugh, maybe something is wrong with me.

He eases me down onto the bed and hovers over me. "What has you fainting and almost breaking my table with your head?" He looks at me knowingly. "How long did you *think* you were with them?"

I want to know how he knows *them*. I want answers, but instead, I open my mouth, and the truth comes out. "Six or eight months, maybe."

He looks at the wall with his usual murderous scowl. I can see rage boiling just under the surface, "You were most likely drugged. The way you have been shaking all over. You could still be having withdrawals. It will take time for all of this to wear off. You may get nauseous or have severe headaches. Body aches are common, and anxiety. If you are lucky, they used a short-acting opioid. The withdrawals begin quicker but tend to dissipate faster." He paces the room and runs his hands through his hair in clear frustration.

I wrap my arms around my legs to steady myself and just take it all in. I may be concussed, I may be withdrawing from drug use, I have been a missing person for a year, and my birthday is next month. The day it happened was a month before my twentieth birthday. We had planned to go eat at our favorite Mexican restaurant and then Mom was taking me to get a cell phone. She was so nervous about me on the roads alone and possibly going off to college in the fall. Radio Shack had a Nokia that was all the rave. I remember how excited I was to be moving from a pager to a cell phone. Looking back on it now, that was such a silly thing to have been excited about.

"Where did you learn those things…first aid and about withdrawals?" I ask while gently touching my sutures. What I really wanted was answers to my very real concerns, but for now, I would settle for anything about this man.

He avoids my question and says, "You need food and rest." He turns to leave without any explanation, as always.

He shuts down the moment I ask for the least little crumb of information about him.

"I am fine and rested. I slept the whole night. What I need is answers." My voice comes out pleading. "I am grateful for the food and the first aid, but…I need to know who you are and why I am here…*please*."

He hesitates at my door, and I notice his muscular back tense up. "You need to eat and rest as much as possible. It's important for healing. When you feel like it, come back and finish eating." With that, he walks out, leaving my door open this time.

We ate together in silence that day for three meals. Other than him checking out my wounds, he kept to himself. Only once did he make it clear that I was not to leave under any circumstances. With each passing day, I was healing, and with each passing day, I was growing more anxious. What reason could he have to keep me here?

This went on for the next three days, during which I made a promise to myself…a promise to escape.

CHAPTER 5

Day six of being in mountain man's cabin and he is still as closed off as ever. We are sitting across from one another in the living room. He leans forward with his elbow braced on his knee as he rubs his stubbled chin. He has on another flannel in blue tones with a white tee underneath and his usual boot-cut jeans. I had just showered and brushed my teeth after finding yet another stack of mystery clothes on my bed. This time it's fitted black jeans and a green tank top.

He leans back, straightening out his long legs and tosses me a muffin that I snatch mid-air. He is drilling me with those intense eyes. My mouth drops open with surprise when he casually says, "My name is Callon Wolfe."

Flabbergasted, I stare at him. Finally, I close my mouth that's hung open. "Okay, Callon…how do you know *my* name?" I press on before he decides to go into silent mode again.

His features soften when he says, "Everyone knows who you are, Maisy Murray…everyone." His voice is low and soothing as if he doesn't want to scare me away. "Your face has been on the news for a year."

My heart free falls into my stomach. All over again, I see the calendar, and the weight of that timeframe is staggering. A year without anyone finding me. A year without any answers. A year of my life stripped away from me. Did their lives go on? I cannot even look him in the eye as I ask the main question burning in my soul, "Then why am I here?" I ask softly, "Why haven't you called the authorities? What took you so long to…even tell me your name?"

Abruptly, he stands and begins pacing the small space, swearing under his breath. His jaw clinches as he stops and pins me with those ocean eyes. "Because I *cannot* call the cops. I was hesitant to tell you anything at all for fear it could put you in more danger. Because…I am a wanted man." He moves into the kitchen and begins rattling around cups, filling two with coffee, as if he didn't just pull the rug out from under me.

I begin fiddling with my braid so as not to look at him directly.

Bringing the cups over, he hands me one and takes his seat across from me again. I bring the coffee to my lips sipping slowly, trying to keep calm whilst my nerves are on end.

A wanted man! My luck is astonishing. I escaped and am now held up in some cabin in the middle of nowhere with a potentially very dangerous person. My hands begin trembling again. At this point, I'm not sure if it's from shock or withdrawals, but it has become a constant in my new life.

Clearing my throat, I try to make my voice come through as earnest as I can. "I don't know what you have done,

Callon, but I promise you can let me go. I would *never* tell a soul! You can trust me. I just want to go home!" I plead.

Setting down the mug, Callon leans toward me and on instinct, I inch back. Holding up his hands in a show of peace, he gently reaches for the cup I'm holding and sets it down. "You are shaking like a leaf; I'd rather not clean up a broken cup right now." Sighing, he runs his hands through his hair. "I can't let you go, not yet. You can call me Cal, by the way."

"So, tell me then, Cal, *am I a captive or not?* You had me tied to the bed after knocking me out with what I presume was chloroform. Yet you fed me and tended my wounds. I don't understand…what is your motive? Are you one of *them?*" He knows immediately who I am referring to. I know my mistake the moment his face becomes savage.

"Do not ever fucking lump me in a category with those shitbags!" He fumes as he points a finger at me. I see the veins working in his neck. "Do not *ever* assume anything. You ever heard the saying, 'assuming makes an ass of you and me?' I am nothing like them, and if I were…you would know it by now." He says as he storms off into the kitchen.

"I'm sorry," I murmur, but it's too late. I can tell he has shut down the conversation. I take my coffee and muffin and tiptoe to my room. A silent tear rolls down my cheek. At the very least I learned a few things during that conversation. I am a captive of sorts. He has done something *really* bad before, I am still a missing person, and I am not going home anytime soon.

The weight of it all is crushing me.

I look over to the bedside table, and to my surprise, a book is lying there. I'm not sure when he put it there, but I snatch it up quickly. To my even bigger astonishment, it's a romance novel by the author Jude Devereaux called *A Knight in Shining Armor.* The boredom of my last few days has me craving anything to occupy the mind and kill the silence.

Silence brings in the negative images that I try so hard to suppress. My parents tried keeping me away from books like this, but I always managed to sneak a few at the library. I open the book and inhale deeply the old, tattered pages. I set down the mug, plop down on the bed, and begin reading right away. I allow the novel to pull me away to a better place and time.

It is extremely late by the time I put the book down, having savored every second of it and successfully ignored Callon all day, even when he would come in and out to offer me food and water. I could see that he was sorry for his outburst, but that doesn't change the fact that he is obviously holding back so much more.

Two can play this silent game.

It must be past midnight, not that time matters now. The book has me reeling, but I can barely hold my eyes open, and eventually, I let sleep take me.

I am in the back seat of my mom's 1970 Mustang. The engine roars as we cruise down the old backroads. I smile, remembering how my mom had to have this car the day she laid eyes on it. She named the car Jovi after her first love, Bon Jovi. Dad and I gave her a hard time about it and cracked jokes, but in the end, the name stuck.

Dad's driving with one hand on the wheel, and Mom is flipping through stations like always. She turns around and hands me a college application to Duke University and gives me her usual wink for encouragement. I had been debating on whether I wanted to go to college at all. I worked in my mom's craft shop all throughout the time I was home-schooled, overseeing the business side of it. I was exceptionally good at it, and so I stayed. My parents were aware of my love for writing and encouraged me, but I just could not bring myself to leave them just yet. I was content. I had a job, my family, friends, and even a boyfriend. I had my privacy staying in what they called the mother-in-law suite which was attached to the main house with a covered walkway.

I was happy, so why leave?

Scanning the application, I glance up as Mom starts her usual rant about the importance of education. I smirk and roll my eyes, absolutely knowing she's a hippie at heart. She opened her own craft shop so as not to ever work for 'the man.' I cut my eyes at my dad in the rearview mirror, about to ask what his opinion is, when he looks back at me, and his eyes widen in shock...

CHAPTER 6

I jolt upright in the bed, gulping in air. I have dreamed of that day before, but never with such detail and clarity. It felt like I was back there in the moment. My dad's eyes, the ones that look so much like mine, haunt me to no end. I remember the feeling when we were rear ended, I can still smell the corn field as if I'm still there where we pulled over. I still see the moonlight casting a shine on a single white heel peeking out from behind the Mustang.

For the first time in a long time, I allowed myself to think about my parents. What if they are alive? I always assumed they were dead based on my memories of that night and the sounds I heard. I never actually made it to the back of the car that night. I know the likelihood of them being alive is slim, but that doesn't diminish the teeny amount of hope that blooms in my chest.

Frustrated, I move to sit on the side of the bed and cup my head in my hands and force myself to recall every detail of that harrowing night after we pulled the car over. Mom and dad had already gotten out to check the damage and talk to the other driver that bumped us, while I stayed in the car.

I absently pick up the application again just to have something to do while I wait. I hear the voices outside and notice they seem to get louder. Suddenly, there's a deafening popping sound, reminding me of fireworks!

Then another…but that sound is not fireworks.

I've shot guns enough with my dad to know. My brain just could not comprehend fast enough. I shove Mom's seat forward, grab the handle and lurch out of the car. I immediately stumbled down an embankment I failed to see in the dark. I hear my dress rip a little on a twig as I regain my footing. My brain is an array of possibilities as to what is happening, but none of it sounds good.

Footsteps are coming toward me. Fast.

I scramble through the brush and bolt into the field of corn to my right. The swishing sound it makes as I run lets me know for sure that whoever is following me will hear me. I stop quickly and get down, hugging my knees to my chest, attempting to disappear within the corn. I kick off my heels and try to breathe as quietly as possible. My mind is running in all directions. I didn't see what happened. Mom and Dad might be okay. I should go back to them.

My fight or flight is screaming at me to run. I can hear someone else swishing through the corn, cursing every breath, and It's the most unnerving sound. I imagine it's what a gazelle hears when a lion is slipping through tall grass on the hunt. My heart hammers away at my chest wall.

Suddenly, my worry for my parents wins the battle, and I leap up, lunging back toward the cars. Even though I am a bit turned around, I make it to the edge of the field. I slow to a walk and ease out of the corn field trying to see if there is anyone around. Behind the Mustang, I see a white heel and what looks like a leg and part of Mom's dress.

Crying out and no longer caring who is around, I scream, "MOM…DAD!" There is no movement anywhere. I hear a snap to my right, like a twig breaking.

Panic takes hold, but before I can make a run for it, something slams into my head.

I let the memories crash over me in waves as I dry my face.

The first month or so of being held captive, I prayed every day and every night. I pleaded to the heavens that my parents were alive somewhere looking for me. I imagined my friend Anna Dawson stopping at nothing to find me. I could see her clearly in my mind printing missing persons flyers and gathering masses of people to search for me.

I grew up down the road from her. She was a bubbly extrovert with a head full of beaming red curly hair. We were inseparable until middle school when my parents pulled me out for homeschooling. And even though life for us went in separate directions, we made it work and she was the closest friend I had.

My boyfriend Thomas Guller was a different story. We had only been dating for four months when I went missing. I liked him very much though. Sometimes, I wonder what became of him. He was the sweet boy next door with blond hair and blue eyes and a brilliant smile. I may have been sheltered as a child, but that did not stop me from longing for love. I think that's because my parents were still enamored with each other after so many years together.

Most people think love like that doesn't exist, but I witnessed it every day. They would steal kisses and looks of longing, especially when they thought no one was watching. The passion they had for each other seemed amplified by the passion they shared for life. They made sure to enforce faith and love into my upbringing. Somewhere along my path, I lost faith completely. I no longer pray.

Has life moved on without me?

I stagger over to the bathroom and turn on the shower. After it's hot enough to melt my thoughts, I step in and inhale the steamy air. I am not sure what is better, real food or showers without cameras around. I get full-body chills thinking about the day I found out that I was being recorded in the bathrooms. I scrub at my skin, though I am certain it may never feel clean.

All wrapped up in a towel, I wipe the mirror to clear the fog and take inventory of my wounds. I brush my teeth, then comb through my hair, working knot after knot out, and then braid it down my back. I press the stitches at the edge of my hairline. They are ready to come out. The old me would have thought this would make a wonderfully cool scar. Now, it's just another reminder. The bruising all over my body is taking on a yellow tone around the edges. The dark circles under my eyes are nearly gone, and color has come back to my cheeks. Healing doesn't happen overnight on the inside or the outside.

On the bed, I find more clothes folded neatly and a glass of water. Cal must have been in here while I showered. I try not to dwell on his proximity to me in the shower and hope he meant what he said about never hurting me. There is a Nirvana tee this time with some worn jeans and undergarments laid to the side. Someone was into alternative and rock. I wonder again to whom these belonged. I dress quickly.

Having had the time to think about my situation, I have produced a solution. If he truly means no harm, then I should be able to leave. I just need to find a way out of here when he isn't watching me like a hawk. There is the chance I may get lost in the woods…therefore, I should stow away some food and water. We can't be that far away from civilization and if that is the case, I would be recognizable. Surly I could get help from someone. I just need to reach a road.

Strength is coming back to me, and I no longer feel any effects from the drugs. It's time to get back to my life, no matter what that life looks like now. I don't know what this guy has done, but one thing is for sure…he has no right to keep me here.

Just then, I hear the locks clinking on the door. Cal enters, appraising me from the shirt down. "Looks like the clothes fit okay. Sorry I don't have anything else."

"They're fine. A little big, but they will do, thanks." I don't bother asking where he got the clothes. It's not like he will answer me anyway.

His eyes land on the book lying in bed. Was that a hint of a smile I saw? If it was, it disappeared just as fast. "You've slept the day away and need to eat. I have some roast cooking if you'd like some." He turns without waiting for me to answer and leaves.

Okay then…I guess we are eating. He is definitely a stickler for feeding me. If only he would come clean about what is really going on.

I take time walking around the small cabin while Callon cooks. I memorize everything down to the old-school quilt with forest colors throughout. I wonder if he has a granny out there somewhere that knitted this for him.

I glance towards the kitchen, but Cal continues to cook and doesn't seem to mind my nosing around. The cabin must be for hunting based on the location, the large deer scene gun safe, the dead animal decor, and the lack of feminine products. It all screams testosterone. Other than the clothes he has given me, nothing indicates a woman has been here in a long time.

"Is it okay if I get a water and snack until the food is ready?" I ask quietly.

"Help yourself…there's some nature bars on the counter," he says without looking over his shoulder.

I smile as I slip a few bars into my back pocket and then grab water. Just as I am about to look around some more, I see a pocketknife on the other side of the counter near Cal and the stove. It is a smooth walnut color wood grain. *This could come in handy;* I think.

"Um, do you have any aspirin or Motrin?" Cal looks back at me with a worried brow. I gesture to my head injury.

He nods in understanding. "Of course." He thinks nothing of it and goes toward the far cabinet above where the nature bars are. I move deftly, swiping the knife once his back is to me. I slip it into my pocket and lean against the counter still keeping my distance from him. I hold my head for good measure.

He hands me the bottle. "Thank you," I say, downing two tablets.

I move through the cabin toward the stairs. There must be a way to sneak out of here. If I run, he will catch me, but maybe if I have a head start, he won't. I decide on some small talk to help build his trust. "Are you a hunter?"

He stops chopping vegetables to look over his shoulder. "Somewhat, yes."

"Care to elaborate?" I push.

"I hunted a great deal as a teenager. I just recently started back hunting…out of necessity."

Uh-huh…makes sense, considering he's a wanted man on the run from the law.

"Can I check out the loft?" I asked abruptly. He looks back at me warily but nods.

Up the stairs, there is a small bedroom with a railing overlooking the living area. The bed and the nightstand are all made from logs, and everything is as basic as I expected.

However, something catches my attention right away.

There is a large window overlooking the stunning forest view. The view means nothing to me. The window is *not* boarded up like the others. That *is* interesting.

I tiptoe down the stairs enough to lean over the railing and peer into the kitchen. Cal is working quietly. Not giving much more thought to it, I hurry back to the window.

"This is a terrible idea," I whisper. He will be after me in a matter of minutes. On the other hand, he doesn't have the right to hold me against my will, no more than Jacob did! I bite my lip as I teeter totter on escaping right this second.

Glancing around the woods and to the sky I can see it is later than I thought. He said I slept half the day away and wasn't kidding. That could be to my advantage. Determination comes over me, or maybe stupidity. Either way, I don't want to waste it. I unlatch the window as quietly as possible. As I swing it open and look down, I see the drop is not too bad. Hope and adrenaline kick in as I slide my legs out and over the edge. I take a reassuring deep breath and drop.

I land with a thud. Not giving myself time to think I dust off my hands, grab my water bottle that fell, and sprint into the wilderness. Above me, dark, ominous clouds are rolling in, but peeking out of the clouds, I can still see the sun.

"The sun sets in the west, moss grows on the north side of trees, and we are most likely still in the Blue Ridge

Mountains somewhere," I whisper as I launch farther into the forest.

There is always a chance we went further away into the Appalachian. Rainer lived deep in the Blue Ridge, a few miles from a main road but a long way from a town. I was usually forced to wear something over my head when we traveled. A few times, I was able to lift the edge enough to see out the window.

One day, I saw a sign for Boone, North Carolina. About an hour later, we were in his home. Who knows where I am now? The night Cal brought me here, I was out cold.

Sweat is raining droplets down my face and my back. The humidity is thick, making it hard to keep running. Once I can run no longer, I ease into a jog and, eventually, a walk. I hear nothing around me. No one is in pursuit of me, at least not yet. I wonder how long it took Cal to realize I was gone. Strangely, I feel a small amount of guilt. He seemed genuine in meaning me no harm, but whatever his reasons for not turning me in to authorities is not my problem now. I need to get back. I try to make as little sound as possible. The terrain has begun a descent. I can just make out the sound of water in the distance.

After a few hours pass, a loud crack pierces the sky. The storm is remarkably close now. Another fifteen minutes and the bottom drops from the sky. I am grateful for the noise. Storms no longer scare me as they did when I was a child…people do. The rain and thunder are gifts to cover my tracks. I push away my wet hair that is coming loose around my face and try to keep a fast pace through the woods. I just need to create enough distance before I rest.

By the time darkness is looming all around me, fatigue does, too. I find a thick outcropping of rock, enough to slip under and block most of the rain. I sip my water and take a few small bites of my bar. I'll be saving most of this in case my trajectory is wrong. I could end up lost in the wilderness. I'm okay with that. It's better than the alternative. It's better than what I've been through. I slip the pocketknife from my jeans and pull the blade out, keeping it in my hand as I lean back against the rock. It is definitely old, but a sturdy little knife.

After a time, my eyes grow heavy, and my head begins to nod. I let the storm lull me to sleep.

"Little bird, do as you are told…today Jacob has many clients willing to pay whatever the cost. If you show out again, he will punish you. No crying this time." Tony is standing in the doorway of the massive luxury bathroom, ever so slowly, trailing his hand down my spine like the creep he is. My body trembles with disgust. Tony is a massive man, tall and built like a wall. He is balding and appears to be in his fifties. His ridiculous gold necklaces shimmer in the lighting. What I hate most is his beady little eyes, which are too small for his large body.

My mind is in its usual foggy state that I have come to appreciate. It dulls my senses for what's to come. On these particular nights, the punishment can be unbearable. Apparently, Jacob makes a lot of money off my humiliation which is why he refuses to sell me outright just yet.

I nod at Tony, making sure to keep my true feelings out of my eyes. He licks his lips, almost making me gag, and backs out the door. Alone in the bathroom, I peer at all the camaras lining the ceiling corners. One at every angle. Closing my eyes and holding back the tears, trying to escape them, I undress slowly. I step into the clawfoot tub in the center of the room, bending, I pick up the sponge. I lather and wash my body all for the pleasure of some nameless creeps on the other end of the monitors. I wash my breast slowly and drag it out for minutes, the way Jacob likes. I dip the sponge between my legs.

Suddenly, I get a glimpse of myself in the mirror across the room. I drop the sponge and just stare at her…me. What have I become? I hear banging on the door. Tony's way of signaling me to snap out of it. Rain begins pounding my face…wait, rain.

Why is it raining in the bathroom? I begin screaming when Jacob, not Tony, comes barreling into the bathroom, pistol in hand, and strikes me across the face.

CHAPTER 7

My screams ring out into the night. Someone is on top of me, and I can't breathe. I thrash and shove, but they don't budge. A hand is pressed onto my mouth, and rain is hitting my eyes, blurring my vision. I grasp the pocketknife tighter in my grip and swing it wildly. It hits something—someone. I hear a yelp before the knife is pulled from my hand.

"Damit Maisy! Open your eyes!" His deep, growling voice is unmistakable.

My breath is coming out in panicked gasps. I squint my eyes open to find Callon on top of me. His weight is crushing, and he looks particularly murderous right now. I catch sight of blood on my hand and realize in horror that I stabbed him.

My body trembles. My eyes dart from my hand to the blood speckling his shirt. Oh my god, I stabbed him!

He eases his hand from my mouth, his face only a few inches away. "You want to enlighten me on where you were going and what *exactly* you thought you could accomplish with a tiny Old Timer pocketknife for protection?"

"I…I was trying to get to Boone."

He raises an eyebrow. "Boone? And what then, huh? What the hell were you going to do? Did you think you could waltz back into your old life? Stab two inches into anyone who gets in your way. Do you think a man of Rainer's stature would ever let that happen? Let you go back…Or let you live, for that matter!" His eyes bore into me with our faces a few scant inches apart.

I do not release his stare; I meet him with equal intensity as tears burn my eyes. "You know, Rainer." It's a pointed statement, not a question. "Then why are you not helping me?! If you truly knew what kind of monster he was, then you would let me go." My voice stays low but holds all the venom I can muster. "You have no idea what I have been through. Why are we not on our way to the police right now…*no*…the day you found me? If you are a wanted man, then just drop me off at the nearest police station. I will never tell anyone about you, nor do I even care what you have done! You have my word and I do *NOT* give that out to just anyone." I lose focus seeing the blood again. "Oh my god…I stabbed you," I murmur.

Cal moves off me slowly and stands a few feet away, giving me space. He runs a hand through his dark, wet hair, looking exasperated. I sit up and then scoot back to where the overhanging rock blocks the rain, wiping my eyes.

"It's just a surface wound, Maisy, nothing more," he says, ignoring my questions once more. To further prove my lack of skill, with the knife, he lifts his shirt, showing a small cut along his side, bleeding but not deep.

With his shirt lifted, I can see his muscled torso. He is way stronger than I thought. I forget how small I am sometimes, but looking up at Cal, I feel exceedingly small. How can a woman ever protect herself? I top out at 5'3, and after the weight I've lost, I can't be more than 115 pounds. He has on his flannel over the bloodied white tee and the sleeve is up just enough to show more of his tattoo. It is an intricate geometric pattern that ends all the way onto his left hand. The words "Death before Dishonor" are strategically embedded in the design on the inner forearm. So, he was most likely in the military. I wonder how far it goes up the arm.

Cal steps a few feet away and pulls something from the ground; it's a duffle bag. He must have tossed it when he found me. He surprises me by walking over and bending to sit under the rock next to me. I feel my entire body tense at his closeness.

Around us, the storm rages on. I wrap my arms around my legs as my rain-soaked clothes begin to take their toll. A deep chill works through my body.

Cal removes his jacket and proceeds to wrap it around me. I remain very still but don't refuse it. His smell envelopes me. It's rustic, like sandalwood, pine, and mint. It is oddly very comforting. He pulls out a lantern and once it's lit, I can more clearly see the blood soaking his shirt. I watch as he takes out a cloth and a jar of something from the duffle bag. He pours a little clear liquid on the cloth and tries to awkwardly hold it to his wound.

I decide at that moment to help him, after all he did stitch me up. "Give me that." I take the cloth without waiting for an answer and hold it to his cut. "What is that on the rag…alcohol?" I ask when I get a whiff of the concoction. My nose scrunches. "It doesn't smell like it."

Cal smiles, *actually smiles,* causing me to stare unabashedly at his mouth. I thought it might be physically impossible for him to smile.

"Here, take a sip," Cal says, still grinning.

I look at him like he's insane. Taking the jar and keeping a hand on his wound, I put it to my nose, taking a sniff. "OH MY GOD, what is that?"

He laughs outright now, and I can't stop staring at his mouth. It is such a beautiful thing, his laughter. Well maybe just laughter and *not* him.

"How are you from the South and have never tasted moonshine before? Especially living near the mountains?" He asks.

I cannot help but smile, too. I haven't seen true laughter in a while, even at my own expense, and it's contagious. "I don't know how I missed out on such a delicacy," I say, my tone dripping with sarcasm.

He holds my stare for a moment, and it's like we are seeing each other for the first time. His smile comes back as he pushes the jar to my lips.

"I never drank alcohol before." Shaking my head, I try to decline.

Taking my hand away from his cut, he hands the jar back to me. "My side is fine, and I am not trying to compromise your morals. I am simply trying to keep you warm. We can camp here tonight, and this," he gestures to the jar, "will help you relax, too."

I feel silly. I am almost twenty-two years old and have never had a drink of alcohol, but I have been riddled with drug use for a year. Shaking away the intrusive thoughts, I glare at him and then turn the jar up. I get two large gulps down before I begin coughing.

"Woah, woah! Slow down. I said *sip* it, not gulp it." Cal takes the jar back with a crooked smile and takes another swig.

Still trying to compose myself, I say, "I feel like my insides have been burned by lava! Why would anyone drink such a thing?" I cough some more, and then there it is…that sound, he is laughing again. It warms me inside.

Cal pulls out some meat and cheeses, handing me a few. "I squirreled these away in case I had to track you for longer than expected." He says through a bite of cheese.

"Squirreled away, huh?" I roll my eyes. We eat and occasionally sip the devilish liquid. It's gross, but I cannot deny I feel warmer and lighter than I have in a long time.

"What were you dreaming about when I found you?" His look tells me he has some ideas.

"I'd rather not say." I look away from his all-knowing stare. Feeling a bit bolder and trying to change the subject, I ask, "So…what is it you've done that has given you 'wanted man' status?" I use my fingers for quotations.

Cal stares into my eyes. At first, his face is tense, then it relaxes. He is so close that I feel his warmth. His expression tells me he has some burdens of his own hidden deep inside. I can see a shift in his demeanor when he decides to talk.

"I've killed people," he says without breaking my eye contact.

A piece of cheese I am holding is frozen halfway to my agape mouth. Stuttering, I ask the only thing I can think of that might make being here alone in the woods with him okay. "Were *they* bad people, or are *you* a bad person, Cal?"

He takes another swig, looking off into the distant woods. "Both, maybe." His voice is deep and grave. "They were very bad people, Maisy…but does that justify killing? I don't know."

This gives me a small piece of the man that I have been living under the same roof with. I reach over, taking the devil jar, and throw some back. I'm beginning to feel the effects. Bravery comes easier after a few drinks of this stuff.

"I need to know more, Callon. I need you to trust me enough to tell me what is happening. Can you imagine being gone from everyone and everything you know?" The moment I ask, I can see hurt briefly cross his face, but he looks away. I realized then that maybe being a wanted man also took him away from everything he knew. "I'm sorry. I guess maybe you do know a little about that." I pause for a few seconds before continuing, "My life is out there waiting on me. My parents could still be alive and looking for me." My heart breaks at the thought. A flash of Mom's heel peeking out from behind the car comes to mind, and I shudder.

"Listen, Maisy, I have a rule that I try not to break, a very simple rule. *NO* serious talk while drinking. *Especially* once you've had too much. It never ends well." His look turns concerned the more he watches me. Finally, he says, "What if I promise that I will tell you more tomorrow?" My mouth opens to protest, and he halts me, saying, "Tonight, we talk about other things."

I contemplate the offer at hand. Not that I have any real choice in the matter. This is the most he has engaged with me since day one, and I don't want to cause him to clam up. I nod my head and blurt out the first non-serious question I can think of, "What's your deal? You are somewhat of a hunter and obviously have picked up some handy medical knowledge. Tell me something about you."

His smile grows wide. It's a beautiful sight.

Ugghhhh! What is wrong with me?

It must be this horrid, poisonous liquid. I'm astonished but beaming when he actually answers me.

"My dad was a jack of all trades in life," Cal says with pride. "One of his many talents included hand-to-hand combat. Another was survival. That's where I learned to hunt, fish, and camp. He was a stickler for a man being able to live off the land even though he didn't have to. He taught self-defense to me and any neighborhood kids willing to learn. We had full-blown boxing matches." He pauses with a chuckle. "As you can imagine, this made for some hot-headed boys who thought they were grown-ass men. I got in my fair share of fights at school. Usually defending someone who couldn't defend themselves."

"That's very gallant of you, considering you are a kidnapper and murderer." The moment I say the words, my mouth drops open. "Oh my god, I am sorry. I don't know where that came from."

Suddenly, he is laughing outright at me…*again.* "Wow, give a lady a few sips of the shine and outcome the claws."

I can feel the embarrassment as my cheeks heat up. "UGH, I'm so sorry. It really was nice that you took up for them…the people in your school." I am, decidedly, a jerk, so I keep talking to move the conversation. "Did you go to college?"

"I did a few years of college before joining the service, then four years as an Army Ranger."

"So, I was right about you being in the military." He looks confused, so I point to his tattoo, peeking out.

"That's very observant of you. Yeah, me and the guys in my regiment all got the same quote, but in different designs before we got out." Abruptly, he takes a long drink and says, "Your turn…I give you a little, you give me a little." He winks and passes the jar back to me. I don't hesitate as I endure the burn and try to ignore what that wink did to me.

"What is your favorite thing to do?" He waits intently, scrutinizing me.

Not a question I was expecting at all. I go back in my mind to who I was before. What made her happy? "I loved two things…horses and writing," I say softly. "I used to ride at a local equestrian center.

"That is a really good answer." He takes a deep breath and the jar. "Have you ever written anything?"

"I started several projects. I was working on a mystery before…well, anyway, it was never finished, but maybe one day. "What is your favorite thing to do, Cal…" I send him the same question.

His crooked smile is back. "Kidnapping women is number one…murder is number two, but a high third is classic cars."

I let my eye roll tell him how poor that joke was but ask anyway, "Which car is your favorite?"

"I would have to say the 1968 through the 1970 Chevelle SS. Those were top for me. I restored several with my dad. His name was Arthur. We did race a few times for fun at a local drag strip growing up." Pride shows in his eyes.

"My mom had…" My throat suddenly tightens. "She *has* a 1970 Fastback Mustang. I helped Dad work on it for her. It's white with deep red racing stripes and louvers on the back." That's as much as I can say without becoming too serious.

"That was an amazing year for the Mustang!" His excitement is apparent all over his face. "I had the pleasure of working on a few." Abruptly, he turns toward me and reaches for me. Instinctively, I pull back, gaining a hurt look from those tropical eyes.

"I was going to pull the jacket tighter. You're shivering a bit." Before I can say I'm sorry, *again*, he backs away and changes the subject. I fix the jacket myself.

"My turn, Maze…what's your favorite food?"

Did he just call me Maze? "Mexican," I say without the slightest hesitation. Which earns me a smile from him. "What is your mother's name?" I quickly add.

Pride shows in his eyes as he says, "Her name *was* Leona."

Was. That one word is heavy. "That's a beautiful name, Callon."

"Thank you. She was a wonderful mother." Moving along, he quickly asks, "If you could live anywhere, where would it be?"

"Well, this is another no-brainer for me. I once went with my parents to the Yucatán Peninsula in Mexico. It was otherworldly, coming from a small town in North Carolina. The beaches were serene, the ocean was so pure, and the natives loved to share their histories with us. It was the peacefulness of the ocean that I loved the most. Yeah, I could live there," I whisper dreamily as I take another sip. "More white devil?" I ask, passing the jar.

"White devil huh…" He grins. "Why yes, I do. Is that what we're calling it now?"

"That is an accurate description of it," I mutter under my breath. "What about you, Callon Wolfe? Where would you live if you could go anywhere?"

He rubs his stubbled chin. "I like your answer, Maze. Yucatán, Mexico sounds perfect."

His sly smile is infectious. Where has this side of him been hiding? I grin back. The alcohol is turning me into an unguarded idiot. At that moment, my bladder decides to tell me I have indeed had too much to drink. As I begin to stand, I say, "Quit calling me Ma—" Before I finish my chastising, I stumble, almost falling onto Cal. Without hesitation he reaches out to steady me with his hand.

"You going to be okay?" he asks.

"Yes, of course." Clearing my throat, I point to the woods. "I need to use the little girl's room." I look down at his hand on mine then quickly move away and stagger off into the woods. Warmth moves into my cheeks.

Strange drunk idiot I have become.

Once we are back under the rock, I notice the storm has completely passed while we were talking. I also come to the realization that I am a lightweight with alcohol. Understandably so, considering I have never had any before tonight. "Cal…I'm sorry I ran today." I don't know what makes me say it. I shouldn't be sorry. He is, quite literally, holding me against my will!

"It's fine, really," he says. He's biting his lip as if he has so much more to say. "I understand why you did it. You have no reason to trust me. I'm just another stranger to you." He clears his throat and continues, "We have to get going early in the morning, and I think you should try to get some sleep. I can keep watch."

"You're probably right," I mutter. Shuffling about, I manage to get somewhat comfortable on my side, using my arm as a pillow. Comfort is a strong word, more like tolerable. Cal pushes the duffle bag over for me to use instead. "Won't you get cold tonight," I ask.

"No, I am fine. Just get some sleep now, Maisy," he whispers.

I find I like it when he says my name. It's comforting knowing that at least one person in the world knows who I am—knows that I'm alive. Even if it's the person keeping me from going back.

CHAPTER 8
Callon

The tree bark is digging into my spine, but I could care less. To see her sleeping peacefully for once is worth it. For every nightmare she has, a piece of my soul breaks. I wish I could take her memories of the last year away from her. There is a fighter inside that small frame of hers. I can see it just under the surface.

I stretch my legs out and enjoy the quiet morning as the sun begins to stream through the trees. Little slivers of light dance across her face and it almost breaks me. Looking at her now, I know I made the right decision, even if it will make me the bad guy in the end. She is worth it.

The slow dawn gives me clarity and the time to decide just how much I'm willing to tell Maisy. While she deserves the truth and nothing less, it's something I cannot give to her completely… not yet anyways. I just need her to be safe before I can do what needs to be done.

I see her stirring and quickly close my eyes faking sleep.

CHAPTER 9

The sun kisses my face, forcing my eyes to come alive. Leaning against a trunk a few feet away is Cal. He looks to be sleeping. I don't disturb him. Instead, I carefully sit up and take him in. He looks at peace when he is sleeping. No stress showing in his square jawline and no furrowed brow. The tough guy exterior is still there, but calm replaces his usual stern features. The Callon from last night comes to mind and I smile.

His long legs are stretched out in front of him. If I had to guess, I would say he was around six feet tall. His stubble has increased in the last week and is well on its way to becoming a full beard. Callon is very handsome in a rustic sort of way. He lacks the features of a killer, or at least, what my mind decided a killer should look like.

What led him out here? What path made him a murderer?

Last night also helped me gain perspective of my situation, but also of the man before me. He, most certainly, has secrets. However, there is another side to him and to his motives. Maybe he has reasons, *legitimate* reasons, for his actions. No matter what I find out today, I must get home, but I also need to give Callon a chance to explain himself. He clearly doesn't mean me any harm. My eyes trail from his legs back up to his body, and when I reach his face, I'm startled to see him looking back at me. My face instantly burns, and I look away.

"Good morning. Nice views out here, huh?" His voice is taunting. All the while, his eyes dance with humor.

As if I wasn't embarrassed already. Ugh! I need to get moving and away from his smug face. "I was just thinking the views around here are quite horrid," I say while standing and dusting myself off. "Let's get a move on. I am looking forward to a shower and the promise you made." I give him a stern look.

"Horrid, huh…that's a little harsh, don't you think?" he says with a wink.

Why is he so exasperating! I stomp off in the general direction I came from yesterday.

"Maisy…you are going the wrong way." His insufferable smirk is back.

I turn on my heel and motion for him to lead the way. We make our way through the dense forest, filling the time with small talk, after deciding to wait for the heavy conversation once we are back in the cabin. "How old are you?" I huff out, climbing my way over a fallen tree.

He looks over his shoulder. "I am twenty-six, and you will be…twenty-one." He continues his climb.

"Yes, that's right." I don't bother asking how he knows. He had said yesterday that I was all over the news. It's so strange to be a missing person when you are right here.

"How old did you think I was?" he asks.

"I thought you were sixty-ish…considering your vast wisdom and grumpy nature," I tease.

Cal stops abruptly, causing me to bump into him. When he turns around, we are almost touching. I back track a few steps quickly. He towers over me, making me wonder why, in the span of twenty-four hours, I am comfortable enough to taunt a killer. "Wisdom and being grumpy are products of my life experiences, not age, sweetheart. It takes time to build this much resentment and malice for the world, not to mention the good looks and brains." He gives me a crooked smile. Heat moves into my blasted cheeks again under the weight of his unrelenting gaze.

After that, I stopped teasing him, and we kept the chats short and to the point. As much as I hate to admit it, this silly banter between us is so much better than the closed-off man from yesterday.

Trying to fill the silence, I ask, "Would you tell me about your mom?"

Callon keeps walking, never looking back, but starts talking about her after a beat. "She was a nurse. Her, combined with my stint in the Army, is where I picked up some medical knowledge. She was a brilliant woman, one that you could never bring down. She always had a smile and was optimistic about life."

"You speak of your parents in the past tense…what happened?" I regretted asking instantly, but my curious mind got the better of me.

"Car accident a few years ago…both died," he says in a clipped voice.

"I'm so sorry." What else is there to say? I know the pain of loss, and only time helps with that. We kept the conversation lighter after that, and I asked about his days in the military. He wouldn't speak much about his time in the service, just that he was an Army Ranger, and he has a best friend named Bowen—whom he met in the service—and whom he still talks to today. When it came to questions about me, I was a bit guarded. I did, however, tell him about my friend Anna and boyfriend Thomas.

Callon's face becomes clearly mocking when he asks, "You had a boyfriend? Tell me about this, *Thomas*." I can tell from his voice this is news to him. So, maybe not everything about me was aired on television.

"Not much to tell, really. We hadn't dated long, just a few months. He lived next door—"

"Wait." Cal grins. "He was the boy next door, and *you* were the girl next door. That is just so…Hallmark Channel, Maze. Wow."

I pick up my jaw and lash out, "Excuse me…there's nothing wrong with a sweet and wholesome boy next door! What exactly is your ideal relationship, Callon Wolfe…a prison guard?"

He's full-on laughing at me now. "While that sounds interesting and very possible in my future…no. I want someone who can lay their head on my chest and make the noise of the day disappear, someone who I can be myself around for the rest of my life."

I was not expecting that response. Why was that such a perfect response? "So…is there someone out there you share that with. Someone who's looking for you, too?"

"No, I can't live the life of a kidnapper and murderer and still maintain a relationship, Maze. I don't know if you realize it, but being a criminal is not easy."

"You are an insufferable pig, Callon and I'm sure no woman out there would want to put up with you anyway, criminal, or not! And stop calling me Maze," I rant. I cannot seem to stop bantering with him. What is wrong with me?

"You know what, you are probably right." His laughter fades after a bit.

I notice, during the walk, that he never asks about *my* parents. He never even asks their names. I want badly to pick his brain and find out what he has seen on the news, but I refrain. Probably out of fear of what I will uncover.

Once we reach the cabin, I make a beeline for the bathroom. Brushing your teeth and showering are some of the most underappreciated luxuries. Once out, I find more clothes folded on the bed, holy jeans, a fitted green T-shirt, and more socks and panties. I slip on the same black boots I have been wearing daily, thankful that they are dry. It takes a considerable amount of brushing my waves to get out all the knots, but I eventually managed.

I stop to take a quick look in the mirror. I am surprised at the process of healing. It has only been a few days, and my face is fuller, and my skin is healing all over. The dark purple is gone from under my eyes. The cut on my forehead is closed nicely and the stitches need to come out. It is the first time in so long that I have begun to recognize myself. I perk up when a strong, glorious smell hits my nose, COFFEE, and BREAKFAST!

In the kitchen, Cal is flipping bacon and stirring eggs. I notice some bread on the counter, so without asking, I start toasting it for us. My tummy growls loudly and I hear Cal snicker.

I roll my eyes as he says, "If you like jelly, there's some in the fridge."

"I most certainly do." I jelly the toast and pour the coffee whilst he finishes our plates.

We eat and enjoy the calm before the storm. I know that whatever I am about to find out will change everything. All I want to do is go home. That is still my ultimate goal. I no longer fear Cal, but I don't trust him completely, either. Just a few short days ago, I was battered, inside and out. I was scared of him and shaken to my core by what I had gone through. Something is growing in me, strength, determination, but most of all…hope. It's like slowly coming out of a nightmare and wishing you could just pinch yourself and wake up instantly, but that can't happen with this nightmare. It takes time.

With the food now gone, we sit across from one another, and I wait patiently.

Callon's eyes are guarded as he asks, "What is it you want to know first, Maisy." It's the first time I have heard such uncertainty in his tone.

"Let's start with the day you found me. Why did you knock me out with chloroform and tie me to a bed?" I go straight for some burning unanswered questions.

Never losing eye contact, he says, "It was to save you." He takes a deep breath and clears his throat, "I knocked you out so that you wouldn't fight me, but mainly so that you couldn't scream. You would have given our location away. I tied you up to keep you from hurting yourself. You still had drugs in your system and were scratching at your arms. I was trying to give it time to wear off."

My face contorts as I imagine that horrid scene. I get this vivid image of my battered, half-naked body being carried lifeless. My cheeks heat with humiliation.

Cal takes notice. "Maisy, you…you should never be embarrassed for what has happened to you. You should be pissed off, sad for your loss of time and family, but *NEVER* embarrassed! You were a victim, simple as that." The venom in his voice is startling.

What he doesn't know is how much I keep locked away inside. I continue with what irks me most, "How were you in the right place to find me at the exact time that I escaped?"

His jaw flexes a bit, and Cal looks down. "I have been staking out certain individuals for a very long time. I have my reasons." He pauses briefly. "When you escaped the house, I was in hiding. I saw you bolt for the woods with Tony not far behind." He sets down his mug and leans back in the chair.

"You were not there to save me; you were there for other reasons." I play through that scenario in my head. "So…you know who *they* are. You know what they do." It's not really a question but more of an observation. However, he does nod slightly in confirmation.

Cal interrupts my thoughts with his own question. "There is something that I have been dying to know. How did you escape that night?"

"It was my last night of 'viewing' before I was to be…sold." I choke out the final word.

"What is a viewing, if you don't mind me asking?" he interrupts.

I'm not sure I can say the words out loud. They sit in my throat like lead. "It's exactly like it sounds." My voice becomes distant from the memory. "I was paraded nude before monitors of men for their viewing pleasure. This was a way to tease potential buyers each week and increase my worth." Surprisingly, I feel relief in letting a tiny part of that torment out of me. "It was like being livestock at an auction."

Cal gets to his feet and hands me a napkin. I didn't realize a few tears had escaped. I blot them away and notice his clenched jaw. "I was purchased that night by someone, though I'm not sure who it was. My fate was sealed. I knew that if I did not escape that night…no one would ever see me again."

I sink back into the memory of that night. Chills break out in my body, but once the floodgates open…I want to tell the story. It just pours out of me. "The buyer showed up a little later that evening, and Jacob had me bathe and pack what little belongings I had. I had thrown on a tank and underwear after the shower but hadn't finished dressing yet. I knew he was waiting for me in the foyer…but through my window, I had seen Tony leave out the back patio door to smoke as usual. I was almost certain no one was watching the side door in the kitchen. They had given me a pill to calm me down, but it hadn't quite taken effect yet.

"I knew if I didn't run for it right then, my life would be officially over. So, I ran without even grabbing my pants. Whoever this buyer was could be worse than Jacob, for all I knew. I snuck from upstairs down to the kitchen, passing no one along the way, but when I reached the kitchen…Tony was standing there. He must have circled around the house." My memory again becomes so vivid. It's like being back in that moment. I tell my story to Cal as if it is happening all over again.

"Little bird…going somewhere?" Tony croons.

His smile lets me know he has waited for the day that I would run. He lunges for me, and I dodge his grasp. As I almost reach the door, I'm jerked backward by my hair and lose balance. My head slams into the counter.

"FOR FUCK'S SAKE GIRL! Jacob will have my ass. Look at your fucking head!

I'm blinking rapidly, trying to clear my vision as the blood streams down my face and into my eyes. I see the door. It's so close. I make the decision that today, I will die or escape. That's the ONLY two options. I struggle with his grip; his hands bruise as they bite into my skin. My face rings when he slaps me, causing me to fall to the floor. Tony's face contorts in rage as he grabs me again, slinging me to standing. He slaps me a second time. I stumble away from him, his hand catching my necklace and ripping it from my throat.

Now, I'm just a few feet away from that door.

Beside me is a vase full of roses, a bulky ceramic vase. I don't give myself time to think, I grab it slamming it against Tony's head, and I run.

Once I'm outside, I realize I don't have much longer before the drugs take effect. I hear Tony's footsteps not too far behind me…

Cal's eyes are distant, as if he is picturing the scene while I tell it. I can feel the anger radiating from him. "That explains the cut on your head and all the bruising." He pauses and I see him become lost in thought. "I want you to know that they will all pay for this. Every single person who touched you will pay."

"I want them to pay." I whisper.

And there it is.

My true feelings. How Christian is it of me to want them dead? But I do want them dead. These monsters deserve the worst kind of torture. If that makes me a hypocrite, then so be it. If it makes me a monster, then that's okay with me, too.

"Why did he call you 'little bird?' I heard him yell it that night you escaped, too."

"When I first got there, the night I was taken, I had on a silver necklace with a small dove pendant. I wore it every day. My parents got it for me on my nineteenth birthday." I sigh, "They never removed it, just used that as my name…little bird. My real name wasn't to be said aloud, especially around anyone other than Jacob. It was ripped from my neck the night I escaped when I was fighting off Tony."

He looks at me sinisterly. "Do you know why you were targeted, Maisy?" Cal says this in a way that makes me think he already knows. He pulls his chair close to me. This time I don't flinch away from him.

I look up to the ceiling and all around the room wishing I could crawl into a hole somewhere. I wanted to have this conversation but now it is taking its toll.

"Maisy look at me." Callon takes my chin making me face him. "If you don't want to talk about this you don't have to."

"But I need to." I whisper. The light touch of his hand on my chin moves away and I feel the loss of his warmth. "Yes, I do know why they chose me. Jacob Rainer said my father was set to demolish him in the upcoming election. My dad, William Murray, was the people's choice. Dad was a decorated retired Naval Officer with an impressive background and more impressive morals. In Jacob's words…he had to go."

Memories of gunshots are in my head, making me shudder. "Jacob had met me before at several events. He had already planned on taking me once my parents were out of the way. He told me that I was basically a bonus. Being William's daughter was one thing, but there was another reason…I could make him very popular with buyers. Especially since I…"

"Since you what?" Cal asks quietly.

I begin shaking my head, unable to say the last words. My face burns.

Cal places a hand on my cheek and looks deep into my eyes bringing back the warmth from before. He seems to notice that I didn't flinch again. He looks as if he can search my brain for the things that I don't want said aloud.

But the problem is, I want to get it out of my head. The guilt I feel for just being me is unbearable. It's festering inside of me like a wound. "The other reason I was valuable to him was that I was…am a virgin." I think my face could catch fire at this point. "I have no idea how Jacob knew it, but he used my body for profit in ways that…people could never fathom. That's also why he kept me for so long. He said that I made him more money in pictures and videos each week with his clientele than selling me outright."

Callon's hand drops from my face and his eyes become haunted. Anger bubbles right under the surface. "That doesn't make sense. How could they possibly know something so personal?" His eyes roam over my face again, "You know deep down there is nothing you could have done to stop what happened, right? Evil people are responsible, and I promise you they will pay before it is over."

Something seems to stop him in his tracks, "Wait, so they didn't rape you?"

Wiping my face, I shrug. "They did plenty but kept me pure for my future buyer, and I have *NO* idea how they could possibly know that about me beforehand." I try clear my throat and attempt to stop the water works. "Is that what you are doing? Making them pay? What dog do you have in this fight, Callon? It could land you in prison or six feet under."

"Like I said before, I have my reasons."

Okay then…he obviously has more content he doesn't wish to unload today. I inhale deep through my nose and brace myself for what I am about to ask. "I need to know what has been released on the news. Where are my parents?"

Callon scoots beside me and takes my hands in his. The calm that washes over me is welcoming. He can't seem to look me in the eyes, which is a first for him. He gently rubs my hands with his thumbs in a circular motion.

I know the truth before he speaks.

"The scene was discovered the next morning by a lady passing by headed to work. The reporter was standing in front of a corn field and…an unmistakable white Mustang. They found William and Victoria deceased."

I feel him squeeze my hands tighter, but my mind has gone elsewhere. I hear the gunshots popping all over again. In my heart I knew when I saw the heel of my mother's shoe behind the car. I knew. Hope…that is what I had. Hope that they had made it that night...hope that they were still out there scouring the earth for me.

Cal tips up my chin. "There is nothing you could have done to prevent what happened."

I squeeze my eyes closed and shakily, I inhale. "What else did the reporter say? What are they saying now? Do they know who is responsible?"

Callon releases me and stands, pacing the floor slowly. I notice his demeanor change in an instant.

What is that about?

Callon finally answers me. "No…Jacob is in the Senate. You have been a missing person plastered all over the news for a year with no leads. Most people believe you to be deceased. Do you grasp what I am saying to you?" He holds my stare.

I know exactly what he means. "It's being covered up."

He nods. "They have reported on the 'likelihood' of this being a robbery gone wrong, amongst other…rumors."

Easing to my feet, I pour another mug of coffee and lean against the counter. "What other rumors?"

"None with any validation. That's not important. What is important is that you understand the gravity of your situation."

"Okay, I do, but what I don't understand is why you are involved at all? You could have let me go at any point or never gotten involved that day in the woods."

"I saw someone who needed help, and I intervened."

There's more he isn't saying, but I decide now is not the time to press him on it. "So…stop me at any point and correct me if I'm wrong. I am a missing person, presumed dead. The people responsible have covered it up. This means they have some pull in the police department, which is not surprising considering we are dealing with a political figure. Jacob Rainer is a leader of sorts in sex trafficking. My parents are gone…" I pause, swallowing the lump in my throat. "We know the truth, but no one else. You saved me by chance, but you can't let me leave because of *your* past. Am I missing anything so far?"

His intense stare is unnerving at times. "I am not just keeping you here due to my past. You need to understand that Jacob has friends in low places *everywhere*. He will never let you live to tell your story. If you go forward right now, he will find you. You will either go back into the sex trade, or he will eliminate you altogether. You are a *serious* fucking threat to his empire right now, Maisy."

He's more right about that than he could possibly know. I have seen the ins and outs of how Jacob moves girls from one location to another. How he picks his prey. I know what most of these men look like, especially those with large pockets. I've met other girls…know their faces but never their real names. Those are the most haunting memories.

Placing my cup on the counter, I run my hands through my hair, and I feel myself losing control. "What now? What am I supposed to do? You are telling me that I could be killed if I go public, the only family I have is gone, and even if I could resume some normal life, where would I go? Is my family home still there, and what happened to everything that belonged to us?"

"Unfortunately, I don't know. If you were a beneficiary, then yes, everything would go to you one day. That is assuming they keep the case open, and the house doesn't end up in an estate sale. I am not the best person to ask about finances and assets, but I am certain that you cannot come forward right now."

"Cal…I *need* to get back to my life," before he can protest, I continue, "Maybe not right away. What if *you* train me to protect myself?"

His eyebrow raises at that. "Train you? You want to learn to fight? And then what…do you think you could kill someone who was attacking you? Taking a life is not that easy and I should know." His lip curls at that. "Last I checked, you were from a very religious family; in fact, I have never heard you even say a curse word."

"You curse enough for the both of us and what does that matter? If I had no other choice…yes, I believe I could do it." I meet his challenging stare.

He scoffs, "It does matter. I don't trust people who don't swear." He ignores my eyeroll and continues, "Even if I could teach you to protect yourself, it would take time. You are but one young woman against a group of untouchable, dangerous men. Your best bet is leaving the US and never returning." His face grows very serious. "I wanted to give you time before I threw that option at you. I had no idea that within a few days, we would be hashing this out." He stops exhaling loudly then continues. "That is why I have been holding back. I didn't know how you would react to giving up a life here. I have unfinished business, but you, *you* get a second chance. It may not look like the life you had before, but it's still worth living. You have made it out of a situation most girls *NEVER* make it out of."

I take a moment to digest everything Cal said. I may have lost my parents, but I still had friends and Thomas. I have the responsibility of taking care of my parents' belongings. On the other hand, I have people who want me dead. I huff out a frustrated sigh, "I have nothing…no money, no clothes, no car. How, exactly, could I disappear even if I wanted to?"

Cal nods in understanding. "Look, Maisy, I could help you disappear if that's what you want. I had planned on it anyway—one day helping you start over. I have the means to do so. However, you are right about needing to be able to protect yourself."

He sees the anticipation in my eyes. "If you really want to learn…I will teach you some basics." He puts up his hands before I can interrupt. "As I said before, this takes time. You would have to be willing to stay with me, here, until you were ready. Once I have everything set up for you to leave, I could help you find somewhere you could be happy."

A desire begins to burn inside of me. Something deep down that I didn't know existed anymore. I nod my head in agreement. "Yes, I will stay."

"Are you sure, you didn't even have time to think on it?" he asks bewildered at my response.

"I'm certain."

He gives a smile, but his eyes seem sad. "It is remarkable that you are standing here alive and well, but more so that you still have this drive inside you. Where does that strength come from?"

My heart warms with his words. "I was blessed with amazing parents who taught me to never give up, no matter the situation. I intend to honor them by living. It's what they would want for me…what I want for myself."

A person cannot go backward and fix the past. One can only move forward and try to pave a better future.

CHAPTER 10

Callon

"How have you been?" I ask as I pull my ball cap a little lower on my face when a few people linger a bit too close to my table.

Bo studies me before answering. His dark eyes bore into me. "I'm good Callon, but are you?"

"Don't get all sentimental on me, damn. I'm fine." I press my lips into a thin line and avert my eyes.

"You don't look fine, and I think we have been friends long enough that you can talk to me." Bo takes a huge bite of his gravy biscuits and stares expectantly at me. "How is she?" he mumbles through a bite of food.

"She will be fine…at some point. She has nightmares every night. I stand there at her door and can't do a fucking thing to stop her pain. It's bullshit. She is strong though, you know? Stronger than she realizes." I nibble my bacon. "She is like a wild animal right now, terrified when I'm near.

I can feel it." I survey the café we are in to make sure no one's stare is lingering too long in our direction.

Bo sees me scanning the room and puts his fork down. "I can see you are on edge, so lets make this quick." He rests his chin against his tawny hands and asks, "Did you tell her anything?"

"I told her what she needed to know. Everything else doesn't matter." I roll my shoulders trying to dissipate some of the tension.

"Has she agreed to leave the country?"

I nod my head. "Oddly enough, she didn't fight me on it. She understands the gravity of the situation now. Will you be able to get her documentation when the time comes?"

"Yeah, that's no problem, but what do you mean *when* the time comes? The plan was to get her out of here and fast." Bo's brows crease as he analyzes me. "She can't stay here Callon."

I clench my jaw in frustration. "Hell Bo, you think I don't know that." I pause for a moment looking anywhere except his face when I say, "she asked me to teach her some survival skills."

He scoffs at me and squints his eyes, "And you agreed to this? So, is it her wanting to stay or you wanting to keep her here?"

"You're an asshole Bo."

Bo's eyes sadden momentarily when he says, "I am right though… aren't I? You can't protect her forever just because you feel guilty."

I drop the bacon I was holding and push to stand, giving Bo the death stare as I say, "Time's up. I need to get back. I have clothes and other shit I bought that she's going to need." I adjust my hat and jacket and just as Bo opens his mouth to speak, I cut him off with, "Do not contact me, I'll contact you when I can…you know the rules."

Bo stands adjusting his long braid as he pulls on his Aztec jacket. His lips are pressed together in agitation. He finally sighs and nods, "I got it man, I know the drill. Stay safe."

"You too brother." I mumble as I tip my head down and waltz out of the café.

He is that to me—like a brother. I shouldn't have been an ass to him. He's just trying to help. If I am being completely honest. He's right…I'm not ready for her to go. I don't trust she will be safe. Not yet.

She needs to stay longer…for her sake.

CHAPTER 11

Why on earth would anyone agree to such punishment?

I've been at the cabin for around six weeks now, and every day, Cal finds new and inventive ways to torture me. I've been training or eating…*non-stop*. He promises me it's for the best, but my achy body says otherwise.

The first few days, he focused on balance and footing. When we are not training, we go into the woods, where he shows me survival techniques. That is the part I'm *actually* good at, thanks to my father. He took me camping a lot growing up.

Cal and I have come to an understanding. This arrangement we have will last no more than six months. And after that, I will flee the country undetected with his help. I don't ask what he intends to do or why he wants to help me so badly. I take the win for what it is. I get a second chance to live, and I will not waste it. My parents lost their lives, and I won't let them die in vain. One day I will have my revenge on Jacob, but for now I just need to live.

Cal tells me there will be times that he has to go into town, amongst other things. When this happens, I am supposed to lock up the cabin and stay quiet until his return. He also finally told me about his truck, which he had stashed somewhere near the cabin on an entrance road. He says it's a 1982 deep-blue Silverado K10. His face beams when he talks about it and… it's kind of adorable. I was beginning to think he walked everywhere, which I knew was impossible considering the amount of supplies he has here. He keeps the keys hidden, probably for fear I'll run again. For now, I have no intention of running. I am tired of feeling weak and vulnerable, and if he can help me get stronger, then I'm all for it.

Life, as unusual as it is, has found a balance for us. I have many lingering questions that I keep locked away. For now, I'm working on healing, both mentally and physically. Dreams still plague my nights, but determination drives my days.

Although, at this very moment, my drive is depleted. I'm lying flat on my back in the dirt after being thrown to the ground for the thousandth time today.

"Get up, come on, one more time." Cal reaches out his hand, which I reluctantly take as he flings me onto my feet. He is wearing gray sweatpants with sneakers and *nothing* else. Sweat trickles down the contours of his abdomen and I have to divert my gaze.

It's intimidating, to say the least. He's all muscle and speed, and I'm…not.

I fan myself which does absolutely nothing for me. My sports bra and leggings are plastered to me at this point. "Come on Cal, I'm done for today" I whine.

"Mmmmm…I don't think so." His eyes are alight with mischief. Before my reflexes even register movement, he has lunged forward, wrapping his calf around mine, pinning my arms, and I'm on the ground. *Again.*

Cal leans over me, holding out his hand again. "Would you let me take you somewhere tomorrow for your birthday?"

My mouth drops open. I'm floored by his question for two reasons: one, I forgot about my birthday, which is tomorrow, July seventeenth, and two…I didn't think I was allowed to leave the cabin.

He moves quickly, dragging me up and off the ground. "It's nothing much, but I thought you needed a change of scenery. It's the least I can do."

"Sure, I guess. What happened to…Do *NOT* leave the cabin," I say in my worst Cal voice imitation.

"I don't sound like that, and I will make an exception as long as we have disguises," he says with a wink.

"Disguises, huh…" Snapping my leg out, I hook his with mine, then off-set his stance with my upper body…just like he taught me. I'm rewarded with him smacking the ground, face in shock. Before I can declare victory, he knocks my feet out, and I land flat beside him with a groan.

"UGHHH CAL! What the heck?"

"Hell, Maisy…it's what the hell! Or shit Cal why did you do that?" He mocks in a terrible feminine voice. He is still intent on corrupting my language.

"I do NOT sound like that, you retch. Can we get back to what you intend to do for my birthday?" I roll on my side brows raised in expectation.

"That…" he taps my nose, "is for me to know and you to find out." With that, he jumps up and jogs toward the cabin. "Come on, let's eat!" he yells back.

He seems really pepped up. How does he have this much energy? Somehow, I manage to drag my sweaty carcass into the cabin to get cleaned up. While showering, I think back to the last couple of weeks, and it makes me smile. I can tell Callon enjoys the company as much as I do. It must have been lonely for him, too, being on the run.

It is an unlikely partnership, for sure.

After showering, I stand in front of the mirror. I am healed everywhere. The cut on my head is turning into a scar, only slightly pink now. And my old self would have been correct. This scar is pretty awesome. My hair even looks fuller. My cheeks are pink and eyes bright.

There she is.

There's Maisy.

During the last few weeks, Cal has left a few times. He purchased some clothes for me, toiletries, undergarments, and feminine products. My face burned like the sun the day he handed them to me, but I was grateful. My menstrual cycle hadn't surfaced in a long time due to malnourishment and stress, but I was thankful, nonetheless. There were three types of clothing that he said were all I needed…workout clothing, hunting clothes, and tactical. He was very close to my size with what he purchased, and I was ecstatic to be out of baggy clothing. Included in the tactical clothing was a *bulletproof vest*.

He is nothing if not thorough and paranoid.

The day he gave me the clothes, he asked me to remove the used ones I had been wearing. I let him take everything except the T-shirts. I had grown very fond of them, especially the Metallica one. He has been 'educating' me on alternative and rock music. He is a country guy at heart but loves rock, too, and I have to say, it's all growing on me.

Another interesting part of my day is finding notes in pockets of my clothing. Cal has been slipping them into the pockets after the wash. The first one I found simply said, "You are stronger than you think, Maze," in sloppy handwriting. Some are sweet, and others funny. The one today said, "If you think you are too small to be effective, you have never been in the dark with a mosquito." I laughed out loud at that one. It has become something I get excited about, but I try not to let it show. It's just one more piece of the complicated Callon puzzle. For a big, tough guy whose apparently murdered people, he's actually a softy.

After stuffing our faces with sandwiches and apples, Cal begins his usual interrogation into all things Maisy. "What would you be doing right now for a living if things were different?" he asks.

It doesn't take long to answer him. I've known since I was a girl what I wanted to do. "I would be a writer."

His eyebrows go up. "That's right, I remember you saying you loved to write the night we were trapped in the rain because of you." He nudges my arm.

"Well, maybe if you were honest with me straight away, that wouldn't have happened."

"Fair enough…you can still do that, you know. This will all be over one day, Maze. You can be a writer."

He's still calling me Maze even though I grumble, but secretly, it's growing on me like rock music.

"What is in store for the rest of the day?" I asked through a yawn.

"I see I'm riveting company for you," he jests. "I think we should take a walk. I have something to show you." His eyes soften a touch.

I watch as his hand slides through his silky hair. It looks like it would be so soft to the touch. I clear my throat and nod a quick yes to the walking idea.

Thirty minutes later we are headed down a sloping hillside in the forest. Cal is dressed in green cargo pants, a black T-shirt, and combat-style boots. He has a backpack slung over one shoulder.

I decided on black jeans with a sports bra and a green tank top for comfort. I have my lace-up black boots on…which I love dearly these days. My long hair is braided again today to help with the heat.

In my "before" life, I would have NEVER dressed like this. I was very girly. My closet consisted mainly of skirts, dresses, white capris, or khakis. With lots of flower prints and heels. I mentally laughed at how cute I was. Life is so strange. Here I am dressed like Sarah Connor from *Terminator*, but she really was the coolest.

Cal interrupts my thoughts with a purposeful nudge, "What is going on inside that head, Maze? You haven't said a word the entire walk."

"Sorry, I was thinking about how different life looks now." A laugh bubbles out of me, "To tell the truth, I was thinking about how I'm dressed like Sarah Connor from *Terminator*."

Cal grins big. "You are, aren't you? You just need some aviator glasses, and you'll be all set. You are way prettier, though." His smile falters a bit when he sees my shock and he cocks an eyebrow at me. "You do know you are in a league of your own, right?" he says, looking at me with honest curiosity in those too blue eyes.

"I guess I never thought of myself in that way." And I haven't. I know I'm pretty, but it wasn't something I placed importance on.

"It's okay to know you are beautiful…inside and out. Confidence is a very attractive quality," he says matter-of-factly.

"Well then, Cal, you must be the most handsome man alive," I taunt.

"So, you are beautiful *AND* smart! Wonderful combo," he says mockingly.

"Please tell me we are close. I can't take much more of your extreme ego today," I mumble. Although the smile never leaves my face.

"Almost there, Sarah Connor," he says in his best Arnold Schwarzenegger voice. "Those were epic movies, though. Which was your favorite, one or two?"

"One," I blurt out rather quickly.

"*ONE*, really? Why one? Two was obviously the better film."

"I liked the love story between Kyle Reese and Sarah. It was beautiful," I gush.

He bites his lip, holding back a laugh. "You are telling me out of all the action, futuristic machines, and badass fight scenes, you liked the love story best. What about the liquid cop? He was insane in the sequel."

I furrow my brow. "I have never heard the cop referred to as the liquid cop."

"He literally melts and remolds himself…liquid cop," he declares.

We both pause momentarily, then burst out laughing.

This right here is what I like about my days. I never realized how much I missed laughter until now.

We bantered some more as we made our way through the dense forest. It's not long before I hear the rush of water nearby. And the more we walk the louder it gets. Soon, I see a winding river coming into view. We hiked along the river, headed against the current. The wilderness in North Carolina is underappreciated. Its dense natural forests are so full of life and character. This time of year, it is hot and humid, and everything is green as far as the eye can see. Ferns and mountain laurels are scattered throughout bringing character to these woods. Soon the greenery gives way to rocks and boulders protruding from the water in various places like nature's statues.

Suddenly, I see it.

A giant, magnificent waterfall rages over a cliff. My mouth drops open as I take in the scene. I feel his eyes on me before he speaks.

"You like it?"

I gain my composure, "Of course I do…it's breathtaking." This gains me a beaming smile as we continue to walk until we are at the base of the waterfall. Cal chunks his pack on the ground and proceeds to remove his shirt, but once he goes for the buttons on his jeans, I interrupt him mid-zip.

"What exactly are you doing?"

"*WE* are going swimming," he says without looking up at me. He's now kicked his boots to the side and has the jeans hanging low on his hips.

"No, I most certainly am not. I don't have a swimsuit, and neither do you."

"I have on boxers, Maze, which is no different than swim trunks, really. And you have stuff on under there, right? Not much different than a bikini, I'm sure. I wasn't planning on going commando on you if that's what you think," he says, biting back a smile.

He's not wrong. I'm wearing a sports bra and black undies underneath this, but I don't think I can move. I am frozen with trepidation. He starts to drop his pants, and I turn away quickly.

"Look, I brought you out here because I thought you would enjoy the waterfall and swimming underneath one. I'm sorry. If this was a mistake, we can go back."

I slowly turn around to find him standing there in nothing but black boxers. My face heats a million degrees. Though, they do look like swim trunks, and I am probably just being ridiculous. It's just that the only times I have undressed in front of men was forced. Cal must see that on my face because he grabs his jeans from the ground intending on putting them back on.

"No, stop. It's okay, Callon. I appreciate this gesture and would love a swim." I smile a little. "Besides, it's been too long since I have."

He nods his head and turns to walk to the riverside, leaving me some privacy to undress. I make quick work getting the sweaty clothes off and follow the direction Cal weaved through the rocks. I watch as he wades into the water ever so slowly. Sweat beads down his muscular back. He suddenly drops down below the surface. He's gone a few seconds, then reappears a little farther away. He runs his hands through his hair, slicking it back as he stands up. I stare a little too long at the water streaming down his body. His full sleeve tattoo reaches up onto the neck a little and makes me watch to trace each and every piece of it.

When I raise my head, he turns toward me but is not looking into my eyes. He, too, takes in all of me.

His gaze doesn't make me feel as uncomfortable as it should.

Abruptly, he diverts his eyes then sends a wave of water my way with his arms, splashing me in the face.

"Okay, okay…" I yell. "You are going to get it!" I cautiously ease into the water, which is like ice coming off these mountains. "Oh my god, this is soooo cold," I shiver. Goosebumps rise all over me. Just when I am halfway in, I look up, and Cal is gone. I see the water rustling near me a second too late, and next thing I know, he's right in front of me, grasping me around the waist and pulling me under.

Time seems to stand still for those few seconds. I should feel the sting of the freezing water, but I don't. I'm painfully aware of the strong arms wrapped around me.

I take in a huge breath as soon as my head pops out of the water and feel his arms release. "Cal! UGHHH," I grumble, which he finds immensely hilarious.

"There's only one way to get used to it and that's by jumping in," he says as he slinks down to where only his head is showing and swims a bit away from me.

With a huff of exasperation, I, too, dip down and submerge myself in the icy depths. Within a few minutes, I am over the cold. It begins to feel marvelous compared to the sticky heat of the atmosphere. I side-glance over at Cal who is watching me intently. His smile is so infectious, and his eyes take on a deeper blue against the color of the river.

I think back to our conversation the day after I ran away as we hiked back to the cabin. He had asked about my boyfriend, and I asked if he had anyone. He joked and laughed it off at the time, but now it worries my brow. He doesn't look like the type to be single. If I'm being honest with myself, he is breathtakingly handsome. He also doesn't look like a murderer but has openly admitted that part of himself to me, so what do I know, really? For the life of me, I don't know why I think murderers come in ugly packages.

We swim for a bit, splashing and joking before I get up the nerve to pry him for more details on his life.

"You joked before about this, but I've been thinking…that, um…there's no way you haven't had someone special in your life. Did you ever have a special someone?" I ask trying to be loud enough over the waterfall.

He wipes water from his eyes and swims closer. Still, only our heads bob above the water as we ease close to one another. "There was someone. My wife," he says rather tersely.

My mind reels at that proclamation, and my eyes bug out of my head. He has…had a wife. He is young, but lots of people marry young. I have so many questions.

"I see that look in your eyes. Before you get sentimental on me, Maze, just know that we are divorced."

Before he can shut down the conversation I ask, "Do you have children?"

His look turns bitter, and he scoffs. "No, although I did want kids…she didn't." He clears his throat, turning to swim toward the edge of the waterfall. He says over his shoulder, "Come here. Let me show you something."

I let him distract from my questions. "There's more than this?" I gesture to the waterfall above.

He waves me over. As I am right near his back, he points to the side of the falls. I see what looks to be a ledge that travels behind it. "Is that what I think it is?" I say with pure excitement. "Can we go behind it?"

"Yes, we can and will." He beams.

We climb out of the river, and Cal grabs his bag before we make our way to the edge of the falls. The mist is a cloud the closer we get. It feels like we are being kissed by the river. We slip behind the falls. On one side of us is smooth-faced stone, and on the other is a wall of water. "This is magical," I say in awe.

Cal sits on a flat rock and pats the spot next to him. It's even louder under here, so we speak up to hear each other. He surprises me by continuing the conversation from before.

"Her name was Brianna…my ex-wife," he begins. His eyes take on a far-off look to them. He must relive things, too, the way I do. "I met her within the first six months of being stationed at Hunter Army Airfield in Georgia. She worked at a local commissary. She was going to school to be a nurse. I guess, in a way, that made me think she was a good person like my mother. A nurse must be good, right?" His jaw clinches, "We were married one year after we met, and she cheated on me within four months of marriage…with one of the guys in my squad." He rustles around in his bag and pulls out sandwiches and water. Handing me some, he says, "Not exactly the sweet romance you envisioned, huh?"

I am dumbfounded trying to imagine what kind of woman could do that to her husband. Another small piece of the Callon puzzle comes into place. I try to lighten the mood a touch. "Definitely not a Kyle Reese and Sarah

Connor kind of love," I say with the most serious face I can muster.

He almost chokes on his bite of sandwich and starts horse laughing. "No. It was more like fatal attraction."

Now we are both laughing aloud so hard tears escape my eyes.

He looks at my tears and shakes his head in awe. "You know…it has been a long time since I have seen someone laugh til' they cry."

"I don't remember the last time I did," I admit. "But I used to do it all the time. Sometimes, it was at the most inappropriate times. Like at a funeral! And once I start…it is so hard to stop." I wipe at my face and try to contain my giggles.

Cal appraises me, "I will make this a personal goal of mine to make sure it happens more often." He motions to the food, and we help ourselves to apples and cheese squares.

I don't know what I did to deserve a second chance in life or what I did to be lucky enough to have met Callon Wolfe, but right now, I'm very thankful.

While we eat, I try to get him to talk about tomorrow. What in the world has he planned for my birthday? It's not like we can waltz into town and have a party. He refuses to tell me anything and the suspense is killing me.

I shiver a little as the mist still sprinkles us. Next thing I know, Callon pulls a blanket from his pack and gently wraps it around my shoulders. He moves intentionally slowly as his fingers linger on my arm.

And now I am shivering for a whole new reason.

Callon leans closer to me, tugging the blanket tighter and says, "You never flinch from my touch anymore." He states. "Does that mean you trust me?"

"I trust you Callon," I say. His face is dangerously close to mine, and it looks like longing in his eyes.

That can't be right.

Suddenly there is thunder rolling in the distance. The brief moment is gone and we back away from each other. Cal looks toward the clouds, "We should get dressed and start heading back."

"What if we get caught in the middle of it?" I ask.

"Don't worry…it's not the first storm we've weathered together, remember…and it won't be our last."

His words hold so much weight to them, but he is right. This is not our first storm, figuratively or literally.

CHAPTER 12

I feel like a child at Christmas as I impatiently wait for Cal to reveal what he has planned. It's my birthday…I am twenty-one years old. I somehow feel so much older.

Today, I'm in my usual black jeans and combat boots. I put on a burgundy fitted tee and let my waves freefall down my back. I stare at myself in the mirror, and it is like my mother is looking back at me. Other than the green eyes I got from dad, I'm a close version of her. It is like having a piece of each of them with me always.

A grin forms when I remember my last birthday with them when I turned nineteen. I made sure they didn't make a fuss. I wanted a party in the backyard with just Thomas and Anna and two other girls, Kelsa, and Mindy, who were mutual friends of Anna's and mine.

Thomas and I were close but still not dating then. Dad put up a huge projection screen out back, and we watched scary movies that night, stuffing our faces with junk food. It was perfect. One of the gifts Mom and Dad gave me was that silver dove necklace that Tony ripped from my throat.

My mood begins to darken considerably. Effectively ruining my good memory with a tarnished one.

I spent my twentieth birthday in captivity at the hands of monsters. The memory is still quite vivid.

I'm not drugged this evening, which is unexpected, considering that's how my days typically end. I lay on the bed looking at the bare walls. I know where I am now. Not the location, but whose house this is. Jacob Rainer. I met this man before and have seen him on several outings with my family. Notably at the governor's ball a few months back. I am not certain yet, but I think that has something to do with my being here.

I've been here around a week, but I'm not really sure. I scratch tallies on the wall by the closet, but some days are a blur. I've begged, pleaded, and cried for help. Trying to find out if my parents are alive only gets me punished. They never touch my face. Which I guess I'm a little thankful for. I don't know what the end game is here. If they wanted to rape me, they would have by now. Other than the first time I was drugged and made to stand naked for those screens, they have left me alone. Another blessing, I guess. My face stays swollen from tears; the real sobbing happens at night. It's hard to be alone with your imagination.

Suddenly, I hear footsteps headed toward my room. I immediately sit up and look at the ground. This is what I was told to do when anyone enters my room.

The door creaks open.

I refrain from lifting my head. Tremors slowly rack my body. A hand grasps my chin, lifting it, and I'm face to face with Jacob himself. Last I saw him, he was tapping a gun against his head in warning. Up close, he looks to be mid-fifties or early sixties, medium build, with short cut sandy blonde hair combed to one side and dull hazel eyes with gold-rimmed glasses.

"You recognize me…I can tell." His hand moves from my chin to caress my neck.

I flinch my head backward, and he grasps my neck with his hand, squeezing enough to make me stay still while allowing me to breathe. When I try to grab his hands with my own, he subtly shakes his head. In fear, I drop my hands to my sides.

He continues with one hand on my neck and the other trailing from my face downward. "As I was saying…you recognize me. That is good, no need for pleasantries then. You are exquisitely beautiful. How did your old man keep you away from the boys for so long, huh? Keep you pure…"

His meaning hits me and makes me want to gag. How would anyone know that I'm a virgin?

"You know I have had my eyes on you for some time. Just waiting for the perfect moment to pounce. You are going to be worth a fortune." He pushes the edge of my tank top down with his free hand and grasps my breast. "What's going to be hard for me is me keeping you pure…" His hand travels from my breast downward, eliciting a whimper from me, which only spurs him on. He tightens his grip on my neck and pushes his fingers into my panties, letting his fingers cup me. "This right here…I wish I could keep to myself," he whispers in a raspy voice.

Tears are streaming down my face onto his hand. He looks at them with disgust and lets me go, removing his hands. Backing away, he places his hand to his mouth and licks the area that touched me, moaning aloud. "Mmmmm, the ripest of fruits. I want to make something very clear to you. At any point, if you fail to be a profit, you become disposable. Don't try to be clever; don't try to run. You are NOT the first and WON'T be the last to grace these halls. So, be a good girl. Do you understand, Maisy?"

I absently nod my head as I struggle to hold back the bile in my throat.

There is a knock on the bedroom door and then it opens, pulling me from my purgatory.

"Maisy, are you ready?" Cal asks, and I glance his way and do a double take. He shaved his beard off, and his hair is slicked back away from his face. My eyes grow round as they trail down to his attire. I slap a hand over my mouth to stop the giggle threatening to release.

"Wow, so… are we going to a rodeo? I have to say, I didn't peg you as the cowboy type." I say in my best, but also terrible, country accent.

Cal is wearing Wrangler jeans with brown cowboy boots and a western snap button shirt with horses galloping across the front. In his hand he holds a Stetson hat. My eyes slowly trail back up to his face, which at the moment is giving me murderous vibes.

"HA, HA, HA, go on, get it out of your system because you are next." He smirks.

I bite my lip and arch my eyebrow at him and ask, "What, exactly, do you have in mind cowboy?"

Thirty minutes later, I am scrutinizing myself in the bathroom mirror, curling my lip as I do. I took off everything I had just put on and dressed in what Cal left for me. I'm wearing a black wrangler skirt with a jean snap button top that I am sure came from the eighties, black cowgirl boots, and a black hat. I sneer at myself in the mirror. The worst part is the blond bobbed wig. I have a ton of hair to get under this thing.

I braid my hair close to the scalp and twist it in tiny balls at the base of my neck in order to get the wig on. Once on, I adjust it in the front and put on the cowboy hat. About that time Cal knocks on the bedroom door before entering. I can feel his amusement.

"Really Cal! This is the best you could do for a disguise?"

His cheek pulls into a half smile as he trails his gaze over me. "I think this suits you Miss Maisy."

"Ugh, go chew on some hay and leave me be." I hear his chuckle behind me as I sigh, looking at myself one last time in the mirror. "Is this *absolutely* necessary? What if they no longer care where I am? What if no one is looking for me anymore?"

"Trust me, people are looking for you. The police department is continuing the investigation based on the paper I read. The local TV station still reports on the case and even some national ones."

I nod and purse my lips, looking down at my alter ego for the day. "Do we get new names for the new looks?" I give him a lopsided grin.

"I like that. How about I pick yours, and you pick mine?" He gives me a side smile that makes heat come to my cheeks.

Now that I'm facing him, I find it hard to look away. The cowboy hat is hung low on his head and those eyes gleam underneath. His strong jaw line is accentuated now without the beard.

I avert my eyes and say, "I'm going to regret this decision, but okay…" I rub my chin dramatically, "I think you look like a Billy Bob."

"Billy Bob, are you serious?"

"Highly serious." I give him a smug look.

"Fair is fair. You look like a…Debbie."

My eyes widen. "Debbie? I don't look like a Debbie." I glance at myself one last time in the mirror. "Okay, never mind," I mutter under my breath.

Cal turns to walk out. "You pick mine; I pick yours remember? Lets go, Debbie!"

"What an insufferable pig," I mumble as I follow him out.

"Heard that," he yells back.

We hike to where Cal keeps his truck. I am smiling from ear to ear. The anticipation of leaving these woods is exhilarating. While I have appreciated everything Callon has been doing for me, I am ready for some normalcy.

My eyes keep wandering to Callon of their own volition. I don't fail to notice how well he pulls off the Wranglers and cowboy hat. I now understand why women love brown patch Wrangler jeans.

We eventually come across a dirt road path which, most certainly, leads to a main road. I realize, with embarrassment, how close we are to the truck from the cabin. It was a fifteen-minute walk at worst. I had no idea where I was going the day I ran.

"We were this close the whole time. Why didn't you tell me how off my trajectory was?"

"You weren't off by much," Cal concedes to my shock. "There are two ways to enter this mountain area. Most hunters come this way and park out closer to the road. Hikers and sightseers come in from the opposite side, where there's a protected forest with trails designated for hikes, not hunting. You were headed in the right direction…and you were correct in thinking we are not far from Boone. You were just taking the long way out."

Once we reach it, I hop into the truck, still thinking about the day I jumped out of Callon's window.

I was right! Which means not only are we *not* too far from a town, but we are also not far from Jacob. What if I had succeeded that night and found my way out of the forest? Would I have found refuge, or something sinister waiting for me?

Cal is quiet as we jostle our way down the dirt road. I was never into trucks before, but I have to admit, there is something about this Silverado. It's a deep blue with larger than normal tires. The seat is one long bench seat. The radio is on low playing some 80's country song. It suits Callon.

"How long have you had this truck?" I ask looking out through the dense forest.

"My dad got it for me when I turned 16. I couldn't believe it. It's an 82' model. It was almost new at the time."

"I like it. It suits you." I glance his way and a tiny smile forms before he looks back at the dirt road.

I wonder what Callon was like as a teenager—what he was like before life dealt us both dirty hands.

Within fifteen minutes, we are out of the woods and on the main highway. My nerves start to get the better of me. I wring my hands together nervously. What if someone recognizes me? What if they recognize Cal? And then another thought hits me.

"What if we get pulled over? The cops would run the plates, right?" I ask quickly.

He glances at me, seeing the trepidation written all over my face. "You don't have to worry about that. This truck *is* mine. However, I had it put in someone else's name for the time being. You remember the friend I was telling you about, Bo?" I nod, and he continues, "He is somewhat of a genius. He was military intelligence for years, but before that, he was just a 'techy' guy. He came from a family of delinquents." He pauses and grins then says, "One of his specialties was fake IDs and forged documents. This truck is in the name of Henry Gates. The ID that I have matches the registration information and has my photo on it."

I look out the window, biting my lower lip. Hearing that does make me feel a bit better. However, it doesn't completely ease the worry from my shoulders. "Why Henry Gates?" I ask, "I mean, how does he pick names when Bo's creating new identities?"

Cal laughs. "Bo used Henry Gates because that is Bill Gates's middle name. His full name is William Henry Gates. Bo is a little obsessed with some of his work. He just reversed the first and middle name for the docs."

"The mysterious Bo seems like quite the character."

Cal's smile fades slightly as he watches the road. He glances my way briefly, "Oh, he is…he will do this for you one day, you know. You will get a new identity."

Why, I wonder, does this make his smile fade? I must be a burden dropped straight into his lap. It should be a relief when I am gone.

We ride for what seems like forever, but as we go, my scenery changes to familiar. We are close to my hometown of Spruce Pine, North Carolina. Cal stops one town over at a Mexican restaurant. I am beaming when he parks the truck.

"Your favorite food is Mexican, right?" he asks.

I could die of glee right now. "Heck yeah!" I say as I scramble out of the truck. His chuckle follows behind me.

"It's hell yeah, Maisy…HELL." He laughs. "And this is just the first stop, not the main one. We have one more place to go later."

Now my interest has peaked. "Mexican food has already won me over, but if you insist…we can go somewhere after." I joke as we head to the large antique double doors intricately painted with exotic birds everywhere. Cal just grins and stops me before I get to the handle.

He gives me a wink as he opens the door for me. "I was going to hold the truck door for you, but you scrambled out so fast."

"And they say chivalry is dead." I give him my best cheeky grin.

Like most Mexican restaurants, this one is very vibrant and full of life. Hand painted Colorful booths line the walls and, the waiters and servers are bustling about. An older waiter with a sweet cherub face comes to greet us and take our orders. His eyes crinkle as he smiles at me admiringly.

"Hola," I say.

"Hola senorita, qué puedo conseguir para la bella dama?"

"Quisiera tamales por favor y—Cal, what would you like?" I ask, turning to face him.

His mouth is slightly open with a flabbergasted look on his face. "I will have the tacos with sour cream and a Draft Miller Lite."

"El quiere tacos con un draft Miller Lite por favor," I finish.

"Y a beber querida," the waiter asks me what I will have to drink, and I don't fail to notice the pink tint to his deep tanned cheeks.

"El aqua esta bien," I order my water and continue mowing down chips. All the while, Cal is studying me with squinted eyes.

"So, you speak Spanish?" he states.

"I do. It's not perfect, but I am fluent enough to get by." He is still eyeballing me, so I continue. "I traveled often and studied languages some when I was home-schooled."

"That's impressive, Debbie. I was not expecting that." He winks. I roll my eyes in return. "I was going to order you a margarita if you'd like one," he adds.

I would love to try one, I think to myself, but… "I don't have an ID, remember? What if they card me?"

"I think that fella taking our orders is smitten with you. I'm pretty sure he would give you the shirt off his back."

I nibble my lip, grinning. "I think you are right…Okay, what the heck." I wave the waiter down as he passes and order a large margarita. The waiter never asks for ID, thankfully and it's not like I'm breaking the law. I am, in fact, twenty-one. I can't help the fact that I am technically a missing person, who's hiding out in plain sight.

The waiter sits the drink down in front of me a few minutes later with a big toothy smile for me before he walks away.

"This thing is enormous!" Cal watches me as I take my first sip, awaiting my reaction. "Oh my god! This is *amazing*."

He gives me a grin. "It is more fun than it should be just watching you be yourself, Maze."

My face heats at the statement.

Cal's clear blue eyes travel to my cheeks and that side smile is back making it hard to breath. What is wrong with me? It seems the more time we spend together, the harder it is to be around him. Shouldn't it get easier? Why does he affect me so?

After we finish our meal, we slink into the truck with our tummies truly sated. I feel more relaxed than I have in a long time, probably due to the margarita.

Cal scoots across the bench seat and reaches for my hand. I don't pull away from him any longer. I know now, deep down, he could never hurt me. Something in me decided that some time ago, I was just unable to admit it to myself.

His large hand envelopes mine. Then, with his other hand, he pulls out a tiny box and places it in my palm.

"It's not much, but I wanted to make sure you had something on your birthday." He clears his throat. "Everyone should have something on their birthday."

I hold this tiny gift as if it is the most delicate thing in the universe. I gingerly open it and I gasp softly. Inside is a gold necklace and pendant. The pendant is a phoenix bird in flight. It's an intricate design with a ruby for the eye. The confusion and shock must be evident on my face.

"Do you like it?" he asks in his deep low tone.

I am speechless as I rub the pendant between my fingers. I finally find my words. "It's stunning, but you didn't have to do this. I am no one to you. You owe me nothing," I whisper.

Cal looks out the windshield and I notice his eyes are distant. Where did he go just now?

"I owe you everything, Maisy."

His words are decidedly confusing me even more. What could he possibly owe me?

"No, Callon...you owe me nothing. You have done more than most people would ever consider for a stranger." I squeeze his hand gently. "But thank you, it really is perfect." I hold it up, examining every detail, down to the swirling feathery tail. "Why a phoenix?"

His thumb begins slow circles along my other hand that is still resting in his. I could have moved my hand from his, but I didn't. Goosebumps spread up my arm.

"To be quite honest...your story about the necklace you had bothered me."

My brow creases. "My dove necklace. Why?"

"Your parents bought that for you, and I can tell it meant something. When you told me what happened the night you escaped, and Tony ripped it from you after hurting you like he did…I wanted to kill him right then and there. What bothered me most was them calling you little bird. You may have been a sheltered girl when you entered that life, but you are no longer a dove, Maisy. You are a phoenix. The old you has burned away, and something magnificent remains. Someone stronger."

Tears burn my eyes as I shift uncomfortably in the seat. Cal put a lot of thought into his gift. I turn my head so that he doesn't see the silent tear dripping onto my cheek, but he gently grabs my chin, making me face him. We are only inches apart. My emotions are all over the place after hearing his words.

He gently wipes the tear away with his thumb. "You are a wonderful person who deserves more than this shit world has to offer. Please don't ever forget that."

This close to him, I lose my ability to articulate. The depth of his eyes are captivating. There is something honest in them. His hand moves slowly to caress my cheek. My mind is fuddled a bit by the stout drink, but I don't care. There is a spark between us that is undeniable. I have tried so hard to ignore it. I thought, after everything my body has been through at the hands of men, that I would never want to be touched again. It's comforting to know that my body also has good sense and knows the difference between good and evil.

I don't know what this man has done, but I trust him with my life. He has kept me safe these last few weeks and he didn't have to.

The last thing either of us needs is something that may derail our plans. My body ignores my brain as I lean into Callon until we are a hairsbreadth away. My eyes travel to his strong jaw and then to his lips. I want to know what they taste like.

Suddenly, his hand leaves my cheek, and he scoots back to his position behind the wheel, leaving me to gather myself. I feel cold. Like he took all the heat with him. I can see his chest rise and fall a little too quickly. A clear indication that he is equally as flustered as I am.

So, what is he thinking? I wish I knew.

"I'm sorry, I shouldn't…I just shouldn't," he stammers.

Maybe I have everything wrong. or maybe I don't really know him.

I mask the hurt on my face, best I can, then say, "It's okay. Really. It's probably just the drinks." I nudge his shoulder, trying to make light of the awkward situation. "The necklace is perfect. Thank you."

He smiles, but it doesn't quite reach his eyes. "You are very welcome." He leans in one more time, taking the necklace from my hands. I turn so that he can latch it. His fingers brush my neck briefly, sending a shiver down my spine.

The moment is over when he puts on his cowboy hat and tips it down in front with dramatic flair. I can tell he is purposely changing the subject. Then he says in his best John Wayne voice, "Well, partner…if you liked the first part of the night, you gonna love the second!"

Glad for the topic change, I pepper him with questions. "What is it? Where are we going?"

"Hold your horses, missy, it's a surprise."

An hour later, we pulled up, dust flying around the Silverado, in front of a large barn-style building. There's a massive rearing horse statue on the outside of the parking lot, and the neon sign across the building's loft says The Stampede. I can hear a band playing and the distinct sound of a steel guitar.

My brows furrow. "You brought me to a country music bar?"

"Don't sound so enthusiastic…and it's more of a Honky Tonk, really. I figured we should keep in character. I thought you liked country music."

"I do, I love it, actually. I just didn't realize you liked it this much."

Cal gives me a side smile and winks, saying, "You don't know everything about me, Miss Debbie." My eyes roll back dramatically.

Cars pack the dirt parking lot, and it gives me pause.

"This is a large group of people; won't someone notice us?"

"The good thing about this place is, it's a bar…people are drunk." He says reassuringly. When he sees my worried look he says, "With our disguises and the amount of alcohol around, I'm sure we will be fine, But NO talking to anyone. Just stick with me."

I nod, but his words do nothing to calm my nerves.

Inside, the place is way bigger than it looks. Straight ahead is an old wooden stage, and to my right and left are resin oak bars lining the walls with saddles replacing the stool seats. Scantily clad baristas are slinging beers and pouring shots. The entire perimeter of the stage is reserved for dancers. Above us is a loft with tables so people can look over the dance floor. The band is playing a Brooks and Dunn tune, and cowboys are spinning cowgirls every which way.

I smile so big I feel my face could split.

I LOVE IT!

It gives me the eighties movie feels. I am smiling from ear to ear when I feel Callon's eyes on me. It is unnerving how my senses just know when he is looking. I pretend not to notice.

"You like it…I can tell."

I shrug as if it's not a big deal, "It's okay, I guess."

"Uh huh," Cal laughs as he grabs my hand and leads me to the bar. I try to ignore that I can feel every cell of his being in that hand.

He orders us two shots of Jack Daniels, and we both throw them back at the same time. He almost spits his out, laughing at my face when the whiskey hits my mouth.

"Wow, does any of this stuff ever taste good?" I groan.

"Nope…but it will make you feel good." He orders two more with two beers and we toss back the shots. Then he leans into me, saying, "Can I have a dance later?"

I feel timid all of a sudden, but then I stare a little too long into those eyes and simply nod my head. Quickly, I look away and change the subject. "What made you choose this place?" I ask, still trying to gain composure from the double shots and being asked to dance. It's like a sensory overload for me, having not been around people in so long.

"I traveled so much in the service that I missed out on the good years when there was a Honky Tonk in every town. They're dying out now. That's why I brought you here, plus I doubted a room full of drunks would recognize us."

"Good thinking." I scan the room, and he's right. No one is paying us any attention. "I was not expecting this but thank you. I do like it." I am quiet for a beat lost in the music when Cal interrupts my thoughts.

"What has given you the far-off gaze?"

I take a sip of the beer and debate telling him, but his genuine smile wins me over. "The sound of the steel guitar playing brings me back to some childhood memories of when my grandparents were still around. My mom's dad used to sit on the porch and play guitar or banjo while my grandmother and mom would sing. I lost all my grandparents relatively young. They were older than most when they had kids."

"Mine were gone too soon also," he adds, "We grew up poor, but I would have never known. They made sure I always had what I needed and what mattered."

That statement tugs at my heartstrings. We quite literally grew up of opposite sides of the tracks, but that doesn't seem to change the fact that we both had good families.

And now they are gone…we have that in common.

We hang out at the bar for over an hour, talking about our childhood. We both kept the conversation light. Callon has that rule of not having serious conversations when drinking.

As we are ordering a couple beers, a woman sashays past us wearing tight-fitting jeans and a pink halter top. Her long blonde hair is curled loosely and flowing around her. She's beautiful, but that's *not* why I notice her. She is checking out Callon unabashedly. Her eyes travel to his rear, and suddenly, I regret these outfit choices entirely.

"I think you have an admirer…Billy Bob." I say, trying to sound nonchalant.

"Oh really, who might that be?" he asks as he scans the room.

The woman has passed us by and now leans against the railing surrounding the dance floor, stealing glances our way.

"Over there by the dance floor, the girl in pink with all the blonde hair."

Callon turns to see her staring back at him. "I guess I've still got it." He grins and winks at me.

"You have something all right," I mumble as I sip the beer.

"Is that jealousy I hear in your tone, Debbie? Surely, I must be mistaken, right?" He goads me.

My face burns. How dare he! I am not *jealous*. To prove the point, I say, "Ew, no! Not jealous. *In fact*, you should go ask her to dance. She looks like the type that would be into delinquents," I smirk.

Cal leans into me until our noses are a scant few inches apart. I can smell the whiskey on his breath, and it only adds to the manly scent of him. What is wrong with me?!

Then he whispers, "Maybe I will."

My mouth drops open as he pushes off the bar and makes his way over to the blonde. I sit up straighter with my shoulders back. I want to slap myself for running my mouth. Why do I even care!

As he gets closer to her, she flips her hair and beams a brilliant smile at him. My hackles rise, and I don't know why. He is a grown man, that I barely know, who can do whatever he wants. I turn back to the bar and try to ignore the ice in my veins. What is my problem? What is *his* problem! We are supposed to be keeping a low profile. What happened to not talking to anyone? I order another shot and toss it back while I'm brooding and stealing glances their way. The moment Callon catches me looking his lips pull back in a smirk, and I want to throw a beer at him.

Suddenly, I feel a presence beside me, and as I look to my right, I am facing a broad chest. I have to lean my head back to see the man towering over me with a lopsided grin on his face. He is good-looking, no doubt, with black hair and even darker eyes. His demeanor, however, is intimidating. And he definitely doesn't understand personal space.

"Would you like to dance?" His deep voice rattles out as his eyes swoop down the length of my body.

The first thing I do is glance toward Callon, who is currently looking our way as if he may murder us both.

Now this…this I can work with. Eye for an eye and all.

"Yes, I think I would like to dance." I take his hand, and it swallows mine whole as he pulls me to the dance floor. As we pass Callon, I arch an eyebrow and give him the same smirk he gave me. I see him lick his lips and then bite his lower lip, nodding.

This can't be good. What was I thinking? We are supposed to keep a low profile, and here I am, being a floozy with the first person to ask me to dance. Well second, if you count Cal.

Big guy pulls me to where I am facing him and leads us in a slow dance. "What's your name?" His voice reverberates against my chest.

"Uhh…Debbie."

"I'm Brad."

"Nice to meet you, Brad." I scan the floor for Callon, but he is nowhere to be seen.

"Are you looking for that guy I saw you with at the bar?" His eyes bore into mine.

"No…I mean, yes, we did come together, but we aren't *together*."

"That's good to know, Debbie." His eyes trail to my lips, and I look away quickly. "I've never seen you here before…you from around here?"

"Uhhhh, no, I'm from…South Carolina," I lie.

"I didn't think so. I would have recognized someone like you. His hand is ever so slowly sliding down my back, and as I am about to move away, Callon is suddenly there at my side, lips pressed into a thin line, and I see his jaw flex.

"Can I cut in?" Cal growls out.

"No, you cannot cut in. Debbie and I were just getting acquainted." Brad spins me so that my back is to Callon.

Cal casually steps to the side of us and looks into my eyes, "I'll have that dance now."

"Back off!" Brad snaps at Callon. He lets go of me to face him fully.

"Woah! No, no…this is not happening right now. Both of you knock it off!" I berate them.

Brad's large hand clasps onto my arm and pulls me roughly behind him as he leans into Cal's face. "I said back the fuck off, she's going home with me tonight."

My mouths drops open at Brad's words and his grip on my arm.

Cal calmly looks at my arm being squeezed by Brad's hand and removes his Cowboy hat.

The next thing I know, he slams his head into Brad's face. I hear the crunch of bone when his nose breaks. Brad lets me go, falling to his knees as he cradles his blood-soaked face.

Before I can even pick my jaw up off the floor, Cal has my hand in his and we are sprinting for the door.

I can hear a bouncer yelling from behind us, but we are plenty ahead of the commotion. We both slide into the truck at the same time, and Cal throws it in reverse slinging the truck around and peals out of the parking lot, leaving everyone in a cloud of dust.

Adrenaline pumps through my veins as we create distance between us and the bar. My chest rises and falls as I try to catch my breath.

"What is wrong with you, Callon? We could have been recognized! What if we got arrested!"

"What is wrong with me? What is wrong with you, Maisy? You picked the biggest asshole in the whole damn place to throw yourself at!"

"How dare you! I didn't throw myself at anyone. He asked me to dance, and I said yes! What does it matter to you anyway? You were over there flirting with the blonde bimbo!"

He gives a fake sinister laugh.

I pierce his soul with my eyes. "What? What is so funny?"

"Girls don't call other girls names unless they are jealous...are jealous Maze?"

My eyes widen and my mouth hangs open. What an absolutely ridiculous thing to say. Then my mouth closes and I give him a smug look. "If that makes me jealous then you must be too...you called him an a-hole."

Callon takes his eyes off the road for a second, and they lock with mine, and I see it clearly then.

Maybe we were both jealous.

It is absurd. We barely know each other. Two lonely people thrust together in strange and unusual circumstances are bound to form connections…right? I'm sure it doesn't mean anything.

Callon has tried so hard to make today special and here we are bickering over nonsense. My shoulders slump and the fight leaks out of me.

"I'm sorry, I shouldn't have provoked you." I admit.

"I provoked you first, so I guess we are even."

We stay quiet for a while until Cal pulls us over, parking at a 7/11. I can see tension in the way he moves. "Wanna come in with me; get some snacks."

"Sure." I slide out of the truck and follow him in.

We mosey around the store, picking out an unhealthy amount of snacks and a six-pack of beer. After Cal pays, we exit the store, making our way to the truck. I am looking down and not paying attention when I bump into a girl.

"I'm so sorr…" I pause, looking over my shoulder. My throat seems to clog. My heart speeds up.

The girl I bumped into pays it no mind, saying, "No worries, babe," as she keeps walking hand in hand with a guy toward a store. I'd know that voice anywhere. There was only one person that I knew that called every girl babe. I know that red hair and peppy walk. I know the tall blonde guy next to her, too. His boyish features.

It's Anna and Thomas.

Cal grips my arm, forcing me to move faster to the truck. "Do not stare. Do not look back at them," he commands in a whisper.

We bound into the truck. I don't realize I'm crying until Cal grabs me, pulling me into his chest.

"I could tell you knew them, but who are they to you?"

"Anna and Thomas," my voice is muffled against his shirt.

"The friend and the *boyfriend* you've told me about. Huh…would you like me to kick his ass? I will, you know."

A giggle escapes through my tears, and I move out of Cal's arms. He has a natural gift of making me laugh, even in bad situations.

He hands me a napkin to dry my face. "I wasn't in love with him or anything…but it is still hard to see that *not only* have they moved on, but they moved on together. I feel ashamed for even thinking about it. They have every right to move on with their lives."

"Maisy, you also have every right to feel pissed off, to feel sad or betrayed in some way. You missed out on dates like that and nights out with friends for a year. Even longer now. Cry, scream, do whatever the hell gets the feelings out, but don't feel ashamed." He tips my chin up forcing me to look at him. "You sure you don't want me to kick his ass?"

I try to cover my smile with the napkin, "No, I'm good. I am already going to have to ice your head from the last one."

Cal rubs his head and flinches, "I'm really sorry I ruined your birthday night out."

Is he serious right now? "Ruined? Are you kidding me? That was the best birthday I've ever had."

His brows furrow. "You really need to get out more, then." This has us both hoarse laughing.

"You are probably right."

Once we are back in the cabin, I pull the wig from my hair, begin undoing the braids, and kick off the cowboy boots. Cal seems to feel the same. He has already removed his boots, too.

"You want one more beer before we call it a night," he asks, holding out a cold one.

"Yeah, sounds good." I was tipsy when we left the bar, but all the adrenaline must have burned some of it off. I take the beer and follow Cal to the porch, where we sit in the rocking chairs.

The night is warm, but a cool breeze blows by every now and again, ruffling my hair. It feels glorious. I lean my head back and enjoy the sound of crickets and rustling trees.

Cal takes a sip of his beer and says, "Are you sure I can't make it up to you for the bar thing?"

"No, I meant what I said?" I laugh. "It was the most epic birthday ever. I could never repay you." Cal's brows raise in surprise, and I turn my body in the rocking chair so that we face one another and continue, "Well, let's see. I had my favorite food with my first ever margarita, a wonderful gift, my first time in a Honky Tonk, and my first time having two men brawl over me, eighties style."

"What do you mean, eighties style?" Cal is trying to contain his laughter but failing miserably.

"You know the kind. Those cheesy eighties movies where the guy and girl fight falling for each other, but when another guy comes around, he fights for the honor." I blush immediately when I realize what I insinuated; that he and I may be falling for each other.

He stares at me with hooded eyes, and heat blooms in my face and pools low in my body. Why did I say that?

I quickly stand up, faking a yawn. I need to get away from him before the alcohol in me says more garbage. Cal stands abruptly, too.

"Are you headed to bed?" Cal asks.

"Yeah, I think I have had enough excitement for one day." It feels like an invisible thread holding me in place. I don't know what makes me do it, but I lift onto my tiptoes and softly kiss his cheek.

When I move away, I can see a war raging behind those eyes, but he just says, "Sweet dreams, Maze," as I back away.

That night, I slept without nightmares.

CHAPTER 13

The pistol no longer feels heavy in my hands. My grip gets stronger each day. I've been here eight weeks now, and for the last two weeks, Cal has been educating me on everything guns. It's late in the evening when we are finishing target practice.

Ever since my birthday, things have changed between us. Grown. We are more accustomed to living together. It has become a balance of give and take with each of us contributing to the housework and fishing. I leave the hunting to him. Not sure that I could shoot Bambi. Somewhere along the way, a friendship developed. I feel comfortable with him…safe.

The skittish girl that he brought to the cabin no longer exists. I feel an ease around him that I can't explain.

"Hold steady like I showed you," Cal's voice comes from behind me. "Now aim for the target in the back first and work your way forward this time."

Cal made a shooting range in the woods from poster board, cast iron pans and cut-out wooden targets. He taught me how to use everything from shotguns and rifles to pistols. He insisted I continue to work with this specific pistol. It's a Glock 17 9mm. He says it's reliable, and I don't doubt him. It hasn't jammed even once, and the aim is spot on.

The cool metal feels good in my hands as I line up for my first target.

The shot pierces the sky when I squeeze the trigger and I can hear the satisfying tings as I get to the cast iron pans. The feeling is euphoric when the gun goes off, vibrating through me. Never stopping, I line up and continue until all seventeen rounds are spent.

"Whewwww," Cal half whistles. "That may be your best yet, Maze," Cal says as he slaps me on the back. "You are badass."

I feel my face blush, which seems to be a normal response anymore. "I don't know about that." I rack the Glock back making sure all rounds were spent before laying it aside. He immediately picks up the pistol, looking it over.

"What is it?" I ask.

"I want you to have it," he hands it back to me. "That's why I've been making you practice with this one so much. I want you to feel like you can protect yourself once you leave here. Living on your own can be scary, especially in another country."

I run my fingers along the barrel of the gun. Once I leave…what will I even do on my own?

"This means a lot. Not just the gun, but all the time you've spent helping me when you didn't have to, so thank you."

My mind tries to picture what the future looks like but fails. Where will I be? *Who* will I be? We originally agreed on no more than six months. However, we both can see that time is moving fast. I still have so many unanswered questions. The desire for vengeance has begun to outweigh the desire for freedom. Cal keeps assuring me that all will work out in the end, but I have this sick feeling in my gut that I can't shake.

"What will you name it…your first gun?" Cal says, pulling me from my thoughts. His eyes are the lightest blue today with the sun shining so brightly against them.

I raise one eyebrow, saying, "I was unaware that it needed a name. Is that a thing?"

"Guns, cars, trucks…if they are good ones, they deserve names."

This makes me think of Mom's car, and I grin. "My mom's car was named Jovi. You can guess who she had the hots for." That brings a crooked smile to his face. "What do you call your truck?"

"Her name is Blue," he says with pride.

"Just Blue…"

"Yes, just Blue! Nice and simple! What are you going to call the gun?" he asks again.

"Hummm…how about *Debbie*."

Cal burst out laughing. "Debbie it is then." He picks up the gun and checks to make sure there are no bullets and then hands it back to me. "I want you to point the gun at me."

"What? I'm not doing that!" I scoff at him and shake my head.

"I'm going to show you a quick way to disarm an assailant. Do it, point the gun at me," he commands.

I huff, but I do as he says, and as soon as the gun tip is pointed at the center of his chest, he snaps one hand against my wrist and another against the gun, moving in opposite directions.

My eyes widen. He took my gun in two seconds! "Wow, show me how to do that, please."

He takes the gun and then steps closer to me, and I can smell sandalwood and mint coming from him. He points the gun at my chest and takes my hands and mimics his movements from before. I'm not sure I can pay attention to anything with him looking like he does today.

"Next, we are going to practice taking her apart. I want you to know everything about this gun inside and out," he says with a wink.

I lose train of thought again when he winks at me. Sweat beads on both our faces and his black tee is plastered to his chest showing every muscle on the way down. I back away a few steps to gain composure while nodding in agreement.

Twenty minutes later, we are sitting cross-legged on the floor of the living room with the gun between us. Cal shows me each part and how to put them together, letting me repeat the process again and again.

"Okay, now let's do this blindfolded," he announces.

"Excuse me…" I gape at him. "You want me to take it apart, put it together, and load it blindfolded?"

"Yes, that's exactly what I want. If you are ever in a situation where it's dark, you'll need to be able to feel your way through."

"Okay, but why would the gun ever be APART to start with?" I grill him.

"The gun probably *wouldn't* be apart, but you are going to know Debbie like the back of your hand, got it?" He dictates, leaving no room for argument. I nod but throw in an eyeroll for dramatic effect.

Cal has me turn around as he places a bandana around my head, blindfolding me. His calloused fingers brush my cheek, causing goosebumps to spread down my body. Once it's tied, I scoot around until we are facing each other again and place my hands flat against the pistol.

"When you pick it up, make sure to keep your fingers away from the trigger and then check the chamber." Cal's voice is low and soothing as he walks me through the process. "Now push down on your side lock lever."

I do as he says, taking extra care to make sure to keep the gun pointing down even though it is unloaded.

"Press the trigger for release, then pull down on both side levers." He must see me trying to locate the levers, so he places his hands on mine. "The slide will move back first, then forward to come completely off. Now, push then pull on this spring." He presses his fingers in tandem with mine, and I feel the spring release. "Now we can slide the barrel out."

He walks me backward through the steps until Debbie is back together with a loaded magazine. Then, he has me repeat the steps without his help.

I slam the magazine in one last time with a victorious smile. I feel to locate the safety, clicking it into place.

Suddenly, Cal's hands slide to my blindfold, and gently, he slides it down. He's closer than I realized and it's hard to breathe when he's this close. It's like he pulls oxygen out of the room. There is so much behind those crystal blue eyes yet to be said.

I wish I could read minds right now.

He has kept his distance lately. I can see him struggle internally with his demons, but I also see him struggle to keep a barrier between us.

An idea hits me all of a sudden. It's something I have thought about before but was too nervous to actually do. That is until the day we wore disguises and went out on the town. If he refuses to tell me more about himself, I will look him up, do my own research.

"How would you feel about another outing maybe… tomorrow?" I ask. "It's been weeks, and I need to see something other than the cabin walls for a day."

"What were you thinking?" He rubs his stubble chin.

"Well, what if we go to the closest library? I could use some more books," and a vacant computer, I think.

He sighs and looks away for a moment. "If we go, you have to wear the wig and *cannot* talk to anyone, okay? Deal."

"Deal." I take his hand in an awkward shake.

If I can't get Cal to completely open up to me, then I will sleuth through the wide web and see what I can find. However, I will need to figure out a way for him to leave me alone long enough to do the search.

The next morning, we head toward the closest library, which happens to be an hour away. I am regretfully pretending to be Debbie again, just not the bar hopping Debbie from last time.

I have on the blonde bob wig without a hat this time with holy jeans a little on the tight side and a white tank top and my back lace up boots. Callon found me a pair of reading glasses the last time he was out so now I sport those with some heavy eye makeup.

If anyone saw me, they definitely wouldn't recognize me.

Callon wears his normal clothing of bootcut jeans and a blue tee but adds a trucker hat and glasses. He is still very recognizable.

His face wavers from scowl to worry. There's clearly something bothering him. "Are you okay?" I ask.

He glances at me, then looks back at the road. "I just have a lot on my mind today."

"Anything you want to talk about?" I ask.

"I worry about you being seen, that's all."

"We went out before, and everything was fine," I say.

"I know, but the meal was secluded, and the bar was full of drunks. This library is in the middle of town during the morning. People will be everywhere living their normal mundane lives, but if you are seen…" he stops, taking in a shuddering breath.

"Look, Cal, if you don't think this is a good idea, we can turn back," I say honestly.

If he is that worried, maybe I should be too.

"We're almost there, and I'll keep a lookout for gawkers. I know you need this," he meets my eyes briefly and I feel guilty for the real motive I have today.

Not long after our conversation we are parked in front of a massive library. The architecture is astounding for a city this small. It's old, but gorgeous and well preserved. It gives me the vibes of a different era.

Cal checks out the surroundings before we enter, then once inside, he winks at me and gives me his best lopsided grin. "Enjoy, Maze, I'll be around." I can tell he is just trying to make me feel better, even though he obviously does not want to be here.

Regardless, I can't help the enthusiasm that must be all over my face. "Ughhhhh, I missed this smell so much," I say as I close my eyes and inhale deeply the worn literature waiting to be explored. I leave Cal to whatever it is he will be doing to keep us safe and unseen.

Whilst the books are calling my name, the real reason we are here is now weighing heavily on my heart. I'm feeling guilty, maybe guiltier than I should considering I deserve answers.

I mosey through isle after isle, showing the pretense of novel hunting. I pick up a few along the way for good measure while keeping an eye out for the computer section. Most of the new, fancier libraries have one, and I am hoping I was right about this one.

Thank you, Bill Gates…or Henry. I giggle, thinking about Cal's bogus ID card.

There, just as I turn the corner, is a computer nook. It's off to itself, and the cubby blocks people from looking over your shoulder. It couldn't be more perfect. I speed over to the cubby and peer around to make sure Cal is nowhere to be seen. I plop into the seat and begin booting up the computer. It takes a bit for the dial-up to get me online, and I nervously tap my fingertips on the desk. I stand again and peer over for one last scan of the area…no Cal.

Finally, I'm online.

I have a sudden, sickly feeling. In one way, this is what I've wanted from day one—an explanation. In another way, I feel I'm betraying the only person who has helped me— The only person that saved me from the horror show I was living.

I take a shaky breath and whisper, "No turning back now."

I type in Maisy Murray first and hesitate for only seconds before I click search.

The first link I see is a nationwide news article with a photo of me. I can feel my heart thumping hard in my chest. This was a photo my mother had taken weeks before it all happened. I'm in a sun dress and sandals, hair curled perfectly and ready for the local craft market. I look young and ridiculous. So absolutely blind to what was about to transpire.

Time is not on my side, so I ignore my thoughts are push on. I skim the article quickly. It is what I expected it to be, a basic recap of the scene. It was released recently and is asking for anyone who knows my whereabouts to come forward.

I roll my eyes.

"I am right here..." I whisper and open a second tab, this time entering Callon Wolfe into the search bar. Immediately, a picture of him in an Army Ranger uniform pops onto the screen. Cal in uniform is a whole other kind of handsome. I appreciate the picture a little longer than necessary. Finally, I pull my eyes from the photo. There are several links, so I click on the first one. Might as well start here.

My breath halts completely. The headline reads, 'Killer Wolfe Still at Large.' I'm not sure what I expected to see or feel, but it wasn't this. I continue reading...

Killer Wolfe Still at Large!

Twenty-six-year-old Callon Wolfe, a former Army Ranger, is still at large. He is thought to have been involved in last year's shooting deaths of senatorial candidate William Murray and his wife, Victoria Murray of Spruce Pine, North Carolina. Their now twenty-one-year-old daughter, Maisy Murray, is still missing and presumed dead. At this time, Detective Sawyer will not discuss the case. However, sources say they have no new leads as to the whereabouts of Callon Wolfe.

My eyes are still skimming the article, but my body is on autopilot as I read the details of the crime scene. All the details except the one I was missing…Callon.

Why are they saying he killed my parents?

I try to breathe. My heart is racing and sweat slides down my back. Suddenly, bile rises in my throat, and I bolt away from the computer and find the nearest bathroom, losing all the contents of my stomach.

After the heaving stops, I just sit there on the floor.

All the questions roll endlessly through my head as fast as the tears rolling down my face. How could he, why would he? I've always known that he was a killer. He admitted as much. How could he possibly be involved in my *parents'* deaths and my kidnapping? Why is he doing this, keeping me out there in that cabin? What is going on?

I am done being under someone's thumb and done being lied to.

I. AM. DONE.

I know by now he is out there combing through the isles for me. I've got to get out of here.

I drop the wig into the trash and roll my hair into a bun. He will be looking for a blonde head. Although, there isn't much I can do about my outfit. I creep out of the bathroom door after making sure everything is clear and make my way toward the exit. Trying to remain calm and look natural, I keep a slow pace. I peer over my shoulder just in time to see Cal heading my way from the other end of the library.

I don't think; I just bolt.

I slam through the double doors and barrel into the street, catching the eyes of several people. I sprint right and head down Main Street, running as fast as my feet will carry me.

I see an alleyway and take another right, never slowing down.

I hear footsteps pounding on the sidewalk behind me. I panic and begin darting in and out of various alleyways. Eventually, I see a door open on my left, and I duck into it stumbling over a box on the way in, but I catch myself on a counter.

It looks like the back storage area of a diner based on the condiments and food packaging. My breath is coming out in gasps, so I try to breath in through my nose and calm down, but nothing helps.

There's a small gap between the shelves. I squeeze myself into the crevasse placing my back against the wall and try again to steady my breathing. Logically speaking, I can't keep running; someone will call the police, or he will catch me. I don't know who to trust and who not to trust.

I was supposed to be able to trust him.

Maybe if I hide long enough for him to lose me, I can figure it out later. The door on the opposite side creaks open and my hope falters. I hold my breath. My whole body trembles and I feel sweat trickle down my brow.

"Maisy, I know you are in here. I need you to listen to me," Cal says through ragged breaths.

I don't make a sound.

"I know what you saw on the computer. You left the tab open. You must know by now that I could never do those things…If I wanted to hurt you, I could have a thousand times."

I close my eyes and try to remain still.

"I did not kill your parents, please believe me. I told you how corrupt the system is. Did you think they wouldn't have a fall guy?" he whispers.

His footsteps get closer.

Suddenly, I am jerked from my hiding spot with one hand, and another is slapped across my mouth, stifling my scream. I thrash and fight with everything I have in me, but he is not budging.

Cal shoves me against the wall, pressing his body into mine, still holding my mouth and hands hostage behind my back. "STOP and listen to me!" he growls at me an inch from my face. "I didn't do those things. Now *we* are going to get the hell out of here before someone sees us. I will take you some place where we can talk. If you scream, it will draw attention to you, and I promise you…I never lied about the fact that Jacob and his guys are still searching for you. Will you go with me, Maisy?"

I stifle the sob that threatens to come out.

What options do I have? If I go to the police, I could end up with Jacob again or killed. If I stay with Callon, I'm living with a murderer, who possibly killed my parents.

I throw daggers with my eyes, but I eventually nod my head slowly.

"I'm going to let go now, and when I do, you will hold my hand, and we will walk out of here, okay? You, Can, Not, Scream."

I nod again as he releases his hold on me and takes my hand in his. He tries to wipe away my tears, but I yank my face back and use my arm instead.

"I'll go with you, Cal, but if you think I will blindly believe you, you are very mistaken. That ship has sailed."

He pulls me along the street back to where the truck is parked. We get in and head out of town without a glance back. The weight of leaving crushes me. Was that my only opportunity to escape this façade of a life…what if I don't get another?

An hour later I realize we are not headed in the same direction as the cabin. Cal has detoured toward my hometown. I haven't spoken to him during the ride, but now my hackles are rising. Why on earth is he heading this way? I soon see something I have both thought about and dreaded.

A cemetery.

Rose Crest Cemetery, to be exact. The place I knew my parents wanted to be buried one day.

"Why did you bring me here, Cal? What game are you playing at?" I spat.

"No games. I brought you here because…this is where your parents are buried."

I look out at the vast rolling hills full of stones. The last remnants of a person's life. "I don't understand. Is this somehow supposed to make up for you killing them? Do you crave forgiveness or redemption? Because I am not Jesus, and I can *neither* forgive nor forget Cal!" I yell.

"I did not kill your parents, and I will explain everything, but I brought you here so that you could say your goodbyes. I thought that maybe it would give you some peace to see their resting place."

Without asking permission, I climb out of the truck the moment it stops and start heading into the graveyard. Cal is on my heels in seconds.

"I know where they are if you will slow down and follow me," he says as he pushes past me, leading the way.

I give him a scrutinizing glare. "You've been here before," I say. It's a statement, not a question. Why else would he know?

Cal absently nods his head and says, "A few times, yes."

I'm seething but keep my comments to myself as we make our way through the graveyard.

Eventually, he stops next to a black marble stone. I move around him and see my parents' names etched there. I drop to my knees, placing a hand on each grave. Anger and pain burns through me as my hands lie on the cold stone.

It's one thing to think they are gone and another completely when you know they are gone. Knowing their bodies are in the ground is too much. They lie here rotting, and for what…it's all so pointless. I feel myself losing it completely. The minuscule thread of sanity I have been hanging onto is about to break.

Growing up I was always told how well I compartmentalize feelings. Dad said I was tough as nails and levelheaded. Right at this moment, I don't want to lock it up in compartments inside my brain. I feel like screaming, raging, and tearing the world apart breaking each and every little box open until there's none left!

Sobs rack my body when the weight becomes too much. When Cal bends down and tries to comfort me, I shrug his hand away.

They were wonderful people, good parents, and so in love. They had more life to live. They died for nothing. They are gone because of ridiculous political rivalries and perverted notions.

I have been thinking about revenge lately, more than any Christian should. Should I even call myself a Christian any longer? I stopped praying after a while in captivity. I lost faith and am finding it hard to get it back. Now, sitting here over their bodies, the need for vengeance is eating me alive. I want Jacob dead, and everyone involved.

What does that make me?

Cal kneels by my side. "If you need me, I'll be over by the truck. I'll give you some time."

"You don't think I'll run again?" I snarl at him. My voice is still laced with venom.

"No, I don't. I think you want more answers, and you still need my help to get your life back."

"I don't have a life, and I don't need you," I mutter. I see Callon flinch at my statement before he walks away, leaving me alone with my thoughts.

I don't know how long I sat there. Long enough that my legs were growing numb. A breeze ruffles my hair, and I get the heady scent of a familiar flower. I look up to see Lavenders in the vase atop their graves. I get the sudden urge to talk to Mom and Dad. It's silly. I know they are gone, but the words fall out of my mouth anyway.

"I'm so sorry," my voice sounds shattered. "You didn't deserve this. If I could trade my life for yours right now, I would."

I bend down and place my forehead on the ground. "We should have stayed home that night. What I wouldn't give to turn back the hands of time. I want you both to know how much you were loved." I take a deep, shuddering breath. "I couldn't have asked for a better life—for better parents."

Suddenly, A man's voice startles me from behind me, sending chills down my body.

"That, unfortunately, is not what you'll have, little bird…a better life."

My body freezes, and my heart picks up pace. I don't have to turn around to know whose voice that is.

How is he here…how did Tony find me?

"Stand up slowly and turn around. Show me your hands," he demands.

Where is Cal! My brain tries but fails to come up with a plan. Very carefully, I stand and turn to see one of the faces that will haunt my nightmares forever. I hold my hands up, take a step back, and look down the barrel of Tony's handgun.

His eyes slide down my body repulsively. "Do you have any idea of the trouble you caused me? HUH! Jacob was not so pleased to find you missing the day you were to be picked up…," He clicks his tongue.

"He blamed me, you know. I'm going to personally make sure you pay for that. You are lucky the buyer was willing to wait for you, or you'd be dead right now."

His voice gets louder, and his face turns red. "I stalked this place for *WEEKS*! I knew one day you would show. I knew you couldn't resist seeing Mommy and Daddy's final resting place." His voice is utterly devoid of emotion.

Tony steps closer, enough so that I can smell his retched old man cologne.

"Hold out your hands." I try to keep my wits about me. I will die today atop my parents' graves before he lays another hand on me.

"I said HOLD OUT YOUR HANDS!" he yells then takes that last step I've been waiting for…close enough that the gun is near my chest.

Without thought of failure or preservation of life, I snap my right hand, grabbing the gun while simultaneously slamming his wrist with my left hand. In an instant, I'm standing there with the gun pointed at his face.

I gasp a ragged breath in shock that it worked.

"*YOU LITTLE BITCH*! You had better hand my gun over now or else! Are you going to shoot me, little bird…I don't fucking think so!" Tony yells.

Everything happens so fast.

I see Cal sprinting between the stones headed our way, his gun lifting to take aim. My body is shaking with pent-up rage and hatred.

Tony takes a step toward me.

In this moment, I know I need to release this rage, or it will consume me. I may have been a good girl at one time, but she's gone.

"Tell Jacob I said hello…" I switch my aim to his knee and squeeze the trigger. The blast, along with Tony's scream, sends birds scattering through the sky. I watch him hit the ground squirming. His curses ringing out through the meadow.

I casually lower the gun and walk toward Cal, who's standing a few feet away. His mouth is hung open and his gun still aimed at Tony. Shock and confusion mar his features.

I hand him the gun and say, "Take me home."

CHAPTER 14

After we bolted from the cemetery, Cal went a different route back to the cabin to make sure we were not being followed. Lucky for us, no one else was visiting dead relatives today or this could have been way worse. Cal tried to speak to me about what happened, but I refused to say a word to him. Inside, I was numb.

Now, back in the cabin, I have decided I *can't stand* these clothes a second longer. There's dirt from my parents' graves and…Tony's blood.

I strip in my room and throw on some green joggers and a black tank top with my boots. I take my bun down, letting my hair fall, then grab my backpack. I sling some soap and shampoo from the bathroom in the bag, along with my toothbrush and toothpaste.

I stomp around the cabin, shoving water and snacks in the backpack along with Debbie the Glock.

I don't think I will *ever* leave the house without her again.

Cal is watching me the whole time. He appears worried, but looks can be deceiving, as I found out today.

I couldn't care less if he is worried. I have had enough today.

Last, I open the freezer and find the other thing I've been searching for…the white devil itself, moonshine.

Cal grabs my arm spinning me around, forcing me to turn and look at him. "Where do you think you are going?"

I jerk my arm away. "I'm not running if that's what you think. I have *NOWHERE* to run to even if I wanted to! I'm going to the waterfall for the night, don't bother following me!"

I head for the door, grabbing the quilted throw blanket on my way out, when Cal grabs my arm again.

Without hesitation, I lash out, slapping him hard across the face.

I stand there seething, hoping he will say something… anything. His eyes are blazing with anger, but he doesn't speak and neither do I. I stomp out of the cabin without looking back.

I thought long walks through the woods were supposed to be refreshing and clear your head, but I guess that's not the case if you just shot someone and found out the one person you assumed you could trust has been lying to you.

At the back of the waterfall, I make a camp for the night utilizing some things I've learned lately. I start a small fire, tie my water bottles in the stream to keep them colder. I pull out the jar of moonshine and take a long swig, squinting through the burn. I set the jar beside the water's edge and strip down. Grabbing the toiletries, I wade into the water. It's freezing, as usual, but feels so good. Looking at the lathered soap in my hands, I start scrubbing my body…hair, everything. The sticky sweat from the Carolina heat washes away, but nothing seems to make me feel clean. I don't realize I'm crying until a sob comes out.

I angrily sling the toiletries onto the bank just as I see Cal walking toward the water. The soap smacks him in the chest.

My eyes grow wide as saucers. I sink to where my head is barely above water, covering my body with my arms.

Cal turns around quickly, placing his back to me. "Maisy, I'm sorry! I didn't know you'd be naked!"

"What did you not understand? I said do *NOT* bother following me!" I yell over the waterfall's noise.

"You know I couldn't do that…I needed to know you were okay."

"Do I look okay to you, Cal? I'm a mess." The truth wasn't what I expected to say to him. I see his back tense.

"I know, and part of that is my fault," he says quietly, tipping his head back. "Can we just talk?"

I sneer at him. '*Part* of this is his fault.' Really?

Right, this second, I want to shoot him in the knee.

The sane part of me knows that's a lie. The sane part of me just isn't home today.

"We can talk…ONLY if it's one hundred percent truthful. No more lies, no more shielding me from whatever it is that you did. I think I deserve that much."

"Agreed," he says as he walks away, giving me privacy to get out and dressed.

The sun is setting by the time I'm clean and clothed. The last rays stream through the trees and make the water dance with color. It would be magical if it weren't for the turmoil raging inside me.

I sit on the quilt, hugging my knees to my chest. Cal is cutting up cheese, meats, and apples with a pocketknife for us. Every now and then, I take another long swig of liquor.

Cal cuts his eyes my way, "You know how I feel about drinking and serious talk. It's never good. You need to be easy with that stuff."

Rolling my eyes, I spat, "No, I don't think I will, Cal…in fact, I think I will get rip-roaring drunk tonight."

He snatches the jar from me, takes a drink himself, and shoves the food to me. "You will eat first!"

"*YOU* don't tell me what to do! Why do you treat me like an invalid? I can handle myself. I don't need you or anyone else!" I feel myself losing it again.

That thread is so thin.

Suddenly, Cal stands and picks me up, cradling me to his chest, I slap and push at him, but he doesn't let go. He squeezes me to him, one hand pressing my head to his shoulder, and then he sits back down with me on his lap.

All the fight leaks out of my bones.

I sob on his shoulder. It's not the first time today that I've lost it, but somehow, this time is like a real goodbye. Goodbye to the old me, and goodbye to my parents. He holds me tight and gently runs his hands through my wet hair.

We stay that way for a few minutes until my tears slow. He whispers into my ear, "I'm so sorry life dealt you a shitty hand. I'm also sorry I wasn't there for you today when you needed me." He squeezes me a little tighter as if I might vanish before continuing, "I walked away to give you privacy and not long after heard a man's voice." Cal pulls my head from his shoulder so that we are face to face, keeping his hand on my cheek. He rubs his thumb in a gentle caress. "My heart sank today when I saw him standing there. As I was running to you, I saw you take his gun, just the way I showed you. I was so proud of you, Maze. You are right about not needing me…I think it's me who needs you."

My heart doesn't know what to do with his admission. His eyes are so blue they seem to glow from within and make it impossible to look away.

I remind myself that I need answers and that I do not really know him at all. Slowly, I remove myself from his lap and sit next to him. I slide the snacks my way even though it feels like I am caving to his wishes. He smiles at that and joins me.

Once our appetites are sated and I have contained my emotions, we each take a long drink of the white devil. I savor the burn this time. The calm is beginning to seep into my bones.

Cal clears his throat, looking off in the distance. "Everything I told you was true about my mom and dad, my friend Bo, and my ex." He leans back against the rock face and says, "It's also true that I'm a murderer." He pauses, looking at me with such pity. "I didn't kill your parents, Maisy. I shot two of the guys involved in their deaths. What I didn't tell you before is that…I was working for Jacob."

My mouth drops. I feel like a rug has been yanked from underneath me. "How c-c-could you…work for him?" I stutter.

He holds his hands up in mock surrender. "Let me finish," he pleads. "Once I was out of the Army, I needed a job. Civilian life was not sitting well with me. I was looking for something that mattered. I wanted to have a career where I could still serve and protect people. A job where my skills wouldn't go to waste. Naturally, I was considering the police department."

He takes a breath and rubs his stubbled chin. "Then, one day, I was personally requested to meet with this public figure who was making waves in political chats everywhere, Jacob Rainer. I learned as much as I could about the man from before we met…didn't want to go in blind. I knew he either came from money or was making it illegal right away. I had never seen anyone that wealthy in this area, but he offered me a killer salary if I would accept a role as one of his muscle guys. He wanted protection, from what, I wasn't sure at the time. You see, I found out later that he specifically wanted single, post-service-type guys to work for him. He looked for people who wouldn't be missed, who didn't have much family."

"But how would he know anything about you?" I butt in.

"Turns out he is friends with many high-ranking officials throughout the country. He can find out anything about anyone… for a price, of course. Anyway, I took the job, thinking that I would make a ton of money, get a dog, and disappear to an ocean somewhere one day."

Cal stops like he is picturing that life he dreamed of. "That is until I started realizing things were not as they seemed." Cal's eyes get distant for a second, then he shares another drink with me and continues.

"One day, he charged me with an unusual task. I was handed a folder containing information on a specific family. He said they were a threat to him and his empire. He made them out to be treacherous. He said the father had threatened his life. He asked me to follow them, document everything they do."

Dread washes over me.

"It was your family. The Murrays." He takes a large gulp of moonshine.

"So, you followed us around like a spy—stalking us…for how long?" My mind spins.

"Two months," he says quietly. "I didn't know what kind of side business Jacob was into, but I knew something was wrong."

Cal's eyes seem lost in this deep dark memory. "I remember the first time I saw you. You were at a press conference with your dad. Your hair was half up and half down, with pieces framing your face. You were wearing a blue dress with silver heels. You didn't fit in, to say the least—like you were more suited to the silver screen." Cal pauses again to look at me. "I had never seen anyone so mesmerizing in all my life…but Jacob asked for information on all of you, so I did my job. I wondered what he could possibly need to know about the daughter of William Murray. The parents, I could understand, but their daughter. I was a fool."

I take a deep breath to try to calm myself. "You were there, watching us for two months. Lurking in shadows."

"You *have* to understand that I was unaware of his motives. I was under the impression that this was life or death for him. I assumed at some point we would either find something on your father or clear him of being a danger."

Cal's jaw clenches like he is struggling to get the next words out. "The night…you left with them to go eat out, it was me who gave them the location of where the car was traveling, and its destination based on wiretaps and a tracker."

He tries to avoid my eyes, but I stare him down. "You told them where to find us…gave them the location." My voice begins to raise, "Were you there when it happened? Did you know what was going down that night!?" I demand, anger lacing every word.

"I was told that they were going to scare your father into backing out of the upcoming elections. It was to be nothing more than a scare tactic and that you and your mother would be fine. They said that this would *end* my current task. That he wouldn't be a threat to Jacob after that night. So, they paid me."

"I hope it was worth it," I throw at him.

"Please, just let me finish. After they sent me the cash, I planned on tailing them. By them, I mean the three guys sent to follow your family, which were Juan Rodriguez, Eric Taylor, and Manny Tillman. They had been Jacob's lackeys for a very long time. Tillman had even been a cop before he turned into Jacob's security and henchman. I caught up to them on that back road, but it was too late. Everything had already transpired."

I take another drink and look at the ground as I ask, "Who shot my parents Cal."

He looks down, fiddling with a stone. "It was Tillman who shot them." his voice is solemn. "Tillman had driven separately and left with you unconscious in the back seat."

Cal grew quiet again. I could see that he was reliving that moment.

"What happened next?" I ask.

"I questioned Taylor about what went down. He was high on something and volunteered more than I bargained to hear. He told me about the real reason they bumped your parents' car that night…to kill, not scare, William. Jacob wanted him to be eliminated. Said he couldn't have William as the second in the senate. Then, he told me the plans for you and said…they could have their pick of any girl at any time while working for Jacob. He told me about the trafficking. I knew right then…all the stalking I did for Jacob was as much about apprehending you as it was eliminating your father." He rakes his hands through his hair and whispers. "I lead them right to you Maisy."

The silence thickens the air as we both sip the alcohol and sink into a dark, murky past. My mind is racing with the information overload of today, not to mention the fact that I shot someone.

Oddly, I don't feel much about that.

"After your newfound discovery of the dark underworld that is Jacob Rainer, what did you do?" I ask with the lack of sympathy evident in my tone.

Cal gets up and stokes the fire, avoiding eye contact with me. "Taylor had already made sure there was no evidence at the scene linking back to them or Jacob. I was a pawn in the scheme all along, you see…They needed a scapegoat. I wasn't brought into that meeting to be a long-term employee. All the lies about protecting and serving a greater good were a façade. No, I was chosen for that night alone. They needed someone to pin the murders on."

"But. I thought you said you *did* murder someone. Which ones?" I ask, remembering his very first confession to me.

"I did." Cal sits back beside me and takes another long drink. "Rodriquez was quiet while Taylor spilled this information, but I kept my eye on him, and when he went for his weapon, I dodged left and slid behind the Mustang, but not before a bullet nicked my arm. I fired a few rounds their way, one barely missing Rodriguez's head. I assumed they planned on wounding me or killing me, effectively leaving a blood trail of my DNA for the cops to find. I was wrong because, within minutes, they fled the scene. I had run out of ammunition by the time they peeled out of there. Like an idiot, I left chasing them. I had no idea that they didn't need to spill my blood. They had already been gathering personal items of mine and left them at the scene."

As angry as I am that he has withheld this from me for weeks, I see now why he feels like he owes me something. I finally understand his odd comments at times and behavior. He feels guilty for his part in all this. I hate to admit it, but in a way, he is just as much a victim as me.

"When and who did you murder then?" I ask.

"I chased them down, I trusted no one after they had me stalking you and your family. I had a tracker placed on Taylor's car, too. They pulled over in an old junkyard, and I waited, watching them dispose of evidence. A switch flipped inside me. I shot them both and left them there…and figured I could use the evidence against them in the morning. I was very wrong…*again*."

I see Cal's hands flexing with aggravation. My own anger from earlier has almost completely dissipated with the realization that Cal is not the enemy here. Not really. I have been treating him like one all day. I have the urge to comfort him even after everything I have learned. I want to grab his hand, I want to lean on him, I want to ease his pain.

I shouldn't want any of that, but I do.

It may be a mistake to take everything he says as fact now, but something has always told me that he would never hurt me. While keeping this from me did in fact hurt me, I can see why he did it.

I lose the internal battle and reach over taking his hand in mine. His brows knit together as he stares at our entwined fingers. After a few seconds, his body visibly relaxes, and his eyes soften. A breath he must have been holding releases.

He clears his throat and continues, "The next day, there was no mention of dead bodies in the junkyard. Somehow, it was never reported on. The news did say that the police department had a suspect in the murders of William and Victoria and the kidnapping of one Maisy Murray…me. Within one day…*ONE* day, Jacob had me pegged as the killer and the bodies of his henchmen missing. When I tell you he will never stop, I mean it. He must have people in the local sheriff's working with him. There is a *seedy* dark underworld that most people don't know exists, but it's there, right under our noses," Cal spats.

I gently rub my thumb over his hand. "Cal…I'm sorry that your life was ruined that night, too." Cal tries to object to my apology, but I stop him. "I mean it. If everything you are telling me is true, then both our lives were taken from us on the same day. If you hadn't got to me first in the woods…" I shudder.

Cal runs the back of his hand over my cheek, then cups my face. Those devastating eyes bore into mine. "I made a promise to myself that one day I would save you. It shouldn't have taken so long. I tried *so* many times to find you, eventually getting Bo involved in the search. I would take a step forward, and ten steps back. It seemed Jacob was always a few steps ahead of me."

His fingers caress my cheek very slowly as if he's memorizing every detail. "It made me sick to imagine what you were going through. There was a point where I hadn't been able to find any confirmation you were even alive. You haunted my every waking hour and my sleep."

I had no idea that he was living in hell right along with me.

"I wondered what condition you would be in if I ever found you. I prayed for you…that was unusual for me, but I did. I prayed for you every night. Do you know how unlikely it was to have survived those men? They use and abuse girls, and then their bodies are never found. How you came out of that still…"

My face burns when I catch his meaning and I back away from his hand. When I came out of it with my purity intact. That's what he means.

"Pass the white devil, please," I say and then take a swig for courage.

"The white devil." Cal's smirk is back. "I forgot you were calling it that."

"It suits, doesn't it?"

"It does. Look, I'm sorry if that comment I said before embarrassed you," Cal adds.

"It's okay. I have just never talked openly about that kind of stuff to anyone except the occasional nurse or my mother. Even then, it was weird."

I take a deep breath, "They didn't, or couldn't get that far with me because Jacob insisted. He used me to make money in other ways. He said he would have potential buyers willing to pay anything by the time he was done. He called it baiting the sharks. I think he just loved torturing me because of who I was."

Call looks at me with sympathy, which I hate.

I stand up and begin pacing the small rocky area, "I need to say this. It *hurts*." I point to my chest. "It is *unbearable* some days to hold these stained memories inside my head. One reason I was taken was because I was a virgin! It makes me sick. If I could go back, I would be willing to give it away to anyone, *ANYONE*, if it meant things would have been different."

Cal stands, too, stepping in front of me. "They would have still taken you, but you wouldn't have survived them."

"Deep down, I know that, but I'm still human, and humans always ask the question what if." I run my hands over my face in utter defeat and exhaustion.

We stay silent for a few minutes, letting the day marinate. Then I ask, "Did you feel bad after killing those men?"

He gives me a knowing look. "No, I didn't. They were the worst kind of shitbags. I felt relief that they couldn't prey on women any longer. And *you* shouldn't feel bad either. What you did today saved your life."

I bend and snatch the jar off the ground for another sip. "You know what…I don't feel bad. That's the issue I'm having. I feel great. He was the KING of *shitbags*!"

Cal has lost all seriousness and has a huge smile splitting his face. "You cussed. Maze, I am shocked and appalled." He dramatically grabs his chest, making me laugh.

"When in Rome, I guess. You *are* a bad influence, Callon Wolfe. I'm drinking, swearing, and shooting people. What's next?" I say a little tipsy, trying not to slur my words.

Cal quits laughing, raises one eyebrow, and leans in close. "I'm sure we can find something absolutely disgraceful to do."

"Like what?" I ask.

"We could rob a bank or become arsonists," he jokes and starts to back away.

I grasp his arm, not wanting to have distance between us. It's probably the drinks and emotional roller coaster, and it's one thousand percent a bad idea, but I don't care.

My heart is racing when the words just come out. "Or I could do something truly awful like…kiss you."

Cal's eyes become hooded as they make a slow descent to my lips. With one hand, he caresses my face and then rubs his thumb over my lower lip. "That would be truly awful." His voice is low and guttural.

My eyes close, and my breath is ragged as he says, "You have no idea how many times I have thought of just that." He looks conflicted even as he says it.

"Then do it," I whisper. I'll blame this on the white devil tomorrow.

"Part of you must hate me." He inches closer and places his hand over my heart. "Do you really want me to kiss you, or is there something more going on inside here?"

That gives me pause for a second. "Both, maybe…and I've never hated you. I just didn't know you." I place my hand over his. He must feel my heart racing under his palm.

"Kiss me before I change my mind."

The turmoil slips away from his face. Decision made. That answer must have been good enough.

Cal takes my face in his hands and leans in. He smells of wood and rain, apples, and moonshine. It's heady and intoxicating. Softly, he presses his lips to mine. The world around me ceases to exist. The waterfall that had been so loud before is silent. The clashing noise in my brain ceases. His hands move into my hair as our lips part in tandem. His tongue sweeps in slowly, devouring me— mind, body, and soul.

A moan escapes my lips, and something in him becomes ravenous. He deepens his kiss while sweeping his hands down to lift me against him. Instinctively, I wrap my legs around his waist, and he presses me against the rock face.

He tastes like cider, excitement, and freedom. I want to crawl into him and become one. He tilts my head back and leaves a path of featherlight kisses down my neck and back up to ravage my lips again. Goosebumps spread along my skin as he pulls my lower lip into his mouth. I reach between us and snag the button of his jeans, popping it loose.

Cal abruptly stops kissing me and leans his forehead to mine. "We can't do this. Not like this."

"Why not?" I ask breathlessly.

Cal's breath is just as ragged as mine as he says, "You've had way too much to drink for one and for two, a very emotional day. You aren't thinking clearly." He slides me down his body until I'm standing.

His eyes are still on my swollen lips. His body is telling me a different story.

"You want me, don't you?" I ask.

"With every cell in my body. I want you," he admits.

"Then have me, please," I beg.

Cal stalks closer, and just when I think this is it, this is happening, he grabs my face and kisses my forehead. I can feel the heat between us cooling as he pulls away from me.

"If you feel the same way after your head is clear and you've had time to process, I'm here, but I can't in good conscience do this." He starts fiddling with blankets and preparing beds.

Silently, I lie down in one of the makeshift beds and pull the blanket up to my chin. He's watching me closely like I may snap again at any moment.

My emotions *are* all over the place. That much is for certain. I am mortified for throwing myself at him. I'm even more embarrassed because the reason is clear. I don't want to admit it out loud, but part of me just doesn't want to be a virgin anymore. Tears slip quietly from my eyes, and it's not long before sleep finds me, and so do the nightmares.

CHAPTER 15

It's midday by the time I'm climbing out of the shower at the cabin. Our walk back was quite awkward this morning. I want nothing more than to crawl into a hole and disappear. To make things worse, I wake up with Cal on top of me, shaking me. Apparently, I was screaming in my sleep…again.

The dream was so real…but it wasn't a dream. That's the saddest part. It was re-living a memory.

My brain must love torture.

These are some of the worst nights. I DESPISE poker nights. Jacob throws these extravagant parties once or twice a month that resemble the nineteen twenties décor and dress. The guests are trusted individuals who partake in this secret twisted life. The worst part is, not just men attend, women do too. That's a slap in the face to see women who are entirely okay with the degradation and enslavement of one of their own.

On these nights, we wear only black thongs, black heels, and a mask over our eyes. Our hair and makeup are fixed to Jacobs' liking, and we aren't allowed to speak. We are the servers for the evening and the entertainment after the games. Apparently, the guests pay Jacob outrageous amounts to join these parties. I always get sick before. Jacob doesn't like us drugged on these occasions. So, we are very much aware of everything that happens.

"Little bird, be on your best behavior tonight; I have many suitors begging for me to sell. I want you to make sure they feel appreciated for their time and money." Jacob leans into my face, and I turn my head away. His hand snaps up grasping my chin, forcing me to look at him. He kisses me, plunging his tongue into my mouth, making me want to gag. Once he has had his fill of me, he lets go. "Tonight, I have a special guest. I want you to only serve him, no other girls. Do whatever is asked of you, and you will not be punished." He must see the fear in my eyes because he says, "Don't worry, he knows he can't fuck you," Jacob whispers into my ear. "He is impatiently waiting on me to let you go. His tastes can be quite violent, though, but no worries, he won't leave any marks whilst you still belong to me."

As he turns to escort me to the poker room, I let myself fall apart inside, if only for a brief moment. My body trembles, and I feel like I can't breathe. All the other poker nights were the same. Serve them, let them look, but no touching.

This...this is something else entirely.

The worst part of doing this sober is knowing how close we are to the doors. The urge to run is eating me alive inside. The room is enormous, with an arched ceiling adorned with gaudy chandeliers. There aren't any windows because of the location of the room inside the house. The walls are a dark burgundy color with black and gold accents.

It feels like a coffin.

There are two bars on either side of the room with round tables throughout the center. Each table has a girl to serve it. Tonight, mine is by the bar to the right of the room and only one man sits there. He is younger than most who attend these gatherings. He looks to be in his *mid-thirties with tawney skin, dark hair, and even darker eyes. There is something sinister in this man. As I make my way to him, his eyes devour my body.*

"You are unexpected," he continues his visual exploration. "When Jacob told me about you, I was skeptical. Many of these girls are damaged goods, one much more like the last." He licks his bottom lip, making me shudder. "You, however, are exquisite. Is it true that you are a virgin?"

I hesitate to answer. My body feels leaden.

"Answer me," he growls.

"Yes," I whisper.

"That is something," he smiles viciously. He has a thick Spanish accent. "I bet you are wondering where the other players are at this table…well, there aren't any. I'm not here for poker. I'm here for you."

Dread pools low in my stomach and I clench my hands to stop them from shaking.

He stands holding out his hand to me. I take ahold of his hand as he leads me toward the exit. I look around the room frantically trying to find anyone who can stop this from happening.

No one cares. They all watch me leave with hungry eyes.

Before I make it to the doorway, I see Jacob leaning against the bar and he tips his fedora hat to me.

A slow rage begins to burn inside.

The man leads me to a bedroom upstairs. Which is much like the décor before, dark and dreary. I decided right then that if I ever survived this, my future house would have NO dark colors, nor would it have the white walls of the room, which is my prison.

He positions me in front of the bed. I try to think of anything to say to stall whatever he has planned.

"What's your name?" I mutter.

"That, I cannot tell you, not yet anyway. When you are mine one day, I'll tell you then." He is caressing my neck with his hand. He is a massive man with a bronzed complexion and soulless eyes.

"Kiss me," he commands

I hesitantly close my eyes and lean forward to gently place a kiss on his lips. This seems to flip a switch in him, and before I can react, he has my throat in his hand, squeezing slightly and pinning me against him. He forces my mouth apart with his tongue and kisses me violently. I begin pulling at his hand and panicking, which only seems to light his fires more.

"When I say kiss me, I do not mean a peck…do you understand?"

I nod, trying to catch my breath.

"You will be mine," he says against my swollen lips. "The things I want to do will have to wait. Jacob can be such an ass, but we can still enjoy ourselves."

He takes me and shoves me to the bed face down, and I feel a rope going around my wrists. I fight with everything in me this time, but then I feel it. A blade is pressed to the back of my neck.

"I like the chase, so…by all means, fight back, but know this. I will have you. My cock will be the first you will ever feel in this cunt and the last." He slides his fingers into my thong. I cry out, but he presses the knife in again. I feel a small trickle of blood roll around my neck to the bed.

There's a knock on the bedroom door, bringing me back to the present.

Maze, are you okay?" Cal asks from the other side.

"I'm fine," I lie. "I'll be right out." I finish getting dressed in my typical Sarah Conner attire and head into the kitchen to face the elephant in the room. Cal has coffee set on the table and breakfast. My tummy growls loudly.

"I take it you are as hungry as I am." He smiles.

"Ravenous," I reply.

As we eat, I can't help but steal glances his way. He is so handsome it hurts, and I am pretty sure he has no idea.

He's wearing black jeans and boots with a fitted gray tee. His beard is growing out a bit and I find that I really prefer the beard. His hair is tousled and unruly today and those ocean eyes—bright and devastating.

I may have had too much to drink, but I remember every detail of last night. I can still feel him on my lips and taste him on my tongue. None of my feelings make sense to me. I should hate him for the role he played. I simply don't.

Cal's not the enemy here.

He catches me looking at his lips, and I quickly divert my eyes.

"Maisy, can we talk about last night?" Cal asks.

I take a big bite of eggs so that I don't have to attempt a response and just nod instead.

He looks at with one brow raised as I shove my mouth full. "I want you to know that…it can't happen again. not right now." His voice is strained.

I stop shoving in food and really look at him. I try to wipe the confusion and feeling of being denied from my brow as he continues.

"We are in a strange situation. We don't know what lies ahead of us. I worry that you, having been traumatized, are doing this for the wrong reasons."

I put down my fork and face him fully. "Whatever you are thinking, just drop it, okay. I was drunk last night. Case closed. It was a mistake," I lie *again*.

I am not about to admit the truth now. He looks skeptical and hurt at the same time. I hate myself for placing that look on his face, but I am not just some damaged girl in need of arms to fall into. I knew exactly what I wanted last night. While part of my reasoning may have been flawed, the other part knows that I have wanted Callon for some time now. This wasn't just some trauma response.

However, I will keep that to myself.

Changing the subject, I say, "Can you teach me how to get out of someone's grip? If someone had me pinned, for instance?" My memories from earlier have me yearning for knowledge and vengeance. Not to mention, training would get my mind off of Cal and the way he is making me feel like stabbing him with my fork right now.

"That can be arranged." He smiles, but some hurt lingers there.

Good. I don't need any more distractions. Once I feel ready, I will be on my own anyways making a new life somewhere far away.

One day, this will be a distant memory.

After breakfast, we begin breakaway self-defense exercises. Cal puts me in different situations and then shows me how to get out of them safely.

I would feel a lot better about it if he would put his shirt on, but here we are. I bite my lower lip and try to concentrate.

"Are you paying me any attention?" Callon asks turning his trucker hat backwards and scowling at me."

"What…yes of course, continue." I wave him on with my hands.

"If someone attempts to choke you, keep calm to save oxygen. Once you feel their hands on you, grab their wrists and pull them down so you can kick them in the chest or groin. You could also hit them or elbow them in the face. If you can do both of those things at the same time, even better." Cal steps towards me backing me up against the house.

My stupid heart rate accelerates. Useless organ!

He grabs my throat only using the slightest pressure.

Panic hits me out of nowhere and my breath becomes panting. I flashback to that moment on poker night.

I begin struggling...hyperventilating!

Cal lets go, grasping my shoulders and shaking me back into the moment. "Maisy, LOOK AT ME! It's me. Hey, hey, come back to me." He rubs my shoulders, trying to calm me.

I take a deep breath opening my eyes. "I'm sorry," I huff out through bated breath.

Cal's eyes bore into mine. There's are war waging between sorrow and burning rage. "You wanna talk about it?"

"No. Let's continue, I'm fine." I shake it off.

Callon shakes his head and looks skeptical, beginning to back away and I grab his wrist. "I am really fine, please, let's continue."

He carefully places his hands on my throat again and holds me gently against a wall. I do as he said and grab his wrist, jerking them down as I fain an elbow strike to the face.

Cal instantly releases me. "Good, that was good. Now, turn around. I'll show you how to get out of a bear hug situation."

I turn and wait for his attack.

In an instant, Cal has me wrapped in a tight bear hug. His minty breath is at my ear. "If someone grabs you from behind, then you should drop your weight and step on their foot as hard as you can. After you do that, you should kick your foot back to hit your attacker in the crotch.

Even throwing back your head to headbutt them can work to loosen their grip on you."

Just as he finishes his instructions, I drop my weight and feel his grip loosen. I throw back my head, but not far enough to make contact.

"That's great," he says, letting me go, then continues, "If someone has you on the ground, then you should pull their head toward your chest and dig your thumbs into the person's eyes."

"That's gross," I mutter.

"Gross, yes, but can it save your life…also yes." He smirks.

We continued with as much training as Cal can remember. By the time I got in bed, I was exhausted but thankful for the sore muscles. They made me feel stronger and more alive.

Not once had I thought about shooting Tony until my head hit the pillow. I wonder if he was treated at a hospital or by someone Jacob has under his thumb. Morbidly, I think maybe he got an infection and died. Maybe bits of my humanity are gone. I wonder what the old Maisy would say to this one. This feral caged version of her.

As I drifted off to sleep, my last thoughts were of what Cal said earlier.

We don't know what lies ahead of us.

CHAPTER 16

Over four months…that's how long we have been here.
Time has flown by like the swift little thief it is. Cal and I
have trained almost every day in some aspect or another.
When we didn't train, we swam or played games to pass the
time. Some nights, I would just sit and read.

Cal began slipping books into my room about a month
ago. It was impressive how well thought out the books were.
It's like he knew exactly what I would read. My favorite so
far is the *Outlander* series. I devoured the pages and became
lost in another time and world.

We have been diligently preparing for the day I leave.
Cal's friend Bo, who I have *still* never met, has been
extremely helpful. He provided me with everything possible
to start a new life. I have a social security card, ID, a
passport and more.

Cal made me a bug-out bag, which is basically everything
I would need in an emergency to disappear. Inside the bag
is all the documentation, several clothing changes, two wigs,
water, protein bars, mini toiletries, a disposable phone with

a card, a knife, two pistols, and ammo. Debbie stays with me, the two he put in the bag are extra.

Cal had Bo stash another car in a specific parking garage of a nearby Hilton Hotel. Inside the trunk of that old Buick is my bug-out bag, along with blankets, pillows, extra shoes, a case of water, and a separate bookbag of cash.

I don't get an answer as to where the cash comes from, but I just hope it is legal. In the dash is the registration matching my documentation with the name Alexandra Marie Scott. I made sure I had a say in what name I would have to carry for the rest of my life. Alexandra was my grandmother's name, and Marie was my mother's middle name. Scott was the surname of my great-grandmother on my dad's side. In this way, I feel I honor those three generations. Giving life to their names again eases some pain in my soul.

One day I will slip away in that old Buick and head towards Mexico.

Long ago, Cal had asked me where I would go if I could disappear, and I said Yucatán. So that's my destination. I will travel there, stopping only when I need gas or food. With everything Bo has provided me, I shouldn't have any issues crossing the border.

Once there, Bo and Cal knew only one person they trusted me to contact. An old Army buddy of theirs, Declan Carter. Declan married a Latino woman he met in a bar while in the Salina Cruz port. After his service, they bought a place together, which happens to be within the Yucatán peninsula. They have informed him that I will need help with purchasing a house, security alarms and cameras.

I'm not picky as to where I live exactly, as long as it is safe. I have decided to work at any local resort or restaurant once I'm established. The Buick is mine to keep, and while it is ugly as sin, I'm thrilled it's mine. I feel my independence is a short distance away now.

Everything is falling into place. Almost everything…

Cal has been emotionally distant from me. When we discuss my future, his future is never mentioned. He won't even let on to any plans he has made…and that terrifies me. I have this gut feeling that he has no plans because he doesn't believe he will need one. He has threatened in the past that they would all pay, meaning Jacob and his men.

Is that what he is thinking…of going in guns a blazing to take out the wicked?

I try to ask him, but he pushes me away. I can't bear the thought of something happening to him. He has literally given me my life back, and I could never repay him.

I want them all dead as much as Cal, probably more so. Even though I lived through hell, I got out. There are others who did not. That's my true hell. It's the guilt that eats me up, the guilt of being the one girl who got away. One by one, the others were sold off. At the time I ran, I was the only one being held in his main house.

I have come to terms with the fact that Jacob is hard to get close to, and life in prison versus life on a beach is no contest. Jacob is too powerful and has too many connections. He's already pinned everything on Cal.

Therefore, if Cal is caught…he's done for.

All these thoughts plaguing me will have to take a back burner today. Because today is Thanksgiving.

I just finished getting dressed. It's bittersweet. On the one hand, I am aware of what I have to be thankful for, and on the other, I remember everything I've lost. Cal's mood has somewhat improved today. He asked me to get dressed up and have dinner with him and that he has a surprise for me. I tried to argue the 'dressing up' part but couldn't refuse when he handed me a bow-wrapped yellow box with the cutest flowery dress folded neatly inside.

I haven't worn anything girly in a very long time.

I now stand in front of the mirror, appraising myself. The dress is a deep teal shade with flowers of burgundy and burnt orange. It has spaghetti straps and a slit up one thigh. The fit is perfect. It's chilly now so I don a warm thick cardigan in a rust color. The chunky wooden heels he left by my bathroom door are to die for. They look like they could be authentic from the 1970s.

Where does he get this stuff?

I leave my hair down in waves, pinning one side back. My body has changed so much. When I got here, I was beaten, malnourished, and a shell of the girl really. Staring back at me now is a strong, confident woman. My toned, curvy frame makes me proud—it tells a story…

Suddenly, I hear an unknown voice outside the cabin. My hackles rise, and I grab Debbie and make my way to the door creeping so as not to make a sound.

Once I am beside the front door, I hold steady, listening carefully. I silently rack the gun back and hold my breath as footsteps approach.

This is it…they've found us.

I try to swallow the lump forming in my throat. My heart is pounding as the steps reach the door and pause.

Just as the door swings open, I grab the man from behind, pressing the gun into his skull.

"Do not move a muscle!" I yell, pressing the gun harder.

"WHOA…WHOA, Maisy, please put the gun down," Cal yells from somewhere outside.

The guy I'm holding doesn't move an inch but very carefully holds up his hands and says, "So, you're the infamous Maisy that Callon can't shut up about…I'm Bo." His voice is soft and calm even with my pistol to his head.

All the tension leaves my body, and I snap my gun away from his head in horror, clicking the safety on. "OH MY GOD, I'm so sorry," I gasp with my hand covering my mouth. My face burns with humiliation. I put a gun to the head of *the* man, making it possible for me to flee the US.

Once he turns around, I finally get a good look at him. He is not what I expected at all. The name Bo gave me the impression of Bo and Luke Duke off the *Dukes of Hazzard* TV show. I was expecting a typical country boy.

I was way off.

Bo has light brown skin and long dark hair plaited down his back. His sharp cheekbones look Native…maybe Cherokee, considering the area we are in. He's wearing a white dress shirt and slacks. He has this big, warm smile that is now turning into a laugh.

Cal takes the gun from me and lays it on the table. "Yes, Bo…this is THE Maisy. Maisy, this is THE Bo." Cal motions between us, also laughing.

Bo sticks out his hand, and I gingerly place mine in his, expecting him to shake it, but he unexpectedly lifts my hand to place a kiss on the back.

I feel like the biggest loser right now. "Bo, I am mortified. Please forgive me," I plead.

He shrugs his shoulders nonchalantly while shaking his head. "There is absolutely no need to apologize. You were doing exactly what we hoped you would. You were protecting yourself. Never apologize for that," he says with all sincerity. "You know Cal said you were beautiful, but I had no idea. You are a vision."

Cal arches his eyebrow and cuts his eyes toward Bo.

Bo shrugs. "What? It's true. He talks about you all the time."

I look at Cal expectantly with my own brows raised.

"Okay, whatever, come on guys, let's have dinner." Cal quickly walks toward the kitchen, shutting down that line of conversation. Bo shrugs again but then winks at me.

I think I like him already.

"What are we having for dinner, exactly?" The smells have had my tummy growling all day.

"Turkey…of course, and green bean casserole, macaroni and cheese, and rolls," Cal says proudly. I finally look at Cal as he's describing the food.

With the chaos, I hadn't noticed him. He's wearing all black, from his dress pants to his button-up shirt. Classic black everything seems to be his favorite. He's dangerously handsome. His blue eyes stand out starkly against the dark attire.

"Sounds yummy," I mumble, still eyeing Cal a little too long for comfort.

Then I come to my senses, turn my head, and quit gawking.

Bo clears his throat, his eyes darting between the both of us. "Yeah, well, I brought a pecan pie."

"Oh, I *love* pecan pie!" I declare. This has Bo beaming at me.

Once the table is set, we settle in to eat. I am just about to take my first bite when I see Bo bow his head. I gently set the fork down, bowing my head too, but with eyes open, staring at nothing.

Saying grace used to be a normal thing for me. My religion has thoroughly been shaken. I feel Callon's gaze on me.

"We give thanks to the plants and animals who have given themselves so that we can enjoy this meal together. We also give thanks to our friends, new and old, who are with us today and to the ones no longer by our side. May this meal bring us strength and health. Amen."

Indeed, I think. To the ones no longer by our side.

Bo finishes with an enthusiastic "Let's eat!"

The meal is something else entirely. We have eaten mainly sandwiches and soup for months. Therefore, *this* is a taste of heaven. Cal is an amazing cook. I savor each and every bite, and I don't fail to notice as Cal watches in appreciation while we devour the meal. In fact, I've caught him stealing glances all day.

The guys joke and catch up during the meal. I stay quiet and just enjoy this side of Callon that I have never been privy to. He is so carefree around his friend. You can tell they have complete trust between them. I've never seen him this relaxed. I have a thousand and one questions for Bo, but I will wait until the meal is over before picking his brain clean. This meal is way too important.

After dinner, I sit on the porch with my piece of pie and listen to the wind whipping through the trees. Looks like a storm may be on its way. Bo leans his head out of the doorway and says, "Care for some wine and some company?"

"That sounds great, although I have to admit, I haven't tasted wine before."

Bo squints his eyes and wrinkles his forehead, clearly bewildered by this confession. "Well, you are in for a treat." He hands me a glass and then takes a sip from his. "This is Golden Scuppernong. It's made locally," he persuades me with that warm smile.

I sip the wine, and instantly, the flavor burst on my tongue. Fruity, bold, and sweet. It reminds me of sunshine and flowers. "I like it…it's different." I take another drink. "In a good way." I add.

"Take it easy with wine. It can creep up on you. People think because it's sweet, they can drink more…not the case," he advises.

"No worries there," I grin. "If I can handle the white devil, I'm sure I can handle some fruity wine."

Bo looks taken aback, "What is the white devil, exactly. Please tell me you don't mean Cal."

I burst out laughing, "Oh, no…no, not Cal. It's moonshine. Have you had it before?"

Bo looks incredulous. "White devil indeed. Cal gave you moonshine, *classy*," he says sarcastically. "Yeah, I have had it before, but never again. That stuff is like lighter fluid." I giggle at the comparison, although he's not far off.

Bo watches me take my first bite of the pie, and I embarrassingly moan out loud.

"It's good, right?" he asks.

"More than good, it's incredible. Thank you for this," I mumble with my mouth full.

Once I manage to quit stuffing my face, I polish off the wine, and Bo gets us another round. Cal insisted he clean up the table and put away leftovers. I think he really just wanted to give me time to get to know his friend.

"What's your full name? I mean, assuming it's not just Bo," I ask.

"Bowen Littlejohn. I know…not a very native name. I was raised by foster parents and then adopted by them later. They gave me my name."

I recall Cal telling me he was in a family of delinquents. It makes me wonder what sort of life he lived. "Did you have siblings?"

"Oh yes, there were three boys counting me, and I had one little sister. Trever, Donnie, then me, then Laya."

His voice is a touch soft when he says his sister's name, and it wasn't lost on me when he said, *'had one little sister.'*

"Are you close to them now? Sorry for prying. I always wanted siblings."

"It's okay. I still talk to my brothers. They live in other states, but we get together whenever we can. They have long since gotten married and had children. Laya was… murdered." He takes a long sip of his wine after the admission. "She was seventeen years old at the time."

Sorrow pools in my chest. "I'm such a jerk, I shouldn't have asked!"

"No need to apologize. There's no way you could have known." He takes a deep breath, looking out through the trees. The darkness has rolled in, and with it, the woodland sounds. "It is something I wanted to talk with you about anyway," he admits.

This has me trying to piece together why on earth her death would be something he wants to talk with me about.

For the first time I see anger in his pinched brow. "You see, she was murdered not far from here. Raped and murdered."

I suck in a breath.

"We believe it was covered up by the police, and not just any cop. We believe it was one of the guys that later began working for Jacob."

In my head, I already know where this is going.

Bo purses his lips and continues, "It happened two years ago. We didn't make the connection until footage was found at a local convenience store showing…Manny Tillman picking her up in the parking lot. I had already been informed by Callon about your parents and what transpired. We couldn't believe that such a tragedy could strike twice in the same area. Let alone to two people who were friends. We knew that it couldn't be a coincidence. It took us a while to realize this operation was much larger than we anticipated." Bo sips his wine, and his gaze becomes distant. "Later, that footage mysteriously disappeared along with all the other evidence. Her body was found in a creek bed weeks later.

"The news channels never even reported on it, no matter how much I fought for her story to be told. She was also Indigenous and from a poor family. No one cared. I couldn't bear to go into her room or part with any of her belongings. Not even her clothes. Manny was the last person seen with my sister…she was wild, and that was no secret, but she would never have messed around with a cop."

My heart aches deeply for his loss but also for the injustice. Her story should have been told! A tear rolls down my cheek, unbeknownst to me. Bo reaches over and wipes it away.

"Hey…I didn't mean to make you cry."

I sniffle and take another sip of wine. "It's just…my heart breaks for you and your family."

Bo sits back in the rickety rocking chair and huffs, "That is exactly why I've gotten so involved. Cal told me everything once he found you. I vowed that I would help you escape the fate that many other women were unable to."

"What you are doing for me…I could never repay the kindness."

Cal walks outside holding a glass of wine and the moment he sees my face, concern blankets his. "Is everything alright?" he says while taking a seat next to me.

"I'm okay. Bo was just telling me about his sister."

Cal nods in understanding. "I would have told you, but I felt that would have made things worse. Plus, I wanted that to come from him, not me."

I understand why he didn't say anything, but it would have painted the picture more clearly about who we are all dealing with. One thing is for certain, I am truly lucky to be alive today.

A realization hits me then.

"The clothes I was wearing before…were they Laya's?"

Both men nod, and Bo speaks up. "I gave them to Callon the moment he told me about you. We figured they were close to your size and could get you by for a bit. I hope they helped."

I remember wondering where those clothes came from that first day and how attached I am now to the Metallica shirt. They belonged to his deceased sister. He said he couldn't even go into her room, but he did to help his friend…to help me too.

"I have one of her shirts that I wear all the time. It's a bit strange that I felt like I didn't want to part with it when Cal brought me the new clothes. It's the Metallica tee. If you want it back."

Bo rubs his chin, grinning from ear to ear. "No way, that was her favorite shirt, too, and it sounds like she wants you to have it."

My chest aches. "Stop, you are going to make me cry again."

"No, really, you may not believe in spirits dabbling in your life, but it happens love. They are out there guiding our way; we just have to pay closer attention."

He has no idea how much I hope that spirits can really hear us.

"I'll keep the shirt, and if you talk with her spirit…tell her thank you," I lean over and give Bo a half hug.

"Enough with the heavy," I sigh. "I want to hear Army stories or girl stories. I want the good, the bad, and the ugly details. You look like men with lots of secrets to tell." They laugh and tap glasses giving cheers to that.

We spent the next two hours sipping wine and laughing so much my cheeks were sore. By the time Bo was leaving, I had learned a great deal about these two soldiers. Everything from traveling with the service to many failed romances. They told stories of their childhoods, and sometimes I told a few of mine. It was refreshing to have a normal conversation with another person besides Callon.

One thing is for certain about these two men, they will protect anyone they care about.

Cal said his goodbyes to Bo and headed into the house carrying our glasses. I turn to follow Cal in, waving goodbye over my shoulder, but Bo grasps my arm, turning me around to face him. Next thing I know, he's bear-hugging me.

I'm not much of a hugger, so I awkwardly pat his back.

As he lets go, he says, "Remember that no matter what, I am here for you if you ever need me." He slips a note into my hand. "This has every viable way to contact me, but it's written in a code. Callon and I came up with this secret code years ago when we were bored and decided to mess with our Staff Sergeant…that's a story for another time. The important thing is no one else can read it other than us. Have him show you how to decode it…just in case."

"Okay…" I laugh. "As long as you promise to tell me the story one day."

"One day…" Bo says as he turns and heads for the trail leading out of the forest.

I stuff the note in my cardigan pocket and stand there for several minutes, relishing the cool night air and the unusually fierce winds. I wrap my arms tightly around me. My thoughts are like this wind, whipping through my mind. How many terrible things had to happen for me to end up here, in this place and time. The strangest part is, I'm grateful. I should be shattered or depressed, or worse.

I'm not.

Life will continue with or without those feelings. I intend to make the best of my situation and not waste the gift Bo and Cal are giving me. I know that deep-seated guilt caused Callon to do everything he has done for me. The same goes for Bo. He probably has some guilt nagging at him for not protecting his sister, which couldn't have happened, but that guilt and vengeance are driving his life now. It drives all of us.

Both men are determined to make right the things taken from them and from me. Does Callon not realize where I would be right now if he hadn't snatched me in those woods? So, yes…I am grateful for being here and being alive.

He has helped me more than he may ever know.

CHAPTER 17

Inside the house, Cal has two glasses of wine poured and alternative music plays on the radio that's perched on the counter. He leans against it, looking every bit like a rugged cologne model. Childish butterflies gather in my belly. I slip off the cardigan, and we watch each other as I lean against the counter beside him.

Sly smiles creep onto our faces. You can feel the euphoria still lingering. It's the first normal day we have had in ages. Minus the gun to Bo's head, which I will be ashamed of until the day I die. Today wasn't much, but it was still everything to me. A warm meal, mundane dinner conversations, wine, and laughter. Not all the talk was light, but it was still needed. It was enough to make me feel like I had family again. My soul was longing for a day like today.

I clink my glass into his and say, "Bo was great, I can see why you two are friends."

Callon's lip pulls up into that side smile that messes with my senses. "It would be hard not to like him. He's much crazier than he looks."

I laugh, "I'm sure you both were a mess in the service…he told me about some code you guys had to torment your Staff Sergeant. What was that about?"

He bites his lower lip and leans in closer. "He's giving away trade secrets. I don't know, Maze, are you part of our club? Are you one of us?" he teases in his deep low voice.

"Yes, absolutely. Now spill the beans."

Cal lights up as he tells me the story. "We would leave notes in specific places in our Staff Sergeant's office once a week. We did it because he was a severely paranoid person, and it was hilarious to see him frantically trying to decipher these notes. Three weeks in, he was convinced there was a major conspiracy going down. The notes looked like absolute nonsense. He got irritated and installed a camera and caught us red-handed, leaving one on his desk. He had me doing everything except my duties for weeks." Cal smiled.

"And what did they say? The notes," I ask.

"That's the best part. Each letter in a word was simply replaced by the next letter in the alphabet. So, like A would be replaced with B. The word cat would be spelled dbu, therefore, looking like absolute nonsense. The letters, once deciphered, were nothing but song lyrics from Celine Dion."

My mouth drops open, and I slap my hand over my mouth stifling a giggle. "You two must have been really bored…why Celine Dion?"

"He would secretly blast her music in his headphones when no one was around. Or at least when he *thought* no one was around. He fell asleep one day with the headphones on, and I saw the tape inside."

"I bet he wanted to kill you two!"

"Oh, for sure, but he appreciated a good prank and eventually forgave us."

We sip the wine for a bit, lost in that silly story.

Cal interrupts my thoughts when he clears his throat and says softly, "I never got the chance to tell you earlier, but…you look amazing."

Heat flushes my cheeks and not from the wine. "Thank you for the dress. It's perfect." I continue sipping my wine not sure what to say.

His eyes are still lingering on my face as he says, "There are some things I have wanted to say for some time now."

"What would you like to say?"

"I want you to know how unique you are."

I roll my eyes, "I don't know about that—"

"You are," he interrupts me. "You continue to have this drive inside, and it lets me know that you will be fine without me, without anyone, when this is all over."

When this is over…why does that wrench my insides? I want this to be over. Of course I do. So why is my heart aching?

Cal continues…seeing as I am lost for words. His eyes soften. "I wanted you to know that I would do it all again."

I seem to be less and less articulate. I feel my face blushing. "Thank you," I mutter. What do I say? He's talking like this is almost over, and we will, what…part ways—never speak again. Where will he go, and what will his life be like on the run? Everyone believes him to be a murderer. How can he have a normal life?

Or does he believe he will not be "around" after…

"Cal…you know you could always move to Mexico too. We could be neighbors," I say jokingly and nudge his side, but I see the doubt there in his eyes.

Cal sighs, swigs his wine, and then begins switching stations on the radio. I halt him with my hand on his forearm the moment I hear the song playing. It's 'Fade into You' by Mazzy Star. The lyrics sound like they fit inside our lives. This life is a type of strange I never knew.

I close my eyes, smiling and swaying slowly to the song. When I open them, Cal is watching me intently. His gaze lowers to my lips and the atmosphere seems to shift. There's a hunger inside him. I've known it for months. He plays it cool and keeps his distance, but there is no denying the looks of longing I get from him.

He exhales deeply. "No Maisy…I don't think I could be *just* your neighbor." His voice is low and guttural.

"Why not?" I whisper as my heart skips a beat in time.

He moves even closer to me and brushes the hair back from my cheek. "I would always be wanting for more."

His admission has my heart acting like a fool. I bite my lip to keep from saying anything ridiculous.

Cal's eyes catch the movement, and he cocks his head to the side, "Don't do that."

"Do what?" I say breathlessly.

Cal sets the wine glass down and reaches over, rubbing his thumb across my lower lip. "Bite your lip…you are driving me insane."

The heat inside me is scorching, threatening to incinerate me. It's an ache I have never known.

Is it the wine, loneliness, boredom, or is this more?

His hand moves back to my cheek and then into my hair, and a slight moan escapes my lips. His eyes bore into mine.

It's a silent conversation between us. The rational part of me knows this could all end badly, but the rebel side has already thrown logic out the window.

Suddenly, Cal grabs underneath me, lifting me onto the counter. Still towering over me, he presses himself against me only inches from my face. He devours my eyes like he's searching for a sign that I may not want this.

He won't find it in there. Any good sense I had left the moment he lifted me onto this counter.

He knows exactly what he is doing to me. I am dying to know what the wine tastes like on those lips.

I lean in, closing the distance between our mouths.

"This is your only warning, Maisy," he whispers against my lips. "Tell me now if you don't want this. I don't think I can back away from you a second time."

A tremor courses through me at the rumble of his smoky voice. "I want this Callon Wolfe…I want you," I whisper.

There's a guttural rumbling sound he makes before he takes my head in his hands and kisses me. When our lips touch, it's sweeter than I imagined, tainted by the wine. His tongue moves languidly and with purpose, sending chills through my body.

I knew it was amazing the first time because I couldn't stop thinking about it every day, even though I pretended not to care what happened under that waterfall. But this…this is different. It's like the wall between us has shattered. It's a unique and beautiful sensation with his beard against my soft skin. He kisses me like a man starving and then pauses to nibble on my lower lip, making me arch my back into him.

Cal relishes in my torment for several minutes and then leans into my ear, "There could never be *anything* on this planet that tastes as good as you. I could eat you up."

My insides liquify, and my breath catches. "Cal, please," I beg, for what I'm not sure. More of him. ALL of him. Even pressed into each other, we are not close enough.

"Please, what? What do you want?" he teases, kissing the side of my mouth.

"All of you…"

He clenches his jaw as if he is dangling on a thin thread, and it's seconds from snapping. He takes my lips again, deepening the kiss. His hands roam from my face to my neck and then to a slow descent from my abdomen to my thighs. His hands slip under the material, bunching it up along the sides, our lips never parting. I feel the cold bite of the counter underneath my bottom. Ever so slowly, he slips the dress over my hips, inch by inch, and then over my head, tossing it to the floor.

I'm left in my emerald lace panties and bra. For the first time in my life, I'm thankful for having good underwear on.

A thousand emotions should be slamming through my head right now, but they are quiet.

The demons are at bay.

My heart is pounding, *not in fear*, but in anticipation. I have never wanted something more in my life, as I want this man right now. The rightness of it washes over me.

His ragged breath fans my cheek. "Do you even realize what you do to me? I should be the bigger man right now. I should be the good guy and walk away. This can't end well." He leans in with his mouth hovering over mine. "However,…I am *not* a good guy."

The heat in his eyes is all-consuming. "I will have all of you, Callon…the good with the bad," I say against his lips.

I reach down and grasp the hem of his shirt, and we break apart long enough for me to lift it over his head. I run my hands down his chest finally getting to savor the muscles rippling down his abdomen. The muscles I have watched work over the last several months. They are mine to explore.

I see the raw pleasure that fills his eyes. His jeans are hung low on his hips, and every inch of him is sinfully wicked. His muscled torso presses against me. The skin-to-skin contact has me moaning into his mouth, but it's still not enough.

His hands roam over my back until he finds what he's searching for. I feel the release of the bra as it falls to the floor. My nipples harden as they brush against his chest. I quickly wrap my legs around his waist closing what little distance we have between us. His hands glide up my thighs to cup my bottom and pull me tighter to him. I can feel his need for me, and it's both scary and exhilarating.

I throw my head back with a moan as his mouth trails down my throat.

All of a sudden my heart jolts in my chest!.

Shock waves tremor through my body as two deafening pops ring throughout the cabin!

I am momentarily disoriented as Cal yanks me from the counter onto the floor, covering my body with his. Then I hear wood crack as the cabin door is splintered open.

It takes me all of two seconds to register that those two pops were gunshots. In those two seconds, I see the dread on Cal's face.

Our guns are on the other counter. Not reachable.

We are on the floor, and footsteps are already upon us.

Without words, Cal's eyes say so much.

Behind him, looming over us, is none other than Manny Tillman. His scarred face and dead eyes haven't changed much since the night he tossed me into the clutches of Jacob Rainer. He's wearing all-black tactical gear along with a bulletproof vest as if he were headed to war.

I guess that should make Cal happy to know that he placed some fear into this shitbag.

"Get up slowly Callon and keep your hands where I can see them." His seedy voice brings back memories of waking up in the back of that strange car. "If you so much as move for a weapon, I shoot her. Do you understand me?" He presses his gun into the back of Cal's head, and I begin to shake with fear.

Cal nods and slowly moves to his feet, never taking his eyes off me while saying, "If you hurt her, you're dead."

I cover my body the best I can with my arms, trying to be strong and not fall apart. My mind is a stampede of thoughts crashing about. The most prominent being, how on earth did they find us? This cannot be happening again!

"It's not me who gets the pleasure," Manny says while looking my body over casually with a sneer. "From the looks of what I walked in on, you may not be worth it to him anymore…but that's not for me to decide."

It's at that moment that I notice the other armed men gathered by the doorway. There looks to be three of them. All are dressed like Manny, except they wear masks over their faces that resemble skulls, and they each have a patch that says G1, G2, and G3. Cal sees them, too, and all guns are pointed toward him.

Manny continues roaming my body with his eyes. "*You* are coming with us, and your beau here is not."

A tear slips from my eye, giving away my façade of being strong. "I will go with you without a fight if you please don't hurt him," my voice cracks.

Cal's eyes widen in shock then quickly turn murderous. He shakes his head vigorously at me in protest. Behind him, the others move closer. Manny puts the gun to my temple and cocks his head at Cal in warning. Reluctantly, Cal stays still. He mouths to me, "I'll find you," as they place duct tape over Cal's mouth. They take his wrists in front of him, binding those with the tape, too. His muscles are taut, and his eyes harden. I see the storm brewing there, waiting to be unleashed.

"That is so sweet." Manny grins, showing his chipped front tooth. I intentionally stare him down refusing to seem weak. My teeth grind together in anger as I turn back to the men taping Callon's hands and mouth.

All of a sudden, my head is snapped to the side as Manny backhands me.

I instantly taste blood.

I can hear Cal attempting to shout behind the tape, but they quickly subdue him.

Before I can muster a word. Manny motions for one of the men to duct-tape my wrists and mouth. I thrash for a second before the gun is pressed harder into my skull. Tears stream down my cheeks.

When they are finished, Manny nods his head, and the man with the G2 patch picks me up and slings me over his shoulder. The one wearing the G3 patch follows behind us. I don't fight back or taunt them anymore for fear of what they'll do to Cal.

I hear his muffled protest as they head for the door with me thrown on a shoulder like a sack.

I can just lean my head back enough to see his frightened eyes watching me go.

One man stays behind with Callon.

No, no, no, no, no. I mentally scream! I said I would go if they didn't hurt him. Panic sits deep in my chest. I try to wriggle, but the guy holding me squeezes me harder. All the while, Manny is humming some rancid 1950s tune as if we were going on a walk in a park. What's left of the door flops closed behind us.

My world is crashing, and my heart is ripping apart in my chest. Where is the other guy…where the hell is he! Why is he not leaving the cabin?

Not far down the trail, I am tossed into the back of what I assume is side by side. It's too dark to be certain, and a bag is placed over my head. They crank it, and I realize how quiet the engine is. They were prepared for this. Prepared to come out here tonight and must have known a good deal in order to find us this far out in the woods. I'm still in shock that we didn't hear them coming at all. Then I recall how loud the radio was and the blasted wind.

Just a few short minutes ago, I was in heaven, and now hell has found me once again.

I'm pulled onto the lap of the one who carried me. He wraps his arms around me tightly so that I can't move a muscle. I can feel how much he is enjoying himself through his pants. It makes bile rise in my throat. He slips his hand under the bag covering my head and firmly holds a cloth over my face. I kick them and fight with everything I have, but it's too late. I'm fading fast.

I faintly hear Manny on the radio saying, "You have the 'go ahead' Ghost 1. Clean it up when you're done."

I hear it then, in the distance…a single gunshot.

CHAPTER 18

My eyes crack open but weakly close again. My mind hazily tries to piece together where I am and what has happened. I shake my head to try and clear it. A voice to my left startles me.

"It's so good to have you back, Maisy."

Chills run down my spine, and the hairs on my neck stand on end. I struggle with fatigue and force my eyes open. I turn my groggy head and there in a black slingback chair is Jacob. Casually sipping what appears to be coffee from a mug. He wears an immaculately pressed blue suit with brown loafers, one leg propped on his other. His face is impassive.

I look down when I notice the feel of the fabric and see that I'm wearing a long white T-shirt and nothing else. I hold my hands up as far as they will go and feel resistance as ropes bite into my flesh. I'm strapped to a bed, and not just any bed. This was 'my bedroom' before I escaped.

"How did you find me?" I whisper.

His sinister chuckle reverberates through the small room. "You have your newfound friend Bowen to thank for that. You see, once we figured out that it had to be Callon who was responsible for snatching you, it was a matter of time before we located the only friend that he had been in contact with over the last year. We followed his movements. Took a long time for him to meet you or we would have been reunited sooner."

"Is he alive…Bo?" my voice croaks out.

"Of course, he is dear. We have no use for him. He was just a means to an end."

I feel a small amount of relief knowing he wasn't another casualty because of me. "What do you want from me Jacob? Why can't you just let me go?" I mumble.

"Why on earth would I do that…" He chuckles again. "You are worth a great deal of money and, strangely enough, even more so now." His smile grows when he sees the confusion on my face.

"Remember that buyer you thwarted. Well…he was quite obsessed with you. He was willing to pay that astronomical fee even if we found you soiled, BUT…he was willing to pay more if you were found to be pure still."

My face cringes.

"Don't get me wrong, dear. He was *pissed* that you got away the day he came to pick you up. What he has planned for you, well that is neither here nor there. What is important is that you are untouched. Manny seems to have interrupted at the right time indeed."

"How cccould you possibly knnnow that I haven't…" I stutter.

"I had one of my ladies check you out. She used to work in a women's center before she came to work for me."

That bit of information curls up in my brain and festers. What kind of woman would do such a thing as to work for a trafficker…exploiting other women.

Then it hits me…

"That's how you knew before. That's how you know if a girl is a virgin—how you knew I was.

He tips his chin down at me with a smirk. "It's also how I weed out girls with STDs and whores. I'm the best for a reason. I have the highest quality girls, and people pay whatever I ask. In your case they paid me to just watch you for months and months. I considered keeping you, you know. But the offer I received was just too good to be true."

"Where are the other girls, you asshole! How many have you done this to?!" I yell.

His eyes open wide, and his brows raise. "You have developed a foul mouth. I'm not sure I like it. I suggest you keep your voice down and watch your tone with me. Emilliano Reyes may be pissed, but me…I am *FUCKING LIVID*!" His voice raises piercing my ears.

I keep my mouth shut, holding back everything inside me. Emilliano. That's obviously the buyer's name. I'll add him to the growing hit list I have tallied on the wall of my brain.

"I had to spend considerable resources to locate you. I had to keep men on the ground in case you surfaced. Not to mention the medical personnel I had to pay covertly to doctor a certain gunshot wound to the knee."

I smile at that.

His lip curls, but he continues, "I have to say…it was very smart not going to the police. That wouldn't have ended very well for you or Mr. Wolfe. Well, I guess it didn't end well after all." He smirks.

I crumble inside the second those words leave his mouth.

I have been silently pushing away the last thing I heard before I was knocked out.

That gunshot.

I can't let myself think about it right now. Later, I can fall apart.

"Mr. Reyes is on his way to retrieve you…*now*," he says matter-of-factly.

"Where will he take me."

"To his house in Spain. I believe he booked lodging at the DelFire Resort." Jacob sips from his mug and sighs. "I need a refill."

He rises and comes to lean over me in the bed. Placing his face way too close to mine. I can smell the coffee and cigars on his breath. He grasps my chin, forcing me to look at him.

"You will be out of my hair soon, and I can only hope that the rumors about Emil are true. They say he is wicked and has an unimaginable sexual appetite. I even heard he likes to cut his girls," he makes false marks along my breast with his fingers as he continues, "thin little slices while he fucks them. Strange indeed."

With that, he turns on his heel and walks out of the room.

I release the sob that's been stuck in my throat. The tears fall freely to the bed.

I can't go with that man. I'll never be seen again. He could use me, then kill me, or worse…keep me locked away for years. I sob more as thoughts of last night come back to me.

Cal can *NOT* be dead. Living in a world without him is impossible. I know that now. My soul was rebuilt because of him, and now it is shattering.

He taught me to forage, to live off the land. He taught me to use weapons and fight. He taught me self-defense. He taught me I could survive on my own and gave me the resources to do that. He taught me something that I never wanted to admit aloud…to love. I never thought I could have those feelings after all I've been through. My trust in men was gone until he came into my life.

My body shakes the bed with the force of my wailing cries. I try to process the fact that he could really be gone, but I can't.

I try to have hope, but two men were in that house, and there was only one shot. Callon was tied up.

I try to breathe.

My chest hurts. Cal can't be dead. He can't be dead. I say it over and over in my head and out loud.

I don't realize I'm hyperventilating until someone comes in the door with a syringe. It's the same soulless brown eyes from yesterday, the guy behind the mask who carried me out of the cabin. Before I can attempt to ask him what happened to Cal, he jabs a needle into my neck. My voice creaks as I try to talk, but quickly, I am pulled into the nothingness.

CHAPTER 19

Callon

The Night Before...

The world around me seems to move in slow motion as I see Maisy thrown over that asshole's shoulder. My vision turns red.

I will rip his *fucking* head from his shoulders before this is over.

"Kneel down," the fake-ops guy says as he steadily holds a 9mm toward my head.

I mumble through the tape annoyingly. It must work because he rips the tape off my face as I smile sadistically, "So this is how it's going to go, huh? You take me out and get some kind of internal promotion with Jacob the jackoff? Maybe get a few girls of your own."

"Kneel down now!" he yells.

"She's strong, you know. They'll never break her spirit." I continue talking trying to buy myself enough time to find a way out of this situation. I slowly lower myself to one knee, keeping the other bent.

The guy pulls his mask up over his head and grins. His dirty blonde hair is plastered to his head and his crooked smile makes me want to bust his teeth out of his mouth. "You have no clue, do you? She *WILL* be broken. Emil Reyes is paying a large amount of money for her tomorrow. She won't even be the same person when he's finished with her. I hear he's a real sicko in the bedroom." He licks his chapped lips and winks at me, trying to push my buttons.

I grind my teeth to bite back the retort. Pure rage burns inside of me.

My body trembles with it.

"Where will he take her?"

"Wouldn't you like to know." He pulls his mask back into place.

"What are you waiting for? You plan on killing me, right?" I test him. He doesn't say a word for several minutes, just watches me. He's probably the biggest brown noser there and wants some kind of acknowledgment and this will give him the pat on the back he's looking for, maybe move him up the ranks.

Piece of shit.

Suddenly, the radio strapped to his side goes off, and I hear Manny's voice on the other end. My brow creases together and alarm bells go off in my head when I hear the words on the other end of the walkie.

"You have the 'go ahead' Ghost 1. Clean it up when you're done."

It only takes my brain a split second to gather his meaning. Shear adrenaline courses through me, and I launch from the floor off my bent leg and slam into Ghost 1's gut just as a shot is fired.

I feel a burning sensation along my shoulder, but I don't stop ramming him until we fall through the already broken front door. His gun hits the ground behind me when he loses his grip.

I land on top of him after we tumble down the front steps and he struggles to throw me off of him.

I slam my head into to his momentarily disorienting him while I pivot to the side and wrap my taped arms around his neck.

His choking gasp lasts only seconds before I squeeze with everything I have, and then give his neck a sharp twist. I hear the satisfying snap as his body goes limp.

I lay there trying to slow my breathing and listen for danger. I hear no one. It's dead silent.

Kicking Ghost 1 off me, I make my way to the side of the house where there's an old rock well. I saw off the tape on the stones. Morbidly, I laugh at the nickname 'Ghost' because now he is one. The irony isn't lost on me.

Standing over him I make quick work of removing all his tactical clothing and weapons.

"These will come in handy," I whisper to his lifeless face.

I want to shout to the heavens and rip the world apart right now to find her, but I have to be smart about this. One wrong move and I'm dead, and Maisy's gone forever.

The first thing I need to do is discreetly reach Bo. He needs to know what happened, and I'll need to stash my truck near Jacob's residence. Chances are he'll take her there under the pretense that I'm a dead man. If Ghost is right, then she will be gone by tomorrow with Emil, the sadist.

I make quick work of cleaning myself up. I bandaged the wound, which thankfully was superficial, where the bullet grazed me. I pack up everything worth keeping and toss the bags outside. I grab Ghost 1's legs and pull him into the house…

"I have the perfect idea for you, buddy." I smile.

CHAPTER 20

I am so sick of being drugged. I awoke a few minutes ago to Jacob yelling for me to get up. It was time. The shackles were removed, and I was yanked from the bed. He gave me thirty minutes to shower and put on a fitted black dress. After some random housekeeper braided my hair, I was given black heels to put on.

My head was finally beginning to clear. My first thought was that I had precious little time to get out of this situation.

The only problem is, there are so many of them and only one of me. The last time I escaped, it was Tony alone. Jacob isn't taking any chances this go-round. He is here in the foyer with Tony mean-mugging me from the corner. He has the two men in black, which I have heard him refer to as Ghosts 2 and 3, and standing guard at the door is Manny.

All are armed.

This doesn't look good for me. I may have a better chance of slipping the grip of Emiliano than trying to run or fight now.

We waited there a few minutes before I heard a car approaching outside. My heart begins to race, and I feel like puking. A radio strapped to Manny goes off, startling me.

It's nothing but white noise, no words.

Jacob nods toward the walkie that Manny is fiddling with. "Is something wrong with your radio?"

"No, Ghost 1 sent me a message last night that his radio went out. It's been coming in as static ever since. He keeps testing it."

"Where is he, and why isn't he here? We have a pickup later tonight?" Jacob asks, exasperated.

"He had the clean-up, says it took longer than he thought it would," Manny replies.

"Well, make sure he knows the timing for tonight. Every second counts."

"Got it." Manny inclines his head.

The clean-up, he said…even though I can't let myself think about this right now, tears still spring to my eyes. I can't do this. I'll lose it again. They'll just drug me if I do. I try to take slow, deep breaths, but nothing is helping. I squeeze my eyes shut and let the tears slide down my cheeks.

Jacob comes over to me, grips my arm tightly with one hand and my chin with the other, and shakes my face. "Get your fucking self together, or we can make this a lot worse." He scowls as he looks at me with disgust.

Just then, in walks Emil. He looks just as I remember him. Tall, bulky, dark hair and soulless eyes. He has a seemingly normal appearance at first glance…unless you have had a moment alone with him.

I know his true nature all too well.

His eyes lock with mine, and a devilish grin spreads across his face. "I am so glad you could make it this time." He turns to Jacob, saying, "I have a meeting in one hour. Sorry I can't linger here, but we must be on our way. I trust the money was counted and was to your liking…yes?"

"Yes, it was. Thank you again for being patient with me." Jacob grabs my hand, placing it in Emil's. "It was a pleasure as usual doing business, Mr. Reyes."

I can't make my feet move.

Emil feels my tension and begins half dragging me through the doors. I look for any opportunity to run, but I'm surrounded as they follow us to a black stretch limo and usher me inside the back. I can see why this car is used once I'm inside. It has custom work adorning the interior, including wrist and foot chains. There is a thick tinted glass barrier blocking the view of the driver. The worst addition, or should I say subtraction, to the car…there are no handles on the inside.

No way out.

CHAPTER 21

Callon

My heart is thrumming inside my chest as I make my way carefully through the forest. Being silent in the woods during Fall weather in the south can be tricky. The only thing keeping me focused is the knowledge of what will happen to her if I don't get there fast. What she went through before was nothing compared to what these assholes will do now that she's caused them so much trouble.

My mind keeps going back to those last moments in the cabin. Maisy offered herself up to save me. That is something she never should have done. It speaks volumes to the kind of person she is, selfless and brave.

I have never wanted anything more than her to be safe and happy. I want it more than I want to live.

We were so close to her freedom. Bo had obtained all the papers she needed. Our old friend from the service, Declan, found a few houses for sale. The plan was in place.

If I was being honest with myself, we had everything ready for her to leave several weeks ago. I wasn't ready to let go.

This is all my fault in so many ways.

I owe her, and she will have the life she deserves.

Last night, after I fled the cabin, I made my way to Bo's house. Once I was close, I went the rest of the way on foot to make sure I wasn't being followed. All the belongings I kept were stashed in a hidden bunker near the cabin. It was small and made more like a cellar for canned goods but worked well for a temporary stash.

Bo's face when I told him what happened is something I'll never forget. It was like seeing him lose his sister all over again. There was no need for convincing, he was completely on board with helping me finish this.

I hid my truck in the woods not far from the end of the Rainer driveway. It's loaded with ammo and a few weapons, blankets, Maisy's bugout bag with all her documentation, some food, and water. I left Bo the Buick. I plan on sending her to Mexico in my truck the moment I get her out of this mess. If…no, *when* I get her back, we have to find somewhere new to lay low for a while.

It's mid-day when I see Jacob's house not far in the distance through the trees. If you can even call it a house. It is a three-story sprawling West-Coast-style mansion. I couldn't start to guess the square footage but knew that today, I would have to comb every inch of this place. I plan on leaving no survivors.

My soul may be damned forever after this, but she will be saved. That is all that matters now.

Once I reach the closest border of trees to the house, I lay low for several minutes, awaiting any kind of movement. Being here again reminds me of the last time I staked out this place.

I had gotten word from Bo that she may have been kept here the whole time. He had followed Jacob's movements, and this house was not his main house, nor was it in his name. However, he was here as much as his house in Raliegh. The difference was the influx of strange vehicles—some license plates from other states, and some not plated at all. That, along with CCTV cams, Bo hacked into gave him places Jacob frequented. He told me to check it out.

I hid in these woods thinking that maybe I would never find her, that she was possibly dead or in another country.

God or fate was with me that day. Maybe both, because after hours of watching the comings and goings of the house, out of the blue, a girl burst through the back kitchen door.

She sprinted into the woods wearing next to nothing, panic clear on her blood-soaked face. I was certain it was her. It was the most sickening feeling to see Tony stumble through the same door seconds later, hot on her heels.

Today I sit here hoping that God and fate is riding shotgun with me again, even though I know I'll be damned anyways.

I'm wearing all of Ghost 1's gear. In theory, I could just waltz in there. I made sure that Manny believed that everything went as planned last night. They think I am dead, and G1 had a rough time with the clean-up and that his radio was having some issues.

"Fuck it…I'm going in. I always did like a good Waltz," I mutter. I sling the AR-15 over my shoulder and double-check the pistols and knives. Making sure I'm ready for anything. One handgun I made certain not to forget is Debbie. If I get to Maisy, she'll need her gun.

I check my surroundings one more time before walking casually toward the back door. My heart beats a steady rhythm along with my footsteps. This is the same door that she ran through months ago. I don't slow or falter when I see someone limp out of the door and light a cigarette.

It's Tony.

He takes a long drag from his cig as he reaches down and rubs his knee, which has a brace from mid-thigh down.

I smile behind the mask, recalling how proud I was of Maisy when she shot him. As I get within ear distance I say, "Knee giving you trouble today, Tony?"

He jumps, bug eyes startled, looking me up and down while holding his chest. "Damn, Kevin! You about gave me a fucking heart attack."

Kevin. So that's Ghost 1's name. He apparently hasn't noticed the voice yet, or the mask is distorting it. Whatever, it works to my benefit.

I smile behind the mask. "Sorry, mate, I was just getting back. Last night was crazy. Took me a while to get it cleaned up."

Tony takes another long drag squinting his eyes in pain. "It's all right. Yeah, my damn knee is killing me today. What a wretched little bitch. I'm glad this is all over. Between you and me, I don't know why Jacob wasted his time and money trying to get her back. Either way, it's done now. The little bird has flown the nest." He grumbles.

My interest has peaked, and my adrenaline is pumping at his words. "What do you mean it's done?" I ask, trying to calm my trigger finger.

Tony slaps me on the back, laughing, "She's gone, thank fuck! Jacob ushered her out the door about an hour ago with that Emil weirdo."

My heart stops for a moment.

I'm too late. I thought I had time. I have failed her. I can feel myself shaking with unspent rage. I have to keep it cool. I take a deep breath through my nose to calm myself, but my teeth are clenching. Someone here will know where he took her. I just have to play this out as planned. No one leaves here alive today.

"That's…well, that's great. Glad to hear it. Where did he take her." I lean against a porch rail and try to act casually.

His face contorts and he scoffs. "Why does it matter? She's not our fucking problem now." Tony finishes his cig and flicks it into the yard.

"Just curious. He's a strange character, I hear."

"Strange doesn't begin to cover it." Tony coughs as he chuckles. "You've heard the stories, man. Besides, I don't know where he's taking her today, but tomorrow they leave for Spain." Tony stops for a split second and cuts his eyes at me. "Take that damn mask off, Kevin. Shit is creepy as fuck."

Spain.

I have to find her before that happens. In the meantime, someone in here must know where she is *today*. I smile as I say, "Sure thing, mate," and I slowly lift my mask to rest on my head, all the while, my hand is on my Beretta M9 equipped with a silencer.

Tony's eyes bug out as his eyes settle over my face.

He doesn't have time to yell before I pull the gun and fire a shot between his eyes.

Not a *single* bit of remorse fills my body.

I make quick work dragging him into some nearby bushes tucked around the porch. Luckily, the blood was hidden in the grass.

Now, onto the next doomed soul to run into 'Kevin.'

I pull my mask back into place and ease into the kitchen, which is the size of three normal ones, and quickly clear it. I check the adjacent rooms, which include a pantry and a bathroom.

Nothing.

The dining area and hallways nearby are also void of life at the moment. Then I hear it…someone's muffled voice is close by.

I decide on the same approach I took with Tony. I am going to walk around like I belong here. I stroll through a door leading to what looks like a small ballroom with its vaulted dome ceilings. The odd thing is the center-raised dais with chains attached to the floor. After closer inspection I see the drop-down monitors at all angles on the walls near the ceiling. It dawns on me what this room is for. I remember Maisy's struggle when she talked about her 'viewing.'

It makes me want to puke.

There, by the adjacent doorway leading out, is Ghost 3. His mask is off, revealing his true self. He has a close-shaved head with beady brown eyes and acne-marked skin.

I guess I'd wear a mask, too, if that's what I had to work with.

He is dressed like me, still in the same tactical gear as before. G3 startles when I enter, and I can see he is just putting away his walkie. That must have been the voices I heard.

He pins me with a glare. "Shit, Kev, where have you been. It shouldn't have taken all damn night. Manny is pissed!" he blurts out.

I keep coming closer, not sure if my voice can fool this guy considering they worked together daily.

"Dude, is everything okay? What happened last night?" He continues watching me but is getting wary the closer I get.

I clear my throat and stop just a few feet from him. "Last night was good, really good." I see creases form between his eyes as he hears my voice. "He's dead alright…," I growl out.

His demeanor changes instantly and I see his body tense. Recognition blankets his face.

He moves fast for the gun on his side, but not fast enough.

I drop him with two rounds to the chest and one to the head for good measure.

I guess I won't be questioning this douchebag. This time, blood is everywhere. I'll have to work fast clearing this house because someone is bound to notice. I move his body into a nearby bathroom and throw a nearby rug over most of the blood, then decide to clear the rest of the bottom floor and basement before moving up.

The lower levels contain entertainment areas, and off to the back it looks to be servant quarters. I see a few staff members milling about cleaning as I walk around still pretending to be Kevin. They are all Hispanic older woman. Most likely purchased not just for work, but because they can be forced to keep secrets. Whether they know about what goes on here or not, I will not be taking their lives today.

I find a door leading to the basement levels. I descend the stairs into another world. There are two options, left or right. To the left, there are several rooms, probably a dozen, with pad-locked doors. All of which are thankfully open at the moment. Peeking into each, I can tell that these are the rooms women are kept in before being sold.

Maisy was kept in one of these.

My heart lurches in my chest and I clench my teeth.

There are ropes at the head and foot of each bed. I scrunch my nose when I get to the last room I have to. It has the smell of fresh paint. Over by the closet, I can make out scratch marks in the wall behind the coat of paint. I run my hands across them. There's so many. I make a quick count in my head, and the realization hits me.

This was likely her room. These are tally marks. I shake my head to clear it. I have to focus, or I'm going to lose my shit.

To the right of the stairs leads me to what looks to be, party rooms. One is huge and has two bars at either end. Round tables a strung about with poker chips in the center.

There's no one milling about down here. I feel dread sink into my bones. What if I don't get her location?

Once I clear the basement areas, I make my way to the stairs that lead to the second floor. This floor has its own smaller kitchen and several sitting areas and bedrooms. They look to belong to the security.

Good. Maybe asshat G2 is here somewhere. The image of Maisy, mostly nude, slung over his shoulder hasn't left my mind. He will pay with his life today.

I see a few more servants who pay me no mind. Then I hear some shuffling and moaning coming from the room at the end of the hall and music playing on a stereo. I creep to the door and listen long enough to know what is happening inside.

I carefully turn the handle…it's unlocked.

I listen once more before opening the door as slow as possible, the moans and grunts of a male continue.

The next sound I hear makes my blood run cold…a whimper from a female.

Quietly, I slip into the room. The music drowns out my entrance. Fate may be with me after all because there's a wall and a bathroom to the right blocking me from seeing who's on the bed…and them from seeing me. I place my back against the wall and ease my way towards the noises.

I've slowed my breathing as much as possible and have my gun by my head at the ready.

"Take all of me, baby…that's it," I hear a man say.

I peek around the corner to see a hulking man with deep brown skin and short-cropped curly hair. He's on top of a girl who is bound, gagged, and blindfolded. She looks to be a young Hispanic girl…*very* young.

I waste no time.

I take a deep breath and move fast into the bedroom and snatch the man's head to the side with one hand and press my gun to his temple with the other.

I make quick note of the situation. He's huge and would be tough in a fight. I keep that in mind and make sure the gun is firmly against his thick skull.

He cuts his eyes a bit to glimpse who has hold of him. "What the fuck are you doing, Kevin!" He yells frantically.

I press my gun harder, and he quits moving.

"Kev, man. I don't know what this is about, but let's talk." He's shaking now. His wild eyes dart around the room. No doubt trying to decide on a weapon.

The girl scrambles and wiggles her way backward, probably scared shitless, not knowing what is happening. I look to my left, and there lying over a chair is the other black ops uniform with G2 on the patch. I found my guy.

Nice.

A manic smile grows on my face, "It's Callon, actually. We do have a few things to talk about. That. Is. For. Sure," I say with venom in my voice.

He struggles a little and spats, "What the fuck did you do to Kevin?"

I take the gun and shoot through the ceiling as a warning, then press it back to his temple. "Speak only when spoken to," I growl into his ear.

Luckily, the girl on the bed can't scream and give us away.

"First question and I suggest you do nothing but answer honestly. Where is Emil taking Maisy?"

He slumps in defeat. "If I tell you, Jacob will kill me."

He's a much weaker piece of shit than he seems. I can tell he is already considering caving in to me. "If you don't tell me, I will kill you. Seems you are in a pickle dick."

He exhales loudly before I see his decision in his eyes. "Okay listen, all I know is that they were headed to the Delfire Resort today and that tomorrow they'll be going to Spain. He's from there…that Emil guy. I don't know where he lives, though."

I was surprised he sang like a canary and so fast.

The Delfire Resort. If I am not mistaken, that is the one a few cities over that all the 'big wigs' go to.

"Question two, did you touch her in any way that was inappropriate?" I make sure he feels my grip tighten.

"No, man! I swear! I would never go against Jacob's orders." He whines.

"And this girl here, who is she?" I feel the need to help her blooming inside me. It's what Maisy would want.

"Look…she's mine. I paid for her." He tries to put a little anger into his voice.

Wrong. Fucking. Thing. To. Say.

"Last question, and I'll release you."

"Annnything, mmman, what is it?" he stammers.

"Who is here in this house today? Name them."

"You are really going to let me go, right?" he pleads.

"Absolutely."

"Okay, okay…um. There's Rick, Jacob, Manny, Tony, and the staff. I don't think anyone else is here today."

"Who's Rick?" I ask.

"That's our other security guy, goes by Ghost 3."

That means two down and three to go.

"Thank you for your cooperation. It's greatly appreciated. However," I could feel him tense up in my hands, "you are a disgrace to men everywhere. The one thing we should do as men is protect our women. I hope you burn in hell." Before he can begin to struggle, I pull the trigger, and he falls limp to the floor. His eyes still bulge in shock on his lifeless face.

Two to go.

The girl on the bed is shaking uncontrollably. I put away the pistol. "It's going to be okay now. I need you to trust me. I am going to untie you, and I need you to promise me you will not scream. Nod your head if you understand me." I whisper.

She nods her head quickly. I untie the bandana from her head and her big, wild brown eyes bore into mine. There's so much damage there. She looks to the bloody man on the floor. "I'm going to remove the gag now. Remember, you *cannot* scream. We must be quiet." She nods again.

I slip off the gag, and she takes in long, ragged breaths as tears begin to fall from those troubled eyes. Next, I remove the ties, freeing her completely. Instantly, she bolts up, slinging her arms around my neck.

"Thank you, thank you." she sobs. Her voice has a thick Spanish accent.

I pull away from her, grab the blanket off the bed, cover up her naked body, and then hold her at arm's length. "Listen carefully to me. There are two more bad men here that I need to take care of in order to save my friend. I am going to hide you and then come back for you when it's over. If, for some reason, I don't come back, you must run from here and do not go to the police. You cannot trust anyone from this point forward." I look around the room, finding a notepad and pen. "This is who to contact if I don't come back. He is a good person, and you can trust him." I jot down Bo's personal information.

She nods and grins from ear to ear making my chest ache. "My name is Maria Sanchez. What is your name?"

Even her voice sounds young...adolescent. It makes me want to shoot him all over again.

I give her a smile even though my heart feels like it's in my throat. "I'm Callon Wolfe. Nice to meet you, Maria." She wraps me in a hug one more time.

She feels like skin and bones.

Just then, we hear a blood-curdling scream from downstairs causing Maria to gasp. It sounds like one of the staff found the body or the blood trail...either way, time to finish this.

"It's okay Maria, I left a mess on my way in. Remember everything I told you." I move away from her to scan the hallway.

So far, I still can't see anyone.

Maria shuffles through clothes thrown on the floor and begins dressing. I turn away and go to the window to peek out. The grounds are clear. From here, I have a view of the driveway. Fire burns in my blood as I see two figures jogging toward a black Mercedes.

It's Manny and Jacob.

They peel out of the driveway, leaving a cloud of dust behind them. They know I'm here then. Either way, I've just lost my opportunity to take them out…for now.

The important thing is to find Maisy. I have one more thing to do here first…

CHAPTER 22

We are headed for the Delfire. Every mile down the road is another mile away from freedom. My mind is on autopilot. Emilliano sits across from me, staring me down with those black orbs he calls eyes. If this is his intimidation tactic, it's working. He doesn't speak. It's as if he is waiting to see what I will say or do. I won't give him the pleasure. I refuse to look at him or talk.

Out of the corner of my eye, I see him remove his suit jacket, leaving him in a fitted button-down white dress shirt. He is a very large man, over six feet and all muscle. Everything about him is menacing. His eyes are so dark they remind me of demons from old movies, and right now, his demonic eyes are devouring my soul.

After a while, he slides over next to me and grasps my chin in his hand, forcing me to look at him. His hand is massive compared to my face, and all I can think is, how will I ever get away from him?

"You seem to be preoccupied in your mind, senorita. What is it that plagues you?" His grip tightens on my face.

I don't speak.

"Well, let me reassure you of a few things. It will make our lives easier together if you understand your situation and embrace it." His tone is condescending.

"You are mine. My property." He releases my chin and moves his hand to my throat, squeezing slightly while moving his mouth within an inch of mine. I gasp, but he continues, "You caused me distress, you know. After the night we spent together at Jacob's, I thought I made it clear that you belonged to me. But you ran away…straight into the arms of another." He stops and squeezes a little harder.

Survival instinct kicks in, and I grab his wrist to try to hold him back. He laughs in my face then releases my neck as his lips snarls up.

"I guess I am fortunate that you didn't give yourself to him. I have so longed to be your first and your last, my love. Now tell me how sorry you are."

My brow creases, and I pause a moment too long.

Suddenly, he backhands me, throwing me into the floorboard of the limo. I lie there clasping my burning cheek. Before I can push away, he grabs my hair and pulls me onto his lap, forcing me to straddle him.

I feel my hair rip in places and tears burning my eyes.

"When I tell you to do something, you do it right then…do you understand me?"

I nod as sobs come out.

"Good, now tell me how sorry you are." He takes his hands, pushing up the end of my dress until it's around my waist.

Even as bile rises in my throat, I say it anyway, "I'm so sorry that I ran awwway." My voice stutters at the end.

He pulls the top of my dress down, exposing my breasts and wraps his hand around my throat again, pulling me to his face. "Kiss me…and make sure to mean it."

I take a deep breath and lean in, placing my lips on his wretched ones. He tastes like cigars.

"I think you can do better than that," he says against my mouth.

I imagine Cal's face and kiss him again. The tears come more freely as I imagine it is Callon that I hold on to.

"Much better. Do you feel what you are doing to me?" He grinds his hips into me. "Don't worry. I want our first time to be in luxury, not in the back of a car, no matter how nice it is. I won't be having you in here. However, I am dying to taste you."

I keep my eyes closed as if I could mentally transport myself to anywhere else in the world.

Emil's hands roam over my body as he continues to grind into me. "I need some gesture from you that you appreciate what I've done for you. I am taking you in and giving you a luxurious life. What will you give me, huh?" he says as he licks my throat.

He takes me and shoves me to my knees on the floor with one hand wrapped in my hair and unzips his pants. Tremors rake my body as I try to push away from him. My head is slammed to the side with the force of another hit.

This time I taste blood and my ears are ringing. Blinking through the stars, I see his putrid face, and he is smirking. He grabs my hair, bringing me back to his waist.

In my heart, I knew right then. This man must die. Someone like him will never stop. Once he is done with me, he will find another girl to warm his bed and sate his sick perversions.

I close my eyes and pretend I'm under that magical waterfall with Callon.

CHAPTER 23

Callon

After seeing them flee the scene, I finished clearing the house and then, with Maria's help, we forced the staff to leave and set off the fire alarms. Maria refused to stay back and insisted on helping me. With a smile on my face, I proceeded to burn the motherfucker to the ground, but not before I located some valuable information for the future.

We snuck off into the forest and made our way to my truck that was near the highway.

The plan is to save Maisy and then once she is out of the US completely, we finish this. Bo has helped me put together some final pieces to make her life easier once she's gone. I'll rid the earth of a few monsters and ensure she doesn't have to spend her life looking over her shoulder. I'm not sure exactly when it happened, but something has changed in me, and it's all because of her. I was a loner who had become content living secluded in that tiny cabin. Now,

I can't imagine not seeing her face every day or hearing her insult me in some adorable way.

Once Maria and I are on our way to the Delfire, the realization hits me that I may be too late again, what if Emil hurts her in some way she can't ever recover from mentally or physically? My internal conflicts must be written all over my face because Maria is staring at me with a worried brow.

"Everything will be okay, Maria." I try to ease her mind, but it doesn't work.

"This friend you are going after, she must be special." She whispers.

"Her name is Maisy, and yes…she is *very* special to me."

I feel her glaring at me as I drive. "She's a very lucky girl to have someone willing to do all this for her."

That made my heart twinge. This girl is far too young to have been through such hardships. "Nah…I'm the lucky one." Maria smiles at that. "How old are you, Maria?"

"Fourteen and a half."

I turned from the road briefly to stare at her, trying to mask the shock on my face. Only children add in the half when telling their age…and she is a child.

It makes me feel better for all the blood spilled back there. I watch the road and stay silent for a bit, but then it hits me. I didn't even bother to ask her if she needed medical attention or if she had any family to go to.

I clear my throat and ask, "Do you need to see a doctor? Are you hurt?"

She shakes her head and holds it high. "I'll be okay now."

Where her strength comes from, I don't know, but it is inspiring. "What about family? Do you have someone I can take you to?"

Again, she shakes her head and, this time, looks out the passenger side window.

Eventually, she says, "My family was brought over to work for Mr. Rainer and in exchange, we would get to live in America. It was just my mother with me. I had no one else. They separated us right away and…I was given to that man." I could see that strength waver in her with that admission.

Scrunching her brow in anger, she whispers, "They used her life as a motivation for me to be good and not fight him. I didn't know until weeks later that they killed her. Mom tried to come for me and fought with the one they call Manny. He shot her." She turns then to glare with full-blown hatred burning in her eyes. "I want them all dead. ALL OF THEM."

She has no idea how much I want that exact same thing.

I nod. "You've got it, kid." I give her the best reassuring smile I can. I hate making promises. Life is full of the unknown, but I ease her mind anyway. "I will make sure they are all punished for what they've done to you. And we don't have to work out everything right this second, but I need you to trust me when I say that I will keep you safe. I have a friend that I'm taking you to. The one I told you about in the house. You can trust him. I can't chance you coming with me to find Maisy. It could put you in grave danger. He has the means to get you a new identity and to help you get back to living."

"Thank you for everything you are doing." She tentatively smiles.

"You're most welcome, kid."

CHAPTER 24

Once we arrived at the Delfire, I was ushered in through a back entrance. It is shocking how everyone bends their will to people of wealth. No one bats an eye at the man using a rear employee entrance instead of the main lobby door to take a girl to his room. Emil just slips money into the hands of the staff, and they turn a blind eye. Where is human decency? Where is chivalry, honor, and integrity?

The suite we walk into is bigger than most American homes. The floors are marble with ornate Spanish-style rugs. The living area has windows along the entire back side facing the city and mountains. In the left corner is a full bar made of walnut wood with bar stools to match. I wrap my arms around myself tightly, feeling the dread of this beautiful nightmare. It feels like walking into a mirage. On the outside, it looks exquisite and inviting. On the inside, it's just a place to die.

Emil slides his hand to my lower back, leading me to the bar. He grabs two whiskey glasses then steps out of the room briefly and reenters with both glasses half full of dark liquid and a bourbon bottle in hand.

"Sit. Have a drink," he commands.

He takes the seat beside me, emptying his pocket contents and laying them to the side.

"Do you like the place?" he asks and then takes a sip from his glass.

I don't answer. Instead, I just nod and sip from the glass. My face contorts, and I wince as the liquor slides down my throat.

"This is the finest bourbon here in the South. Is it not to your liking?"

My memory of the first taste of moonshine comes back to me and punches me in the chest.

The white devil.

What I wouldn't give to be sipping that retched gasoline right now with Callon. I can feel my eyes welling up, even as I struggle to hold it back.

Apparently tired of me being silent, Emil takes my face roughly in his hand and makes me look at him. "I suggest you answer me, or if you'd rather skip the small talk, that can be arranged."

"I am not much of a drink connoisseur," I whisper.

He lets go and nudges the bottom of my glass for me to take another drink. "No worries. I'll teach you everything you should know. You will have a luxurious life. We shall travel the world together."

"As long as I behave…right?" The words come out before I can stop them.

His smile is condescending, and his eyes become even darker. I didn't think that was possible. "That is correct. Obedience is rewarded, defiance is punishable. Turn around." He commands and motions his finger in a circle for me to swivel the bar stool.

When my back is to him, he begins undoing what's left of my braid, letting my hair fall to my waist. My skin crawls at his touch.

"Your hair is beautiful. I want you to leave it down for me unless I tell you otherwise." He says as he trails his fingers through it. He grabs a handful, bringing it to his nose as he inhales deeply. "You are quite intoxicating."

I swivel back quickly and down the rest of the bourbon in one gulp.

He chuckles menacingly. His eyes bore into the side of my face as I continued to stare at nothing. He picks up the liquor and pours both of us another half glass.

"I will provide your clothing and such once we get to my home. You will be happy there…as long as you are a good girl."

Emil stands and forces my stool toward him as he towers over me. Looking down at me, he licks his lower lip and says, "I will have you in every way possible, but first, I must break you in." He leans down, taking my hips and lifting me until I'm flush against his body, then letting me slide down slowly until my feet touch the floor. "Now…I will be right back." He motions toward what I assume is the bathroom. "I need to freshen up. When I get back, the fun begins," he says as he runs a finger down my cheek.

He begins walking away but says over his shoulder, "I have my best man outside this door. Just in case you get any ideas about leaving me again. I don't recommend it."

Once I am alone, every cell in my body screams at me to run, to flee this hell, but I stand there frozen with fear of what will happen if I do.

What happens if I *don't?*

I know the answer to that question. I am not ready to find out how crazy he really is. My body begins trembling as my mind races as fast as my beating heart.

Then I see it…

There, at the end of the bar, is a bottle of pills. I paid no attention before when he emptied his pockets. It has no label on it, but it looks like the same ones they used to give me.

I tiptoe to the pills and pop them open quickly. Taking out several, I smush them with the bottom of my glass. Then, I scrape the powder into Emil's bourbon, stirring it vigorously with my finger. I dust off the bar and my hands, move back to my stool, and have a seat. I cup my glass in hand and try taking deep breaths to calm my nerves.

What if he doesn't take another drink…or what if he *tastes* it in his drink? What if it was Motrin or some other mundane pain medication?

My resolve is all but gone, and I am just about to switch glasses when he saunters out of the bathroom with a devious look in his eyes. Emil is shirtless and wearing only his suit pants from before. His massive form stalks toward me.

I've made a huge mistake.

I look down at the small blade he carries in his right hand then my eyes dart back to his. "What is that for Emil?" I ask nervously.

He moves to the bar and leans against it. His bourbon is within inches of his hand, but he doesn't reach for it.

"This is a tool." He says casually.

"A tool for what?" I ask breathlessly.

"This tool helps reinforce a submissive nature." His thick accent has taken on a predatory tone. "It is also a tool for pleasure. Did you know that pain and pleasure go hand in hand?" He reaches for his glass, bringing it to his lips while watching me intently. Abruptly, he places his glass on the bar without a sip and cocks his head to the side.

It takes me a moment to realize that he is waiting for me to respond. "No…I didn't know that" I whisper.

This seems to placate him, and he lifts the glass again and, this time, takes a long gulp, drinking more than half of its contents, then sits it down.

My heart stops beating as I wait for him to have any reaction to the taste. Emil moves until he is in front of me. He seems oblivious to the drink.

I release a breath that I didn't know I was holding.

"Drink," he commands.

I do as he asks and down the rest of my bourbon. My mind is a jumble of possibilities. What if he did taste it and isn't saying anything? Lord, give me strength, I plead inside my head.

Emil holds up the small silver blade, inspecting it. "This, my dear, is for your sacrifice to me." He ignores my frantic look as I question him with my eyes.

"I require you to give yourself over to me, mind, body, and soul. Your life force is your blood, you see; therefore, I need to make you bleed for me."

This does me in. *"Please don't,"* I beg. "You already have me. There's no need for this." I reach up, cupping his face in my hands to try to convince him. "I'm here. I am yours…*Please* don't do this!"

His voice grows darker. "This is what I require from you. It was not a request."

Before I can respond, he wraps his left hand in my hair and pulls me into a deep kiss that makes me squirm. Then he yanks my head aside. I struggle but quickly stop as the blade is pressed to my neck.

"Do *NOT* move," he spats in my ears.

I squeeze my eyes together as a tear slides down my cheek. Emil leans down and licks the tear as a moan escapes him. He moves the blade down until it is at the juncture between my neck and chest and presses in hard enough to make a thin slice. I whimper and try to pull away, but he has my hair wrapped tightly in his hand with my head held firmly. He moves his face closer to mine and forces me to watch him slowly lick my blood off the blade. He then moves to lick the blood from the cut. He forces my mouth to him when he is finished and kisses me roughly.

All I can taste is copper. I gag.

Pain explodes in my head as he slaps me hard enough to knock me off my feet. I cry out as I smack the floor. My hands pull at the rug trying to drag myself away, but I feel his hands grip my waist as he flings me to my feet.

I can't contain myself and instead bury my face in my hands as I sob.

He stops momentarily and grabs his glass, downing the last of his bourbon. He moves to stand before me and suddenly picks me up, carrying me to the bedroom. His eyes never leave mine. "You are exquisite. Your pain and tears are intoxicating. I can't wait any longer to bury myself inside you. The two of us will become one."

Everything feels like it's in slow motion. A nightmare where you try to move but can't.

He tosses me onto the bed and stands there, hovering.

If my pain gets him off..., what lengths will he go to?

I take my shivering hand and place it against my neck, then take it away. It's covered in blood. It's hard to tell how deep the laceration is.

Emil grabs my legs, pulls me to the end of the bed and, at the same time, my dress drags up and around my hips...

Losing all sense of pride, I beg and plead for him to stop. "*Please*, Emil, don't do this. *Please*! Let's just go slow."

He lets out a low chuckle, "No, I don't think we will." He pulls the top of my dress down until the whole garment is gathered at my waist, and I'm bare to him. He leans down, grasping my breast and placing his face inches from mine.

"Please...continue to plead. I love the sound of you begging." He forces me into another kiss. I turn my head from his devouring mouth, and he moves to my neck.

Just as I am about to give up all hope, he stops and shakes his head as if to clear it. He pushes himself back to standing, and I see his eyes. They are heavier than before, and he wobbles a little on his feet.

I hold my breath, not moving a muscle.

His face is contorted in rage. "*WHAT DID YOU DO?!*" he yells.

"Nothing, I swear..." I say as I scramble backward toward the headboard.

"You little cunt..." Emil lunges for me, and I dart to the other side of the bed, sliding onto the floor. Scrambling to my feet I make a beeline for the living room.

Before I reach the bedroom door, I feel his hand latch onto my arm, slamming me back into his chest. Callon comes to my mind instantly. His warm chest pressed against my back as he taught me how to escape a bear hug attack.

I drop my weight in Emil's arms, and it forces his release long enough for me to slam my elbow back into his nose.

Blood sprays everywhere.

Emil drops his head cupping his nose. "You are *FUCKING DONE!* Do you hear me?!" he shouts. *"FUCKING BITCH!"*

I race out of the bedroom with Emil on my heels. I turn to see him stumble. The drugs finally doing their job.

He won't last too much longer. If I can just hold out.

I am almost to the door in the living room when I remember the man outside. I make the quick decision to run the opposite way and try to lock myself in the bedroom until he passes out. I can figure out an escape later.

I'm almost there when I feel his grip on my arm. Emil catches me just as I am passing the bar.

This time I fight with everything I have left in me. I slam my fist into his nose and blood sprays again as he yelps. He doesn't let go and when I swing again, he dodges the blow and wraps his free hand into my hair.

I feel my body tipping backward as he slams my head into the bar.

There's a loud cracking sound and I see stars as I hit the floor, limp. I hear something hit the ground beside me.

The last thing I see is Emil's face on the floor in front of mine before I am out cold.

CHAPTER 25

Callon

Maria is safe with Bo, and he is diligently working on a plan for her like he did for Maisy. I left my truck behind and took a rental Crown Victoria Bo had ready for me.

This will all be over soon.

I am outside the resort, watching and waiting for the right opportunity to arise. This place is definitely out of my league. However, I just have to find the right schmuck to 'borrow' a change of clothes from.

Thirty minutes into the stakeout, I see a man in a three-piece suit headed to the parking garage in his Jaguar E-type. He looks like a man who would rather park his own car than allow some kid at VIP do it. With that car, I don't blame him, but this isn't going to be his day.

I make my way through the garage awaiting 'Jaguar guy' to get out. The moment he does, I grab him from behind and press the barrel of my gun against his temple with my hand clasped over his mouth. He struggles and mumbles, but I hold firm.

I growl into his ear, "If you value your life, you will shut the fuck up and stop moving." That gets me the response I'm looking for, and he stays still, holding up his trembling hands.

"This is simple, I need your clothes and key card. You give me those, and you live. Then I will tie you up and leave you to be found. You will not be hurt. Got it!"

His eyebrows crease with confusion and distrust, but he nods vigorously.

"Do not look at me. Keep your eyes down and do not scream, or it will be your last act on this earth."

I release his mouth and push his head to face the concrete as I wrap a blindfold over his eyes. He is shaking and sobbing, makes me *almost* feel bad, but not that much. I hold the gun to his head the entire time he undresses. As he reaches to pull down his tighty whities, I halt him with a tap of the gun to his head.

"Hell no…keep those on. I don't need your undies. Ugh, gross, man."

Once he is fully bound, I leave him in his car as promised. Bo was instructed to make an anonymous call to the police once I'm gone. They'll find him safe in his car. I don't make a habit of killing innocent people.

I don the suit and shoes quickly and dump the contents of his briefcase into the car. I place my clothes inside the case and head toward the elevator entrance with the key card in my breast pocket. Then a thought hits me…the windows. Don't want this guy to die from suffocation in his favorite car. That would be shitty of me. I crack the windows and head out of the garage.

Show time.

Once inside, I take a pamphlet I pass by that has all the five-star venues and restaurants in the area. I keep my head down and fain interest in the brochure, trying not to be noticed. I have no clue which room they will be in. However, I know who will, the kitchen staff. They know who orders what and when it needs to be delivered. That's my best chance of finding her.

It takes me a while to locate the kitchen and wait until the doors leading in are clear of people. I creep in and quietly slip into the pantry closet I find in the back. Looking through the glass square in the door. I wait to see whose day I'm to ruin next.

Five minutes feels like a lifetime until, finally, someone pops in the door. A tall and gangly man with large bifocal glasses…doesn't look like a fighter.

I wait until he is walking right past the door, and I slam it open, hitting him in the back and thrusting him to the ground.

"*What the hel—*" he starts to yell as I slam my knee into his back, holding him down and pressing the gun to the back of his head.

"Don't move, don't speak, and don't look at me." I knew I had to be quick in case another employee came waltzing in. "I need to know the room number of a well-known douchebag that happens to be staying here, and if you don't tell me…well, then you are about to have a VERY bad day."

"If I do that, I'm fired," he whines.

"If you don't, you are dead, and I get someone else to do it."

He sighs and lays his forehead on the floor, mumbling a silent prayer then says, "Who is it?"

"Emilliano Reyes."

The chefs' eyes bug and he begins shaking his head side to side. "That man is bad news. If he finds out, he'll have me killed!" he pleads.

"Then be a smart man, give me the room number and don't tell anyone we had this conversation. It's a win, win situation don't you think?"

His head is nodding as he cries, "You promise you won't hurt me, right?"

"Promise, now out with it!" I push my knee into his back a little deeper.

"Okay, okay, okay! He's top floor. Presidential Suite 4."

"When I release you, stay down for two minutes until I am good and gone. Go about your day as normal. Like you said, if you tell anyone, he comes after you and…so will I." I slowly move away, keeping the gun on him until I am out of the room. I wait at the door for thirty seconds, listening, but hear no movement. I'm just going to have to hope that he keeps his mouth shut long enough for us to get out of here. Because there is no other option.

I will leave with her or not at all.

My nerves are on edge and the damn elevator seems to take forever to reach the top. The elevator door opens finally, and I quickly notice the suit inconveniently standing outside of Presidential Suite 4.

He looks like a smaller version of Vin Diesel, but stocky as hell, nonetheless. This may be harder than I thought. Then I notice the earpiece he has in and the cord running to his pocket. Dude is listening to music on the job. He's nodding his head along to a beat. He was *not* the best choice for security detail.

Good for me.

I smile and casually glide down the hall, seeming to be having the best day ever. As I pass 'Little Diesel,' I let my pamphlet drop from my pocket.

On cue, he bends to retrieve it, saying, "Excuse me si—" I spin fast and grasp him in the sleep hold before he can finish his sentence. I squeeze as hard as I can as our bodies slam into the wall.

He struggles and reaches for his gun, but I slam us to the ground and wrap my forearm tighter around his neck. I hear the gun clang on the floor. He tries to pry my arm from his neck with one hand and reach for the gun with the other.

He is stout as an ox, but I don't release pressure until he finally stops moving.

I lean over him trying to catch my breath and check for a pulse. It's good and strong. I snatch the room card he has in his pocket and his pistol fitted with a silencer. NICE.

This guy may or may not know what Emil does, but I don't feel right taking his life if there's a chance that he may be innocent.

I drag his heavy ass into the closest bathroom, prop him in a stall, tie his hands, and place a gag over his mouth.

Cleaning staff will find him…eventually.

Now…my plan could be foiled by two people, him being found too soon and the chef. Shit, shit, shit!

Back at Suite 4, I listen with my ear to the door.

Nothing. Not a sound. Not even a television or stereo.

My gut wrenches at the silence. What if something terrible has already happened? A new fear invades my mind. What if they are not here and all of this is for nothing?

I swipe the keycard and say a silent prayer of my own as I slip into the room.

I shut and lock the door behind me as slow as possible. Everything is too quiet here. I inch my way from the foyer to the living area. Sweat trickles down my spine.

My body freezes as my head tries to understand what I'm seeing.

There, by the bar, are the bodies of two people.

I rush over, pistol drawn, seeing right away that one is Maisy. It feels like the breath has been knocked out of me when I see her lifeless bloody form on the ground.

I briefly glance at the other body. This must be Emilliano. I drop to the floor, feeling for Maisy's pulse. My heart stops while I hold my fingers over her carotid.

Thu-thump-thu-thump. I feel a steady rhythm and release a thankful breath.

Whatever happened here had been bad. Real bad. Her dress is around her waist, and there's blood on the floor and in her hair.

My body begins shaking with rage. I clench my jaw looking over to the piece of shit beside her.

He is still breathing.

She must have fought back. "That's my girl, Maze." I whisper.

And I feel that statement to my soul. My girl. That is what she is. But how the hell did they both end up knocked out cold on the floor?

I look around to try and decipher what has happened and what my next move should be, mumbling, "Maisy, I've got you. you are going to be okay." I lean over her, fixing her dress. She doesn't show any signs of waking up.

"Now, how am I going to get you out of here without being seen…?"

To the side of the room, I see a large luggage cart. My brows raise. "Oh, you would hate this idea, sweetheart."

I carefully roll her onto her back. I pause when I notice the cut along her chest. "What did he do to you?" My vision goes black as I look at her bruised face and sliced chest. The back of her head still leaks blood, and so does the chest wound.

I remove my suit jacket and work it on her to help keep her warm. I lift her off the floor and lie her on the cart and then proceed to place jackets, blankets, and suitcases around her curled body; anything that will hide her. I make sure her face is in the center and not covered. I walk around it at least three times, ensuring no one passing will see a body on this cart. Then I turn my attention to the lump of shirtless bile on the floor.

"I know exactly what to do with you." A sinister smile splays across my face as I drag his carcass toward the large glass doors. He is huge, and it takes considerable effort to cart his big ass to the balcony. Once we are through the doors, I pull him near the banister. "This is not going to be easy," I mutter as I look at the size of him again.

The sun is setting, which will make it hard to see what is going on up here, but not impossible.

I lay down beside him like I was taught in the Army, grab an arm, and leg, and roll with him until he is in position. Once I have him just right, I stand with him on my back.

Suddenly, I feel his hand twitch, and he moans.

"Oh shit, oh shit," I whisper.

I spin around quickly, taking a few steps backward and thrust him over the railing.

Time slows as he is falling away from me.

I see his eyes open wide in horror.

The last thing he sees is my grinning mug. I continue to watch until his body smacks into the pavement stories below.

Good riddance. The world is short, one massive asshole. As I make my way back to Maisy, I hear commotion and screams from the street below.

We have to get the hell out of here and NOW!

I roll Maisy through the hall to the elevator, then punch the button for the ground floor. Once inside, I fix my suit and wipe away the sweat. I crack my neck and knuckles a few times to release some tension.

I've made it this far. Now to reach the fucking Crown Vic.

I casually roll through the hall that leads to the parking garage, passing several people along the way.

Once in the garage, I hear sirens in the distance and pick up my pace. I pass by the random, unfortunate soul I tied up in his car. He will be fine; I'll make sure of it, but for now…she is my only concern. I ease her into the back seat of the car, cover her with a blanket, and toss the rest of the bags in the trunk. My heart aches at the sight of her battered body.

It makes me want to toss Emil's ass over that railing one more time.

Luck is somehow riding shotgun with me today as we exit the garage. It happens to be at the opposite end from where police and ambulances are already gathering around Emil's lifeless corpse. Some people are walking and others running up the street toward the commotion. Nosey people wanting to be the first to see what is happening. Nobody is headed left out of the garage other than me.

All my original plans fly out of the window as I realize how uncertain our future is now. She needs medical attention, more than I can give her. I try not to think about it, but the worst possible brain injuries flutter through my mind. Best case scenario, she has a mild concussion or has been drugged, and her head is fine.

The fact is simple and also complicated, she has to go to the hospital.

The obvious problem is that once she is there, the media will get wind of it fast, and so will Jacob, wherever he is.

This was not the plan! She was meant to disappear and live out her life in peace. I squeeze the steering wheel so hard my knuckles turn white. I will burn the world down if that's what it takes.

Maybe there is a way we can use this to our advantage…I think as I monitor her breathing in my rearview. It's nice and steady—strong like her.

She has me completely consumed and doesn't even know it.

CHAPTER 26

"UGGHHHH," I groan loudly as I awake to the pounding inside my skull. I feel like I have been struck with a sledgehammer…repeatedly. My eyes blink a few times before I can bear to open them fully. The lighting around me is blinding, and my mouth is parched. My surroundings come into focus. There's a steady beeping on my left.

It's an IV pole. I follow the tubing to see the IV in my arm.

"What is going on?" I say aloud as my voice cracks. A monitor on the wall displays a steady heartbeat rhythm and blood pressure readings. A chair in the corner is empty, although a blanket lays haphazardly on it as if someone were there.

I'm in a hospital room.

I rise quickly, feeling a tug of resistance and realize my arms are strapped to the bed with padded white wraps. The kind that is usually placed on crazy people.

"Well, doesn't all this seem slightly familiar," I whisper, somehow managing sarcasm.

Panic builds slowly in me the more alert I become. With every passing second, my last memories begin to wash over me. I fought off Emil and drugged him before that. I remember that it wasn't enough because he caught me and slammed my head into the bar. I remember his face as he fell beside me right before the darkness took me.

My last worrying thought was which one of us would wake up first.

How did I get here? How am I alive?

I hear voices muffled outside my room door but can't quite make out what's being said. Whatever has happened, one thing is for certain…I cannot trust anyone with the truth. As of right now, there's only one person I need to reach, and that's Bo. He will know what to do, and maybe, just maybe, he will know what happened to me. The only problem is the paper he gave me with his contact information is long gone.

My heart begins to ache in my chest as a lump forms in my throat. Cal would know what to do. I close my eyes and picture his face. I wish we had more time. So many words were left unsaid. How can I move past the only man I have ever loved and to have had him for such a fleeting time. He was my savior, but more importantly he was my friend.

What I wouldn't give to go back to that moment with us making out on the kitchen counter but for things to go differently. It's the purest form of torture to dwell on what could have been, but I let myself anyway as tears soak the pillow.

I never really grieved him properly.

Now, I want to scream and shout at the heavens for answers to *why* he was taken from me. *Why him?* He sacrificed everything to find me.

Those were his last mouthed words to me as they carried me away. He said he would find me.

Cal was right about Jacob; he would never stop. If Jacob thinks for a second that I'll turn him in, then I'm number one on his hitlist, and I have to get out of this hospital! What is the news saying, I wonder? At least now he will want me dead and not a slave, I think morbidly.

The doorknob to the room turns, and I take a shaky breath, trying to gain control over my emotions. A nurse walks into the room with a weary face as she eyes the monitors, not yet realizing I'm awake. Then, she turns to look at me and startles. Her big brown eyes widen.

"Oh honey, you're awake! That's wonderful." She leans over me, and her eyes linger on my wet cheeks. "You are safe now, Ms. Murray." She pulls a tissue from a drawer and dabs my cheeks lightly. "How do you feel? Does anything hurt?"

I ignore her questions, wet my lips the best I can with my dried-up tongue, and manage to ask, "How did I get here?"

She sees my struggle and holds up her finger as she walks out of the room and, minutes later, returns with ice chips.

"Here, sweet girl. Suck on these, it will help." She puts a piece in my mouth.

It is so soothing, and I am immediately grateful. Once my mouth has moisture again, I repeat the question, "How did I get here?"

"To be honest, hun, I am not supposed to be talking to you about anything. However, keep this between you and me, okay?" Her curly brown hair hangs in ringlets around her round face. Her deep southern accent somehow brings me comfort as she looks around the room as if someone might be listening and continues, "You, my deary, must have a guardian angel out there because you were anonymously dropped off here. The police had already checked the emergency entrance camera footage, but unfortunately for them, that *particular* camera was down. Strange huh? No other cameras were down in the hospital except the ones that faced the parking entrance and ambulance bay."

I scrunch my brow at that. "Yeah, strange," I mumble.

One person comes to mind, handy with computers, who has a gift when it comes to making things disappear. Could it be Bo who brought me here?

My nurse's name tag is dangling in front of me as she checks my IV and continues talking in her sweet Southern voice about what I am hooked up to and why. It reads Tammy Washburn.

"Mrs. Washburn," I interrupt her, "Why am I strapped down?"

She visibly frowns before answering, "Well, you came in with a head injury and unconscious. Once we did the head scan and established that you didn't have any major brain trauma, just a concussion, we did a blood panel and found a certain…drug in your system. You were slightly out of it, calling out a name in your sleep. You were…pulling at your IV. I'm sorry, we had no choice but to do that to ensure you got the fluids and medicine you needed."

"What was the drug?" I asked, even though I knew the answer.

"Rohypnol."

I think back to the bottle sitting at Emil's bar. The label was rubbed off, but I could make out the R. It was a date rape drug used on me several times when I was with Jacob. The odd part is that I drugged Emil and all the while, he was doing the same to me with that first drink of bourbon, and I never realized it. That is both sick and twisted. The problem was he didn't realize I had quite the tolerance for it. It must have taken longer to hit me this time, or he didn't use enough.

Tammy reaches down, unlatches my wrist on both sides, and smiles as she fluffs my blanket. "I'd say it's plenty out of your system now. Would you like the TV turned on and some food?"

Wait, did she say I was calling out a name while I was out?

"What was I saying…when I came in?"

She averts her doe eyes and fiddles with the monitor. "Honestly, I couldn't make it out."

Something tells me she could, but why would she not say?

She turns on the television, and as she's about to leave, I stop her. "How bad is it out there?" My eyes pierce hers, and she gets my meaning.

"We have succeeded in keeping the leaching news reporters outside. However, the police are everywhere. The detective on your case, Detective Sawyer, has been patiently waiting for you to wake up." She stares at me a bit longer, and her eyes soften, "But no worries, he doesn't have to know you are up…just yet." She winks.

I tell her thank you and give her an appreciative smile. I could hug her if it wouldn't be awkward. I think I really like her.

I sit up in bed, munching on ice and flipping through stations until I reach the local news. I almost choke on a chunk of ice at the face I see before me.

There, on the news, is Emilliano Reye's face. The screen switches to a reporter on the street in front of the Delfire.

The streets in front of the historic Delfire Resort have been blocked off today as an investigation is now ongoing into the death of forty-five-year-old Emilliano Reyes. His body was found lifeless on the pavement stories below his high-rise suite. According to the resort manager, his stay was to be brief, and he was going to head back to Spain today. It is not apparent, at this time, whether or not this was a suicide.

In a strange turn of events, a man was found bound and gagged in his car with nothing on but his undergarments in the parking garage of the Delfire shortly after an anonymous call was received to the resort manager. He was found to be unharmed. The police are not commenting on anything at the moment; however, they did comment that they are not certain if these two incidents are even related.

My mouth hangs open with the ice melting in between my fingertips. "What the hell happened while I was out," I whisper.

Looking at the bottom corner of the screen, I can see that it's noon. I listen to the reporter cover everything she knows, which isn't much, while I scramble through it in my head.

Yesterday, I was with Emil; today, he is dead, and I am in the hospital. I think about the hospital cameras that were mysteriously not working when I was dropped off. Did Bo do this? It's hard to imagine him murdering someone, even someone as sick as Emil. I need answers and fast before I am grilled by that detective.

Just as the name skims my mind, the room door opens and in walks a police officer. One look at the badge tells me I summoned him up somehow. He is tall and lean with brown, short, cropped hair and blue eyes. He rubs his fingers over his mustache, smoothing it out as he enters the room. His eyes look kind, but is he really?

Behind him, rushing in, is my nurse hot on his heels with a food tray in tow. "Sir, she really needs more time to recoup, and I just brought her lunch, which she desperately needs!" When she looks at me, I can see the 'sorry' she is trying to portray with her eyes.

I struggle to sit straight up and feel the aches and stings in various parts of my body. I take the tray from her and tell her it's okay. Might as well see what he knows. She purses her lips and gives him a nasty look but finally sighs and walks out.

"I do apologize for the intrusion. My name is Detective Sawyer. I was assigned to your case when you went missing." He pauses and takes a weary breath. "I have to say…we were not prepared to find you, especially not alive. I'm sorry if that sounds harsh. It's just that you have been gone a considerable amount of time, Ms. Murray."

"Yes, it was," I say quietly.

"We don't have to do this all today. You have clearly been through a lot, but I just wanted to introduce myself and ask if you wouldn't mind answering a few questions for me?

I shrug instead of answering. This…this right here, is what terrifies me. What do I tell him? Can I trust him? He takes the chair in the corner and pulls it up to my bed. He reminds me of Robert Redford in a way. Outward appearances can be deceiving. No one knows this better than me.

"I want to start by saying that I am sorry for whatever it is that you have been through. I am here to help you, not make it worse. If you looked outside right now, you would see a circus of vultures ready to peck at you. I will not let that happen. We will discreetly take care of you and then get you somewhere safe. I don't want the reporters anywhere near you."

He pauses, waiting for any indication of how I feel. I give him nothing and instead pick up my tray and begin nibbling on a piece of toast.

"Okay, listen…just nod yes or shake your head no. We don't need a full-blown conversation just yet. However, there are bad people out there who deserve to be brought to justice. Maisy, do you know who brought you here?"

I shake my head.

"Do you know where you have been all this time?

I hesitate, but then nod.

"Were you with your parents the night…" He changes the question. "Do you know what happened to your mom and dad?"

I nod.

"Were you there when it happened?"

I nod.

"Do you know who is responsible?"

I don't move. I can't tell him anything without placing a beacon on my head. Cal was trying to save me from this type of scrutiny. It would be so nice to tell the world and tarnish the names of all the scum involved, but I could never be free of it. I would be haunted and hunted forever.

He seems to realize I've shut down and so he moves on. "Was this man there the night it happened?" Detective Sawyer pulls a photo from the folder he carries by his side. The moment he flips it to me, my heart squeezes in my chest.

There is Cal's face. It's the same photo I found online the day we were in the library. His ocean eyes stare back at me. Now *he's* haunting me. I try to clear my expression, but it is too late. The detective caught something in my gaze.

I shake my head no to his question.

His eyebrows pinch together. "Do you know this man?"

I shake my head. Lies.

He cocks his head to the side, pursing his lips, like he's trying his best to read me. "We received several tips claiming this man was seen leaving the scene that night. Certain items link him to the crime. He has made it to the most wanted list in connection with your parents' deaths, and you are telling me you never saw him?"

"That's right," I mutter.

"That *is* strange." He taps his chin with the folder. "The Chief of Police has made it very clear that Callon Wolfe is to be brought down. He will be conflicted for sure to hear that you don't recognize him. I guess it doesn't matter now, seeing as we got word of a body found two days ago that is believed to be him."

My mouth drops open, and my heart beats faster, but I try hard to hide my turmoil. I quickly cram another bite of toast in with a shaky hand.

He wants to see my reaction. Mentally, I block it out and try to focus on anything except the words that just left his mouth. I continue munching on bread, but it tastes stale in my parched mouth.

I nonchalantly ask, "What happened to that guy…Callon was it?"

Detective Sawyer's brow raises. He is definitely not buying what I'm selling. "Do you have a weak constitution, or can I be candid?"

"By all means, be candid," I mutter through a bite of food, keeping my eyes locked on my plate.

"We found a burned body in a cabin. After some research and fingerprinting along with DNA samples collected. We believe that Callon Wolfe lived there, or rather, was hiding out in those woods. The body could not be identified, seeing as how it was burned beyond testing capabilities." He pauses, watching me.

I feel my face pale as the blood leaves it.

"You know, I am surrounded by mysteries right now." He props his hands under his chin and continues. "I have an up-and-coming senator murdered along with his wife, a daughter thought to be kidnapped, and months go by with nothing more than tips left anonymously regarding this Army Ranger—who by all accounts was quite a remarkable soldier. That's not even the strangest part. I have a dead body…burned inside a cabin believed to be Callon. Another house not far away caught on fire the next day. It was a sprawling mansion that we have yet to find out who the owner is.

He sucks his teeth then continues, "Yesterday, I found myself standing over the apparent suicide of a prominent businessman from Spain…and guess what…he shows signs of a struggle. *Even stranger,* he had the same drug inside him that you have. A bodyguard of his was found knocked out in a bathroom but refuses to cooperate. Then, there is a man tied up in his own car after someone stole his clothing and briefcase. More has happened in this town in forty-eight hours than in the last ten years that I have been a detective." His lips form a thin line as he leans back in the chair.

"That is all very strange," I concur.

He smirks. "It can't *all* be related, right? That's what I keep telling myself, but for a small area, it sure is an awful lot of excitement. Not to mention, someone called in to report that guy in the car. Now, who would steal from someone but feel obligated to make sure he was okay?"

"That does seem odd," I mutter.

"Maisy, is there anything you want to tell me about what has happened to you, or do you need some time?"

I peer up at him then back to my plate. "I need time…please."

His jaw flexes. The detective shows restraint for whatever he really wants to say and gets up to leave instead. "I'll be back tomorrow, but until then, can you look this over and see if you can enlighten me on why this would have been in your jacket pocket when you arrived at the hospital?"

He reaches into the folder, pulls out a note, and hands it to me then heads for the door. He stops, and without turning around, he says, "That jacket you were wearing happens to match the description of the suit taken from the guy bound and gagged in his Jaguar in the Delfire parking garage.

"Strange indeed," he mutters as he walks out of my room.

I stare at the folded paper, too stunned to open it right away.

Could that have been the same jacket? What is going on?

I gently open the note as if a lion would burst out of it. Instead, I am met with pure nonsense. It's not a note really, more like a child had written random letters over and over on the page. After a few minutes, I crumple the paper with frustration and toss it aside.

I have more questions now than before. I let my mind drift to the cabin. He didn't just die; they burned his body. I push away the tray, feeling like I might be sick. "I can't get through this without you, Cal," I whisper to no one. "Just give me a sign, something, *anything.*" As I say the words through unspent tears welling up in my blurry eyes, I see the note lying there, bawled up on the floor.

"OH MY GOD," I say aloud.

I scramble off the bed, pulling my IV pole along with me, and snatch the note from the floor. I ignore my pounding head. Pressing and flattening the paper out, I take a second look.

It's their code. The silly story Bo was supposed to tell me but didn't get to finish. Cal told me that story about the prank they pulled. Cal said each letter was a replacement for the one before. Instead of A, it would be B. Hope starts blossoming in my chest. "Okay, I'm going to need a pen…" I say whilst I shuffle through every drawer in the room. I hear my doorknob turn and pause, pretending to stretch my legs while covering the paper.

My nurse walks in and gives a start when she sees me. "Honey! You need your rest and shouldn't be up walking about!" she chastises.

"I just really needed to move around." I fake a few grunts and continue stretching.

"Okay, but only for a few minutes. Can I get you anything?"

I smile sweetly. "Yes, actually, can you get me some paper and a pencil…I like to draw when I'm bored."

Her cheeks dimpled. "Oh, sure thing." She leaves quickly and returns soon after with a pad and pencil.

Once I have assured Tammy several times that I am fine, she huffs but leaves me be. I quickly flatten the note onto the bed and look it over again, praying I am not wrong about this.

NBJTZ
JG ZPV HFU UIJT MFUUFS
UFMM UIFN OPUIJOH
UIFZ DBO OPU NBLF ZPV UBML
JO UJNF BMM XJMM CF SFWFBMFE
J XJMM LFFQ ZPV TBGF FWFO GSPN B
EJTUBODF
FWFO EFBUI XUMM OPU LFFQ NF GSPN ZPV
TFF ZPV TPPO

XIJUF EFWJM

After deciphering the first word…I know I am not wrong. Hope blooms in my chest. If this is their code, then it must be Bo looking out for me.

Maisy.

That's the first word on the page. My heart begins to race, and I exhale loudly. I go slow, doing each word carefully until I have it all written down in front of me.

MAISY
IF YOU GET THIS LETTER
TELL THEM NOTHING

THEY CAN NOT MAKE YOU TALK
IN TIME, ALL WILL BE REVEALED
I WILL KEEP YOU SAFE EVEN FROM A
DISTANCE
EVEN DEATH WILL NOT KEEP ME FROM YOU
SEE YOU SOON

WHITE DEVIL

Tears drop onto the page.

I read it over and over a hundred times. Is it really him? Is it really Callon? It must be, right? It's signed white devil, which is our inside joke. Bo is the only other person to know about it, but would never pretend to be Cal. My heart is exploding in my chest. I want to run from this place and find him. Every part of me is saying to do just that. Every part except this minuscule slice of my brain that says to stay still and be patient. He said all will be revealed.

If this *is* really Cal, if he *is* alive…I need to trust him.

Later that evening, after an emotional breakdown, I ripped the papers to shreds and flushed the pieces down the toilet. The detective has copies, I'm sure, and it's only a matter of time before he figures out how simple this code really is. I will continue to play the traumatized young woman in hopes that I can hold the wolves back until I know for sure that Cal is alive. Until then, I will wait for him.

Even death will not keep us away from each other.

CHAPTER 27

Today is December 5, 1999. It has been one whole week since I received the coded note. I was released a few hours ago from the hospital. Turns out I was dehydrated, needed stitches for several lacerations, had a concussion, and exposure to drugs. Therefore, the doctors wanted to keep an eye on me.

I think my nurse, Tammy, was actually trying her best to keep me out of the media's grasp a bit longer. I am certain I was calling out for Callon in my sleep and for whatever reason, Tammy never said a word. I will forever appreciate the kindness she bestowed upon me every single day that I was there. She gives me hope in humanity and proof that good people exist.

Nurse Tammy wasn't wrong; the media frenzy had gotten out of hand on the outskirts of the hospital. I refrained from watching the news and instead let Tammy fill me in on all the speculations. And it was just that…speculations. No one really knew what happened to me. The only thing they knew for sure was that I was back and safe in that hospital.

I often sat in that room, thinking about Jacob, and wondering where he was and what he was doing. He would have known right away that I was found, and that Emil was dead. He must be waiting me out to see what I will say. Maybe he's been stalking me the whole time.

I wasn't as concerned at the hospital due to all the cops required to stay near my room, but now I am being released. The fear is real and embedded deep in my bones. It stems from such uncertainty of what I will have to face in the public's eye and who could be lingering in the shadows. I still have every intention of moving far away from here, but first, I have some unexpected responsibilities to handle.

I had somehow stored certain things in boxes in my brain to pull out at a later date and time. I am known for compartmentalizing when I get stressed. That trait helped me survive captivity. One of those boxes in my brain stored the knowledge that one day, I would have to deal with my family's belongings *if* I were ever free to do so. My family's property, like the house, the land, the cars, would have all been placed in my name, since I am the only child.

When I was living in the cabin, I had resigned myself to the knowledge that one day I would leave, and those things would just be left behind along with all the memories. Maybe they would go to auction and be sold off to various people who would love to own something from the famous Murray family murders.

The plan was to stay a missing person, but now…here I am. I never imagined that I would be headed back to that house.

To my home.

I'm riding shotgun with Detective Sawyer, still not convinced I can trust him, but here we are. It's not like I had much choice in the matter. He was able to get me out of the hospital discreetly, with the public unaware.

We're on the way to my parents' house…well, my house. The amount of time that I was missing would have normally pushed a bank into taking the house. Lucky for me, a friend of my dad's happens to be a lawyer and a good one. His name is Jack Olsen and while I was missing and the investigation continued, he took it upon himself to do some pro bono work in making sure my belongings remained mine for as long as he could. I also learned that he had been at the hospital the day I was dropped off. It was his blanket on the chair. It is comforting knowing someone was there for me at that moment, even though the police refused to allow anyone else in due to the investigation.

I later found out that Jack was having none of that and claimed status as my attorney and, therefore, could see me when he pleased *and* that they were not to ask me any further questions. Jack stayed in contact over the phone with me the last days I spent in the hospital.

The detective speaks up, breaking my train of thought, "I want you to know that we will have someone patrolling this area until we can establish whether or not you are in any immediate danger. I will give you time today to sort through things, but I will be setting you up somewhere off the radar to stay."

"I need to go home," I grumble while looking out the window.

"That's fine, but one night only…the reporters will find out soon enough where you are. We can't have that right now. Especially when we don't even know what we are protecting you from." He looks over at me pointedly. "This would be a whole lot easier for everyone if you would let us in on who is responsible."

I nod. Knowing that he cannot directly question me now without Jack present. "I get that, and soon I will, but right now, I just can't. I'm sorry."

"Would you at least agree to see a therapist? You are not expected to deal with things alone in life. It is perfectly normal to need help." He glances at me briefly while driving.

I sigh and decide that this may feel like a step in the right direction for him. So, I give him this win and I say, "Sure, I'll do that."

His cheeks pull back in a grin. "That is fantastic, Maisy. I'll ask around the department and get you some recommendations and it will be at no charge, okay?"

"Thank you, Detective."

"Just call me Sawyer. That's what everyone else calls me."

"Okay, Sawyer." I fiddle with my nails nervously the closer we get to my home. Slight bruising still mars my knuckles from punching Emil.

I wish Cal could have seen that.

He notices my anxious fidgeting and says, "Look, I made sure to divert the reporters. They were given false information on where you would be headed after the hospital. No one will be here other than you and I and your attorney. I will keep you safe." His eyes crinkle as he gives a sad smile, "but one day is all I can grant you to stay in that house."

I take a shaky breath and nod as I see that we are taking the last turn that leads me home.

He intentionally slows the car down as if he is trying to buy a little more time. "Maisy, before we part ways, I have a question. Did you have a chance to look at that paper found in your jacket pocket?"

I refrain from looking his way since I am a terrible liar. "I did. It just seemed like gibberish to me, so I tossed it."

"Well, per protocol, I made a copy. It sounded like gibberish to me too…at first."

My heart rate picks up pace. "At first?" I ask nonchalantly, scrunching my brow and trying my best to look intrigued.

"Yes, well, the more I looked at it, I noticed some repeated letters grouped together. It seemed like repeated *words*. For instance, ZPV was written several times. The letters are positioned as words would be, and it's laid out like a note."

"Really, why would someone do that?" I watch him closely.

"For the obvious reason—to get a message to someone without anyone else being able to read said message." He stares me down.

What does he know? Has he already deciphered it?

I sit up a little straighter, ignoring his insinuations, and glance out as we roll into my driveway. I feel numb looking out over the house. "Thank you for everything you are doing to help me." I reach for the handle to get out of the car, and he halts me.

"It's what I do, no need to thank me," he smiles. Just as I step out of the car and shut the door, I hear him through his lowered window mutter… "In time, all will be revealed."

I whip my head around with my mouth hanging open, but he is already backing out.

So, he did decipher the note.

My heart thumps wildly in my chest. He figured that much out. Which isn't much, really. I need to stay calm. He knows it was to me, but not who it's from. I don't know what to make of this revelation. If only I could trust him. It would be nice to have a detective on my side. I shake off the trepidation and move to the door.

Before entering the house, I peek down the street and see two patrol cars on either end near my house. I was told they cleared the place prior to my arrival. Parked across from my house is Jack Olsen's unmistakable M5 BMW.

For a few minutes, I just stand outside and take it all in. My childhood home looms over me; a 5,000-square-foot white Victorian-style home. To the left, toward the end of our property, sits my dad's shop, where he would spend most every evening tinkering with cars. For a political man, he was quite handy with a wrench. The lawn is mowed, and bushes manicured which leaves me conflicted.

It looks like we never left, like time stood still.

I eventually get the nerve to go inside.

I am just as shocked seeing the inside as I was on the outside. Someone must have kept this place up. It's clean and tidy, with *everything* in its place. I smell coffee brewing and turn left to make my way into the kitchen, where I find Jack in front of the pot with his back to me. He is in his usual navy three-piece suit.

Jack is probably in his mid-fifties in age but doesn't look it. He is shorter than average and stout, but his face seems to just age slower. He still has a head full of thick dark hair, and from the side, I can tell he has a five o'clock shadow going on. He glances over his shoulder and freezes when he sees me.

"Maisy, my god, you are here. I thought I may never see you again." Jack's smile doesn't quite reach his downturned eyes. "Can I make you a cup?" He lifts his mug as he asks.

"That would be great, Jack," I say softly.

He nods and begins making my cup.

I have known Jack most of my life. He and my father played golf every other weekend, and our families even vacationed together when I was little. My dad was fortunate to have a friend like him. He's as genuine as they come, and for a lawyer, that is saying a lot.

"Have a seat, sweetheart." He passes me the mug as we sit together at the dining table. He reaches over and places his hand on mine, and I see unspent tears lingering in his eyes. "I want to first say that I am sorry for the loss of your parents. They were amazing people and deserved so much more."

I try to swallow the lump in my throat. "I'm sorry, too, Jack. Dad was your best friend."

A single tear spills from his kind hazel eyes, and he clears his throat. "That he was. I am not sure that many people get to have true friendships in this life. I had that and will forever be grateful even if our time was cut short."

He moves his hand away, sitting back in the chair, and I do the same. He sighs heavily. "I guess you are wondering why I am even here or why the house and property look like they do."

"Um, yes, actually. I kind of expected a mess when I arrived, not that I'm complaining." I cock my head to the side and wait for the explanation.

He clears his throat and runs a hand through his thick puff of hair. "I could not let it go...the hope that you were alive. I can't explain it, but I felt like I owed it to William to do this for you. He would have done the same for me if it was my Lora. So, I took it upon myself to start a charity in your name, a charity that would fund basic billing expenses, while I petitioned for the estate and your mother's car to be put in a holding status until you were found or declared deceased. The landline to the house was turned off months ago, but power and water are going…of course." He gestures around us.

The light from the kitchen window streams in like a halo around his head. I give him a lopsided grin. "Jack, you are an angel. This place would have been seized by the bank if it weren't for you."

He frowns and shakes his head, "Not so fast. I'm not that great. The funding has been run through and is a week away from being depleted. I lost the battle with your parents' other cars and the craft shop. They were auctioned off."

"What about the Mustang?"

His eyes grow solum, "It was…it *is*, part of the ongoing investigation. They will not relinquish it as of yet."

I nod once, staring blankly into my cup.

Jack being Jack, he jumps right into the grit of things and says, "What do you need from me? Do you want to talk about what happened? I can ruin whoever's life you need me to ruin."

That brings the corner of my mouth up. "I may take you up on that one day. For now, I just want peace, but peace seems so far out of reach."

He presses his lips together and nods. "Take all the time you need to gather yourself but know that I am here for you all the way."

I take a minute to bask in the warmth of the sun streaming in and finally say, "I appreciate that, and I did reluctantly agree to see a therapist at the recommendation of Detective Sawyer."

He beams in approval. "Good! I think that is wonderful. Have they lined you up with anyone yet? Anyone I know?"

"No, he just mentioned it in the car. I'm sure he will tell me soon. He is picking me up tomorrow and dropping me at some hotel," I say with distaste.

Jack groans. "I know. I was informed about that yesterday. Trust me on this. It's for the best. Those reporters will do anything to be the first to get pictures of you."

Jack looks at his watch and then checks his cell.

"Do you need to be somewhere?" I ask.

"No, well, maybe. I have a complicated case coming up, and the client is breathing down my neck, but you are what matters. They can wait."

I grasp his hand again and beam at him.

We spent the next two hours laughing about old times. He told me stories about my father that I had never heard before. The funniest being when they got drunk on a golf course at North Myrtle Beach and crashed the golf cart into a pond.

I was hoarse laughing, imagining my dad drunk and disorderly. He always seemed so put together and never drank to excess around me. It made me feel cheated out of having those candid conversations with Mom and Dad that you only get to do once you are older.

As Jack was preparing to go, he stopped and handed me his card containing all manner of ways to reach him. We agreed to talk every day once I was in the hotel, and he promised to help me with the business side of moving on.

The emotional side…well, that is a different story.

"One more question Maisy…I have a friend who's a realtor and a very good one. If you are serious about selling and starting fresh somewhere, I can help you with that."

"Thanks Jack, I may be taking you up on that sooner than later." I throw my arms around his neck, hugging him tight, and hear him sniffle. I squeeze a bit tighter, not quite ready to let go.

Once Jack pulled away from the curb, I was left with nothing more than my thoughts and this big empty house full of memories and nick-nacks. I tip-toe up the stairs. The creaks seem so loud in the quietness of this place.

In the master bedroom, at the end of the hall, is Mom and Dad's room. The room is just as odd as I remember. While the rest of the house is old Victorian style with everything just so, their room is filled with my mother's quirky personality.

She always said that a couples' bedroom was a sanctuary and that it is the one place where together you can be who you truly are. It should make you feel serene.

It does quieten my soul a bit as I look around. The room is painted a deep dark shade of hunter green; the ceiling is black, and the curtains are deep gold with black velvet crows along the edge.

Bookshelves line one entire wall, and spaces between books contain nick-nacks and large gemstones. A chaise in mustard, along with a rattan ottoman, sits in the corner for reading. The walnut solid wood floors are covered by woven

Tibetan rugs in funky colors. The other wall holds art and various unique collections from their travels.

My mother was eclectic, to say the least, and an amazing artist. The canvased piece in the center of the wall was my favorite as a child. It's a painting my mom did of a couple dancing in the rain. The woman's hair is plastered to her head as she looks longingly into the eyes of the man she's with.

Mom always said she could feel the love and even the raindrops on her face when she looked at it.

I turn away from the painting so as not to wallow in self-pity and decide to be productive instead. I have today only to gather any belongings that I want to keep, because, unbeknownst to the good detective, I plan on being out of the country very soon. I can have Jack do his magic for me even if I am no longer around.

My mind is made up, and I am determined to start a new life elsewhere. I have no idea how to locate Bo. I assume, at some point, he will find me. As for Callon…I am starting to believe that note may have been left by Bo, or was it made before they found him. I have cried myself to sleep every night, wondering if he is alive or dead. The unknown is killing me, but it has been a week with no contact. By now wouldn't Callon have come for me if he was still alive?

Several hours later, two peanut butter sandwiches and two more cups of coffee, and I have a small pile of things that I intend to take with me when I leave this place.

In the pile, I have a chest of old movies and photos, a suitcase of clothing, cash I found stored in the safe, my dad's 1911 Colt pistol, and a second large suitcase that holds some of my parents' most treasured items. The painting of the two lovers in the rain is propped against it all.

I somehow manage, through aching fatigue, to shower, shave, floss, and brush my teeth. The day has weighed heavily on me by the time I pull on my old Bruce Springsteen T-shirt and some panties and prepare for bed.

I flop onto my parents' mattress and sink into the plush covers.

I decided against sleeping in my old room seeing as how it is a mother-in-law-suite, detached from the house. My parents' bed just feels safer.

Within minutes I am out cold.

CHAPTER 28

I see a meadow of lavender flowers. _I remember this day clearly. Dad had a business meeting in Charlotte, North Carolina, and we tagged along for the ride._

Mom, being Mom, wouldn't stop nagging at Dad to pull over when she saw the field of flowers coming up. He scoffed and complained but pulled over anyways. He could never tell her no.

Mom walked through the field, pulling flowers, and sticking them in my hair. I was ten at the time, but I recall in such detail how beautiful she looked with the sun beating down on her dark hair and her pink skirt flowing in the wind. She was magical.

My mind becomes lucid, and I realize…I am not a child. I look down at the jeans and combat boots I wear. Why am I here?

I panic and start to move away, but suddenly mom is there by my side, her blue eyes turned down with sadness.

"She's gone. They are dead. This has to be a dream," I whisper to myself.

"Everything will work out in the end, my sweet girl," Mom whispers into my hair. My heart clenches in my chest as she continues,

"One day, you will ride away into the setting sun on a horse with a wolf at your side."

She stops and holds me at arm's length. Tears roll steadily down my cheeks, but confusion is still written all over my face when she says, "It is so beautiful here."

"Mom, I miss you both so much. Please don't leave me."

She gently wipes my tears away, shaking her head. "It's beautiful here, but it can be beautiful where you are too."

I hear a creaking sound that doesn't make sense with our setting. I look at the ground and around the field but see nothing amiss. Mom and Dad begin fading away. I hear the creaking get louder…

"Stop! Wait! Please, No! Don't go!" I shout, but they are gone, and I am left in the field. The creaking continues. I hear someone walking through the flowers…

My body bolts upright in the bed and I try to catch my breath.

It takes my brain a split second to comprehend what I am hearing.

Creaking! The stairs!

I scramble onto the floor and snatch my dad's pistol off the side table. It's dark, and I can barely see, but I feel the cool metal and find the thumb safety clicking it off. I'm thankful I loaded the magazine earlier. I cock it back, putting one in the chamber, and try to slow my breathing as I tiptoe my way to position myself behind the bedroom door.

The creaking has stopped. Whoever it is may have heard me cock the gun.

My heart is hammering in my chest and my body trembles.

"Don't shoot…" I hear a voice say from behind the door. "It's me, Maisy. I'm here."

I don't move or breathe for a few seconds. Am I still dreaming? Is this real?

All logic leaves me as I grab the door, swinging it open wildly. I aim my pistol.

Callon is standing at the other end of my barrel.

My lip trembles in time with my body.

There he is…my mouth drops open, and a cry escapes me as I lower the gun and launch myself into Cal's arms.

He catches me as I wrap myself around him. His woodsy scent surrounds me, and something in me immediately begins to heal. A broken part of my soul slips into place. A piece that I didn't even know was missing.

Cal buries his face between my collar and jaw, and his breath shudders against my skin as he inhales deeply. Then we are moving as he carries me to bed. He turns to sit with me still wrapped tightly in his arms—my legs around his waist.

He eases the gun out of my vice-like grip, laying it to the side. He still doesn't speak, and neither do I.

He holds me for what seems like forever as I sob. Cal finally places his hands on either side of my face and forces me to look into his eyes. I am not prepared for the sheer amount of pain I see in them as he scans my face over and over, examining each healing wound. Even *more* shocking is the unspent tears lingering in his eyes.

"I thought you were dead," I whisper.

"Me too," Cal says as he leans forward, kissing each tear and each scar.

We stay silent and wrapped in each other's embrace for a few more minutes. I praise the steady heartbeat I feel against my chest, reassuring me that he is really here…alive.

He continues kissing my head and cheeks. I close my eyes and savor the feel of his lips. As he nears my mouth, he pauses never taking his ocean eyes from mine. I lean in, closing the minuscule distance between our mouths and kiss him with every bit of pent-up emotion I have inside of me.

All the unsaid words will have to remain that way for now. This is too important. This invisible thing between us is all that matters. I press myself against Cal, feeling like we are still a world apart. I long to have every single fiber of his being and to never let it go. To give him all of me in return.

A guttural rumbling escapes his mouth when I deepen the kiss, exploring him with my tongue. The minty taste of him is intoxicating. Cal catches my bottom lip and nips it. The heat coursing through me threatens to burn me alive, and suddenly, the clothes are suffocating.

I want, no, I *NEED* to feel his skin against mine. To know he is *really here*, safe, with me. Cal places his hands on either side of my face. The yearning in his hooded eyes matches the one in my soul.

I lean back, breaking our contact, and frantically pull off my top, flinging it across the room. His eyes flare then darken.

Everything takes the back burner to this need we have right now. A silent conversation plays between our eyes.

Cal takes his time, gaze trailing down my body as if he wants to memorize every inch. I see anger for a fleeting moment mask his face when he sees the raised slice on my chest now healing and stitches removed. I take his hand and place it over my heart.

"I'm okay now…now that you are here."

He lifts his arms as I ease his shirt over his head, and before the shirt can even hit the floor, his mouth is back on mine. He devours me with a need I have never known. I can finally feel his chest against mine. I have longed for the warmth he brings and to feel the steady beat of his wonderful heart in time with mine.

Right now, our hearts are playing a beat even Metallica would envy.

Cal never breaks our contact as he lifts me and spins around to plant me on the bed, hovering over me with heavy eyes filled with desire and something much more.

I am afraid he will do the 'good guy' thing he does and try to slow down. I can feel how much he is holding back. His restraint is balancing on the edge of a cliff, and I am about to toss him over.

I slide my panties off and fling them to the side.

Something snaps in Callon as his heated eyes move down the length of my body. His chest rises and falls as his jaw clenches. He moves to stand before me, wearing nothing but his tactical pants and boots. I have never seen anything more perfect. Every curving muscle defining him is taut with anticipation.

I see the way he keeps his eyes locked on mine as he unzips his pants then slowly removes them, almost daring me to look away.

I do not give in.

I let my gaze languidly roam down his frame, and my heart races at the sight of him. He is perfect. Butterflies flit around in my stomach.

Callon climbs on the bed and leans over me, trailing kisses along my cheek and then down to my neck. I lean my head back giving him better access. When he reaches my chest, he slows and, with devilish eyes, looks up at me as he takes the peak of my nipple into his mouth, causing my back to arch and me to moan loudly. I push my hands into his hair and relish the silky strands.

He continues this exquisite torment with me writhing underneath him until I can't take much more. He kisses his way slowly back to my mouth.

His kiss is all consuming. His body presses into mine, grinding in time with the kiss.

I run my hands over his back and up into his soft hair again while pressing my body firmly against his. The taste of him is so delectable.

He stops kissing me and watches me with his heated gaze, seeking my reaction as I feel his hand slip down my body until it rests between my thighs.

My breath stutters, but I don't look away as he slides his fingers over my center.

I gasp loudly and Callon only increases the torment as he takes my mouth with his, kissing me in time with his fingers movements. I feel a knot of pleasure coiling inside of me and I break away from the kiss as my head arches back.

He continues the sweet torment until I can hardly take it anymore. My hands tighten in his hair as I move against his hand.

My mouth falls open with a cry as waves and waves of pleasure rack my body and I surrender to them all.

I finally come down from that high and look into Cal's eyes and it is my undoing. His lips are slightly open, eyes dark and feral.

I pull him in for a sensual kiss and then suck his lower lip into my mouth. I relish the loss of control in him as I feel the rattle of his groan through his chest against mine.

I want *all* of this man, and I want him to have every piece of me until there's nothing left. There's something to be said about loss and perspective. I never knew I could have this moment with Callon, and I'll not waste it.

Callon gently kisses me one last time before he shifts his body completely over mine. The weight of his body is a whole other sensation that I never knew I needed so badly.

He runs his fingers through my hair as he says, "This will be the ONLY time I'll ever hurt you, Maisy," Cal whispers against my lips right before he presses himself inside me.

I gasp and then Cal's lips are on mine, muffling a loud moan. Cal moves slowly.

The pain is there, but something more, so much more.

"Don't stop…please," I beg against his lips. My words are his undoing because he takes my mouth, the kiss becoming carnal as he thrusts himself inside me.

He moves his hand into my hair again, gently pulling my head back as his tongue dances with mine. I arch into him. His stubbled chin against my skin leaves goose bumps all over my body.

Even this close, skin to skin, it's not close enough. I want to stay like this forever, wrapped up in each other's body and soul. The pain eases and becomes a dull ache as two people become one. Nothing has ever felt more right than this moment with him.

I can feel my core tightening with every thrust. A crescendo building higher and higher. I wrap my legs around his waist, needing more of him.

He leans into my ear with his deep low voice and whispers, "I want to watch you come undone."

His words are just that, my undoing.

Heat pools low in my stomach. I arch my back just as Callon takes the peak of my nipple into his mouth…at that moment, and I cry out with the force of the spasms. Cal muffles my cries with an all-consuming kiss as he thrusts hard into me one last time.

I feel his body shudder with release.

We lay there spent side by side for several minutes after, not taking our eyes off each other. There are so many things I want to say.

Cal drags his thumb over my bottom lip and simply says, "Hey, Maisy."

A smirk pulls at my cheek, and I reply, "Hey, Callon."

CHAPTER 29

We stayed awake for hours, catching up on what transpired after that fateful night in the cabin. I learned that Callon Wolfe is not a man to be messed with. He told me all about what happened the night I was carried away. It was G1's body burned inside. That was brilliant because now Callon is the one presumed dead.

He also told me about Jacob's house and crew and about finding the young Maria. My gut felt like it was twisted when he told me her age and how he found her. Hearing that Maria was not only okay, but staying with Bo was a relief. They are lying low somewhere until Cal reaches out to them.

When he told me about the Delfire, I was speechless. Not only was he the one to find me, but he tossed Emil over the balcony! That's an image that would make a normal person shudder, but me…no, I feel nothing other than relief. If that makes me a monster, then so be it.

Callon has, apparently, been stalking me in the shadows from the moment I was 'anonymously' dropped off at the hospital. He said he was so worried about my head injury that he had no other choice than to take me there, even if that meant the public finding out I was alive. Bo did, in fact, screw with the cameras. I was not surprised by that information.

We had a good laugh over the coded note left in the jacket pocket.

I told him *everything*…and I mean everything.

Once the floodgates to my brain opened, my mouth seemed to let it flow out of me in an endless stream of confessions. Words that I never wanted to be said aloud from the time I was taken until I was handed over to Emil. Secrets I once thought would go to my grave. As embarrassing as it was, it was also so very cathartic to release those demons.

Last night, I slept the most peaceful sleep I have ever known. It is the slumber of someone truly sated and safe.

The morning creeps over us. There's a hint of light streaming through a crack in the curtain. That solitary beam is gracing the most handsome face I've ever laid eyes on. The face of someone who has saved me in so many ways. My hero of the day and night. Pieces of last night flash through my mind, bringing heat to my cheeks and other areas.

What has this man done to me?

I feel like I am still me, but not. It's like being suddenly transformed into who you were meant to be all along. This is the version of me that I didn't know existed. The version of me that can be happy and loved again, but as a woman.

My mind drifts back again to every single caress and every single kiss in an attempt to cement it into my memory. Everything from the minty taste of his mouth to the way his weight felt pressing me into the mattress.

"You are adorable when you blush…what has your cheeks turning pink?" Cal's deep voice brings me out of my headspace to see him grinning as if he knows exactly what I'm thinking.

"Last night," I say honestly. "It was perfect." I reach over to trace his strong jawline slowly over the short beard until I reach his lushes lips.

Cal takes my hand and places kisses along my knuckles and then my palm. "Are you sore?" he asks in between kisses.

"A little." I see the worry cross his face briefly, so I quickly add, "In a good way." That brings a very proud smile to his handsome face.

Pounding on the downstairs door has us both bolting upright in the bed.

"Shit, Cal, you have to hide. It could be the detective," I say franticly as I jump from the bed, pulling on some jeans and my discarded Springsteen tee.

I scramble about the room. "I didn't think he was coming until much later."

"Shit, Cal?" he mocks. "What a dirty mouth you have."

I give him a dramatic eye roll and toss his pants at his face. "No jokes right now! Stay out of sight, okay?"

He gives me a devastating side smile. "Sure thing, sailor mouth."

"Really, Callon…ugh, I forgot how frustrating you are. By the way, you are the one with the sailor mouth…I can't help being around a delinquent caused some bad habits to rub off on me."

Suddenly, Cal grabs me and tosses me onto the bed, covering my body with his, making it impossible to move. "Delinquent, huh? Well, you are attracted to this delinquent," he says in a low, sexy voice. "What does that make you?"

I playfully smack his bottom. "Makes me question my intelligence. Now get off of me." Cal nibbles and kisses my throat and then suddenly sucks a spot on my neck hard.

I pull away with a gasp, and my eyes widen. "Did you just leave a hickey on me!" He licks his lips devilishly and grins.

The door pounds again as I finally push the big pain in my A-hole off me as his laugh rumbles behind me.

I bound down the stairs and stand on my tiptoes to look through the peephole. I feel for the Colt I stuck into the back of my pants before I finally see who it is outside.

My mouth drops open wide when I do.

What is *she* doing here?

I open the door and stare into the eyes of my old friend Anna, with my ex-boyfriend Thomas at her side. Tears are already forming in her eyes, and she wears an astonished look on her face. I see her lip tremble. Anna hasn't changed a bit, from her bright red hair to her kind blue eyes. Thomas looks the same, too, standing by her side…other than all the blood has drained from his face as if he's seeing a ghost.

I guess he, kind of, is seeing a ghost.

"Maisy…you are really here." Anna's childlike voice cracks with emotion. She carefully looks me up and down. "We thought you were dead, but then the news this week blew up with all this talk of you being found." She doesn't make a move to come near me. She looks at me like I may flee at any moment, and maybe I'm giving those vibes because I wish I could flee from this conversation. I don't feel ready for it.

They look me over from head to toe again, making me feel exposed. I'm sure my appearance is cause for alarm. The old Maisy was prim, proper, and always dressed immaculately. Here I am in torn jeans and a band tee, barefoot with disheveled hair, healing bruises, and scars.

"I'm here," I say, looking between them biting my lip. "Would you like to come in? I can make coffee," I ask and immediately want to slap myself for offering.

Cal lingers somewhere in here and I hope he stays hidden.

"Sure, that would be great." Anna walks past me giving me a wide berth and heads toward the kitchen she knows too well, having spent countless hours with me growing up. Thomas creeps past me with his head lowered, and he is obviously trying not to look into my eyes.

I start making a pot of coffee while they take a seat. I say over my shoulder, "So, two cops are watching my house from either side. Did they not give you any flack for coming here? I was told no one was allowed to come here," I ask.

Anna gets a lopsided grin. "It's a small-town Maisy, as you well remember. Everybody knows everybody. I know Gerald and Conner...that's the cops working the street. They went to high school with us. They also knew we were best friends and let me come to check on you."

Wow, so much for protection. I do recall those names from school, but I was young when my parents switched me to home school.

It didn't escape my notice that she said 'were' best friends. "Well, here I am," I mutter, not knowing what to say to these two. It feels strange being around them. I don't relate to the person I was before. She has been reborn...transformed. They seem unchanged, and that's not a bad thing. In fact, it probably means they have led normal mundane lives not filled with tragedy.

"Look, Maisy, I know this is weird for us all, but I needed to see for myself that you were okay."

"I'm good, look at me…all in one piece." I can't hide the sarcasm that laces my tone. I pour three cups of coffee with milk and sugar and pass them around the table before sitting across from them. Thomas takes a sip, still mute, and eyes intentionally diverted.

Annas eyes soften a touch then she asks, "Do you want to talk about it? What happened?"

"No," I blurt out a little too quickly.

"Maisy, we missed you terribly, and I don't know what you went through, but for me, I grieved for you. We thought you were dead! I just needed you to know that I never stopped thinking about you. I never gave up hope." I look at her then and her eyes are pleading.

I take a shaky breath. I can hear the honesty in her words. I'm sure she did grieve, but she sits here now in front of me, dating my ex, and that still doesn't sit right with me. She doesn't know that I know they are dating. I remember clearly how it felt to see those two outside the 7/11 hand in hand.

I can't quite put my finger on why I am being so defensive, but I lash out anyways.

"Tell me this, Anna," I stop and look to Thomas, then back to her, "how long after I went missing did you two start seeing each other?"

There's an audible gasp from her as she flushes red in the cheeks. Thomas looks like a deer in the headlights, and I'm driving the truck that's about to smash into him.

"How did you know?" Anna asks in a shaky voice.

I stare her down. "That doesn't matter, just answer me."

She looks away, swallowing hard. "It was around Halloween last year." I see her hands trembling as she attempts to sip the coffee.

I purse my lips in consternation. "So…let me get this straight. Your best friend in the entire world goes missing, her parents are shot execution style," I pause, watching her shift in her seat uncomfortably, "you wait a few short months before moving in on her boyfriend? Or was it you, Thomas, who moved in on her?" I glare, making him break his silence.

Thomas exhales and finally finds his voice and says, "I did ask her out, Maisy. We thought you were dead…and we were hanging out all the time after you went missing. Anna had me help her put posters all over the city. We organized all the big searches." He takes another sip of his coffee and runs his hands through his blond locks, looking like he wants to bolt from this house.

My heart aches as I see a solitary tear roll down Anna's flushed cheeks.

I suddenly feel foolish. It wasn't like I was in love with Thomas. It's hard to be angry with two people who fell for each other in dire circumstances. I know a thing or two about that. What did I expect…for their lives to stand still when I left?

I shock them both when I finally speak. "I'm sorry Anna…Thomas. I shouldn't be giving you shit right now."

They both stare at me with bugged out eyes and mouths hung open.

Then I realize it's because I cussed. Was I really that innocent and sheltered…geez. I smile at that, and it becomes contagious as I see both their mouths pull up into a smile.

Reaching over, I grab Anna's hand and squeeze it. "Thank you both for your efforts in trying to help find me. I really am sorry you had to go through that." I take her hand and place it in Thomas's. "I am also glad you had each other to lean on. I was gone…a very long time, and things change. People change."

Thomas visibly relaxes. I see the tension leave his taut shoulders. "We never meant to hurt you. I never meant to hurt you."

"I know that" I say softly.

And deep down I really do. She would never have looked twice at Thomas had this never happened. She was a good friend.

"So," Anna breaks up the heavy conversation, "what's with the new look, babe? People do really change." She cocks her head with her gaze traveling my outfit.

I chuckle. I missed the sass in Anna's voice and hearing her call me babe. "Well, I thought I would try grunge for a bit. What do you think?" I say as I flip my hair over my shoulder and lean back, sipping the coffee.

Anna clears her throat purposefully. "It's 'different' for sure." She laughs, then adds, "Honestly, it kinda suits you. You have this whole mysterious, dangerous vibe going on…I like it."

"Glad you like it. I was shooting for badass. So close enough, right?"

Anna opens her mouth wide dramatically, "Maisy Murray…who are you, and what did you do with my meek friend?" She chides.

"I am afraid she's dead and gone, and this is what's left," I say jokingly, but Anna sees the truth in that statement. She gives a slight nod.

"I'm starving. I have no clue what's here, but would you like something to eat? If there is anything, of course?" I jump up and begin rummaging through the cabinets.

"Sure, babe. I'll help." Anna goes to the fridge and starts taking inventory.

It feels so normal for a second. Just two girls raiding Mom's fridge like old times. I see a hair tie on the counter and flip my head over to bind the mass of hair up into a ginormous, messy bun. When I stand upright Anna and Thomas are staring at me with pinched brows and worried eyes.

I follow their gaze to the back of my hip, where the Colt is peeking out of my jeans. I fling the hem of my shirt to cover the gun and, without addressing it, turn to look for food.

Anna's voice chimes in behind me, "Are you still in danger, Maisy?"

Turning to face her, I huff out a long breath. "It's just for my peace of mind, okay? Nothing more." I can see she's wary as she and Thomas make eye contact. She doesn't buy it, but she lets it drop.

I turn back to the cabinet and spy some muffins above the microwave. "Ohhhh, thank you, Jack," I whisper. He must have left these yesterday.

We share muffins and coffee as we catch up on lost time. I give nothing away about my life over the last year. However, it is strangely nice to hear theirs. Both are taking college classes online and working. The awkwardness I thought I would feel around Thomas is non-existent.

Looking across the table at him now, it is hard to imagine the attraction we had back then. He looks wholesome and kind, cute even…nothing like my feral mountain man hiding somewhere in this house.

Thinking of him now makes me desperately want to share him with my old friends. I hope that one day, I can do just that.

As they gather to leave at the door an hour later, we hug and hesitate before releasing each other. Anna looks me over one last time and stares knowingly at the red spot on my neck and then into my eyes.

My face burns.

"Listen, babe, when you are ready to talk to someone, I'll be there. If you never want to talk, that is okay too. Don't shut me out, though. I am here when you need me." She hands me a paper with her contact information and new address. "I mean it, don't shut me out, okay?" she squeezes my hand.

"I promise one day we will catch up for real," I say, squeezing hers back.

"I'm going to hold you to that," she says over her shoulder as they walk away.

I see the police officers in the distance, keeping a close eye on my house…and me.

I shut the door behind me and jump when I feel strong arms suddenly wrap around my waist. I smell Callon's distinct scent and immediately relax and melt into him. "Were you privy to the whole conversation while stalking the shadows?"

"I was." Cal's voice is low and deep against my ear.

"And…? What do you make of it? Was I wrong for so quickly forgiving them?"

"Maisy, you already know the answer to that. She was your close friend; she *is* your Bo. The old you did die and burn to ashes…but that is exactly how you became a phoenix. You are stronger than most people could ever fathom. It is okay to realize they deserve happiness as much as you do."

His words bloom warmth in my heart. "Since when are you so perceptive, sir?"

"I have many talents, Maze." He flips me around and throws me over his shoulder as I cackle out loud. He bounds up the stairs carrying me like a sack of potatoes. We enter the large bathroom, and he sets me down in front of the ornate clawfoot tub.

With deviously heated eyes, he starts the water, dropping in some oils my mother has on a shelf.

Callon slowly raises my arms and slips my shirt over my head. He takes the gun, placing it on the counter directly beside us.

Neither one of us will ever make that mistake again.

He unbuttons my jeans and slips them from my hips, grasping my underwear at the same time.

I stand before him and don't feel the need to wrap my arms around myself. I don't feel the need to hide anything from him. He is my person, the one I can bare all to.

"Now, get in the tub," he commands.

"Bossy, are we?" I joke but climb into the tub as I'm told.

"You relax. I'm going to find snacks." He points a finger at me.

After a few minutes Cal returns carrying crackers, cheese, and ice water. "This is the best I could do," he says, handing me a small tray.

"This is perfect. It reminds me of our snacks under the waterfall…but it would be much better with you in here with me." I pin him with lowered lashes.

His side smile has my heart fluttering as I watch him undress slowly. His body is sheer perfection. He slips into the tub opposite me.

"You know what I like most about this?" I ask while taking a bite of my cheese.

"What is that." He asks in his deep guttural voice while taking my foot in his hands and massaging it, making me fumble to remember what I was about to say.

I regroup my thoughts and continue, "How natural it feels to be with you. I don't feel judged. I just feel…I don't know…I—" I suddenly struggle with my train of thought again.

"It's loved…the word you are looking for is loved," Cal says softly.

I pause with cheese near my lips. I have felt it for a long time now. I knew what we had between us was special. It is hard to put what we have into words so simple. This connection is a palpable thing.

"Is that what it is, Callon?" I grin.

"Of course, it is. I love you, Maisy Murray. Don't you know that by now? You have enveloped me in your web, and I have no desire to be free of it."

I nod slowly. His words are pure and raw.

"I know," is all I can manage to say as a tear slides down my cheek.

CHAPTER 30

Two hours later, we are dressed and seated at the kitchen table, looking over sweet tea glasses at each other. Both of us thoroughly hot and bothered. Cal refused to take me to bed, saying we needed to wait a little. I can tell he's worried about causing me pain, but he doesn't see how much I want him.

I couldn't care less about the pain.

"We need to discuss what happens next," Cal says, dragging my mind from the gutter.

"Okay, *you* are the mountain man prepper. You tell me, what is our next move?" I smirk at him.

"Mountain man…" Cal drags his hand through his short beard, laughing. "So, I am a mountain man and a delinquent and again, I ask…what is wrong with you? *You* seem to find this mountain man attractive. You have been undressing me with your eyes ever since we put our clothes back on." He grins annoyingly.

"Ugh, you are insufferable." I ignore those straight facts he is speaking. "Okay, I'll be serious. Do you have a plan?"

"I want you out of this country and away from danger. That is number one. That is…*if* you still want to leave." He pauses for a minute as he analyzes my face for any sign that I may want my old life back. "I know being here must bring up all kinds of memories and feeli—"

I interrupt him, "Yes, I want to start a life somewhere far away. As much as I will miss this place, I am not the girl who grew up in this house and never will be again. I'm ready to move on." I can feel the rightness in the words as they leave my mouth.

Cal nods, contemplating our circumstances. "Will there be anyone here that you will miss; any family that will come looking for you?"

We had talked briefly about our past lives, but I could see where his mind was going. Most people have extensive family trees. "There's no one except Jack, and I will stay in contact with him."

Cal looks uncertain but continues, "Okay so we get you out of here, then I stay back and finish this."

My heart twinges at the thought, and my hackles rise. I glare at him. "Absolutely not, Callon! You can't stay here. You are a wanted man, and Jacob will never let you live. We disappear together!"

Cal looks at me sternly. "There's no way in hell that I will leave until Manny and Jacob are dead. They ruined both of our lives! They are the big players in this, and once they are eliminated, we can truly stop looking over our shoulders."

"And there is *NO WAY* I'm leaving you," I spat. The pain of losing Callon boils up from deep inside. I can't go through that again.

"You will do this, Maisy, if I have to force you!" Cal growls. "I cannot…*stomach* the thought of something happening to you." Cal curls his lip in anger then a flash of pain takes its place.

"You don't understand Cal…"

"I understand, trust me. You need to know the pure hell I went through, wondering what was happening to you after they carried you out of that cabin! It was like a raging inferno inside my brain. I would have burned the world down to find you. I should have protected you that night!"

There it is. I can see it then, what I didn't see before. He still feels guilty, maybe even more so now. He blames himself for me being taken *both* times.

I set down my tea as I nibble my lower lip. "Cal…it was not your fault. What happened with Jacob, and what happened in the cabin. You cannot take the blame for what they brought upon us."

Cal runs both hands through his hair, and then takes a calming breath. "I love you more than myself, more than the earth, more than life. I will not lose you; I would not survive it."

His words pull at my heart strings. "I know…neither would I." "What if we compromise a little? What if I stay here just long enough to give the detective something to go on and to see a therapist? I think that will appease him for a bit. *You* can be looking for Jacob and Manny while *I* get my affairs in order. But, if during that time you don't find them, then you leave with me."

Cal looks wary and averts his eyes from mine. "We need to be gone sooner rather than later. Jacob is out there somewhere and desperate to shut us up for good. We are the only thing that could bring down his whole underground trafficking empire. People kill for a lot less. At this point, he is going to have it out for you first, not me. I might have burned his house down, but he is rich…it can be replaced with ten more properties just as shitty as that one. *You*, however, have made a laughingstock of him. You are the one girl that couldn't be broken. The one with a spirit far wilder than he could have ever imagined.

"The little bird that burned away into the phoenix."

My mouth slightly opens, and I immediately fiddle with the pendant Cal had given me on my birthday. I've never taken it off since that day.

In the beginning, I felt defeated and every bit the victim, but he was right. I am here today because both of us, not just Cal. I am no longer the victim but the survivor who has the knowledge and power to take down the filth infecting my home.

"Okay Cal, I can contact Jack today and work out the details to sell the house. I will have him help me with filing the insurance and moving any belongings to storage for now. What I need to know is, what do I tell Detective Sawyer? He will *not* let this go."

"He's like a dog with a bone, that one," Cal says, rubbing his chin. "Why not tell him part of the truth?"

"Which parts, though?"

"Tell him it was traffickers and even tell him what happened with Emil. Just do not disclose anything regarding Jacob or your location for the time being."

"I don't know, Cal. What if he doesn't stop pushing me?"

"He can't question you without Jack there anyway. Have Jack by your side the whole time and only give him a piece of the puzzle. Besides, I have Bo digging deep into the good detective. If he is trustworthy, we will know soon enough."

"I think he already assumes Emil was involved because we had the same drug in our system." Thinking of that moment makes me question something. I cock my head to the side when I ask, "By the way, how did you get me from that suite to the parking garage without anyone seeing you carrying a lifeless woman?"

Cal cringes and bites his lip before saying, "I hid you on a baggage cart with suitcases around you."

My eyes widen. "Oh my god…while clever, that is a disturbing image." I shake my head, "and the note you left in that jacket was also clever, but the detective figured it out quickly." I add.

Cal's face shows some worry at that revelation. "I didn't know that, but it doesn't matter. I left nothing incriminating in it and didn't use my name."

"True, and the body found in the cabin is believed to be yours for the time being. Maybe we can find a way to clear your name, too." My mind goes back to the question Cal asked me earlier.

"Do you have any reason to stay Cal? Don't you have any family or friends that will miss you?"

He shakes his head, and his eyes look solemn. "I have been a missing person as long as you, remember? The few scattered family members I have left are estranged, and Bo is the only loyal friend I have."

I sip my tea and try to calm the uneasy feeling I have deep in my chest. It's like this is all coming to an end finally, but to what end?

Cal reaches into his pocket, saying, "By the way, I have something for you." He pulls out the small Old Timer pocketknife. The very one I stabbed him with, and my face flushes. "I thought you may want to carry this." He smirks at me.

I take the knife and feel the coolness of it in my palm. I can't help the smile that blooms on my face. "Thank you, Callon."

Cal's turns serious, "I want you to carry Debbie at all times, too, but I thought the knife may give you comfort."

I can see there is something under the surface he is not saying.

"What is it? Is there something you haven't told me?" I ask as I slip the knife into my pocket.

Callon leans his head back and huffs out a long breath. "Jacob was on TV over the last week…still attending his banquets and debates."

I'm sure the shock is evident on my face. "How is that possible? You burned down his house. There must have been, at least, some kind of an investigation."

"I'm not sure, maybe there was, but if the house wasn't in his name and he's lining pockets…who knows." Cal sounded exasperated. "He is acting like he is invisible, Maisy…and I believe he is absolutely certain that you will not turn on him."

"Maybe he is…" I whisper, dread filling my mind in waves.

Cal seems to see right through me and says, "We are going to make it through this."

After our conversation, I had Callon scour the house with me to make sure I had everything I needed or wanted stored away for the day I would leave. We stacked the last remaining items in the living room for Jack to pick up and retired to the kitchen to await the detective.

I have been watching Cal all day. The memories of last night are never far from the forefront of my brain. Right now, he is lounging in the dining room chair across from me. The long table putting too much distance between us. I'm shuffling through old documents of my parents' when I raise my head to find his blue eyes on me. The air around us shifts with the intensity of his stare.

Suddenly, I feel I have no self-restraint. He wants me as badly as I want him. His whole body tells me so. He's just afraid I need time to heal.

Well screw that!

I stand casually without breaking eye contact and shove all the papers on the table to the floor.

Cal's eyes widen as I climb onto the table and crawl towards him, dropping down to straddle his lap. His lids lower as heat fills his gaze. He watches me carefully, still not touching me as I slide my T-shirt slowly over my head and toss it aside.

His voice comes out shaky as he asks, "Are you sure you aren't too sore?"

I lean in closer, "A thousand percent sure," I say against his lips.

He takes my hips with his hands and slides me forward as he grinds into me. The friction pooling heat low in my stomach.

Our mouths come together slowly at first and then turn more demanding as he slips his tongue against mine. He deepens the kiss and makes me breathless. The rumbling groan that leaves him skitters along my body. Goosebumps rise all over my flesh as he leaves a trail of kisses from my mouth, across my jaw, and down to my neck.

Abruptly, he lifts me as he stands and lays me back across the table. He makes quick work of removing my jeans and then drops his followed by his shirt.

He grasps my thighs, pulling me toward the end of the table and then pressing his weight into me as our mouths clash again more violently.

This is raw and real.

I flex my hips against him earning me a groan against my swollen lips.

"You will be the death of me, and I would go willingly." He growls as he shifts his hips.

I brace my hands on the table as he pushes himself inside me. My mouth opens wide as a moan escapes. I lean forward, catching his lower lip in my mouth as he thrust into me.

Every cell in my body is on edge as we move together.

Callon takes my hair and pulls my head back and trails his tongue down my neck and back to my mouth. I'm shaking with the need for release.

He no longer tries to be gentle, like last night. The frenzy of our need outweighs his worry.

My body quivers under the skill of Callon's mouth and hands as he ravages me.

I can feel my body cresting, and I sense it in Cal, too. He takes my lips in a passionate kiss, and I lose all control as spasms rock my body. Callon grips my hair tightly as he finds his release.

We finally pull away enough to stare into each other's eyes. Sweat gleams on our faces, and our chests rise and fall rapidly together.

My heart has never felt this full. It could burst.

CHAPTER 31

One Week Later...

I stand in front of the full-length mirror, adjusting my army-green canvas belt. My hair is thickly braided down my spine which now reaches my lower back. I am wearing slim-fitting black jeans and my...Bo's sister's combat boots. My long-sleeved green T-shirt is tucked in. I slip the Old Timer into my pocket and Debbie into the back of my jeans.

"I really do dress like Sarah Connor these days," I say while smiling at the woman looking back at me. I gently touch the scar on my head.

I have been living in a top-floor suite at a local hotel for a week now. The last time I saw Cal's face was that day at the dinner table.

That table shall live in infamy.

While we were getting back dressed that day, we were interrupted by a knock on the door. Callon hid as he listened to me talk with the detective. He had set up a safer place for me to go before the reporters flocked in to devour me.

As I packed my things, Cal waited in my closet, almost giving me a heart attack when I went to gather my remaining clothes. We got only a brief moment to say our goodbyes and one swift but passionate kiss, and I was gone.

At first, I worried he would be discovered, but then I realized that Callon Wolfe could take care of himself. Our plan wasn't thorough, but I still had that hope that it would all end as it should. I held onto every kiss and every touch we had shared together, keeping it fresh in my mind until the day we were free.

The detective had sent word earlier that he would be waiting for me outside at four o'clock to take me to the therapist. He has shown great patience with me, considering I have yet to talk about what happened a year ago. I decided against telling him anything yet, even a partial truth as Cal suggested.

Outside my door I hear knocking and the detective's voice, "It's Detective Sawyer. Are you ready to go?"

I take in a deep breath and yell back, "Be there in a minute."

I'm as ready as I will ever be.

I don my long black winter jacket, one long enough to hide Debbie. I nod in the mirror and head toward the door. I grab the room keys off the counter, and as I drop them in my pocket, I feel a piece of paper crinkling against my fingers. Gingerly, I pull it out and unravel the small pink post-it note.

My breath catches, and tears well in my eyes.

Burn them all to ashes my Phoenix.

I have been waiting with bated breath for a week straight, not knowing where Callon has been and wondering when…or if I would get a message from him. I should have known he would plant something in my clothes before I left. It is but one of the quirky things I love about this man.

Love. The realization hits me then at how fiercely I do love him. I should have said it to him. I should have screamed it from the mountain tops. Why had I held back the words that day in the tub?

Right then I hear another knock on the door and mumbling about being late. I stuff the note back into my pocket and leave with Sawyer.

We had small talk along the way as we drove through town after town and ended up in the middle of a run-down area of long-since abandoned brick buildings. I recall from childhood that there was once an ice cream shop through here that Mom and Dad would take me to on Sundays after church. I found it odd that anyone would be able to keep a business going on this side of town these days.

We park in front of a two-story block building with bars on the windows. The shrubbery around the steps is overgrown and the walkway cracked from age. The only thing modern here is the black Mercedes parked on the curb with tinted windows.

"Who is this Therapist you are sending me to?" I inquire with skepticism in my tone.

"I don't personally know her." The detective puts the car in park and starts surveying the area himself and rubbing his mustache. "Beats me why she would have an office out here. We had received several names of qualified and highly recommended individuals. However, this one was placed first and foremost, stating she was the best when it comes to individuals with trauma. Her name is Eilene Everly."

"Hum," I look around one more time with scrutiny.

Jim must notice my nerves because he says, "It will be fine, Maisy. I know it feels like an invasion of privacy, but I have seen a therapist before myself and was glad for it afterward."

That *is* shocking. Most of these hard core detectives put up walls. They don't knock them down and spill feelings to strangers. "Why…if you don't mind me asking?"

"I have been in this business a long time and seen things that no one should ever see. Some kept me from sleeping at night." He looked out the window and collected himself before saying, "Either way, it will be good for you, and maybe then you can find your own closure."

I knew that I was making his life harder by keeping the truth to myself. I intend to rectify that, but not until Bo reaches out to me. I cannot blindly trust anyone.

I move for the door handle, but he stops me with his hand, "You can trust me, Maisy."

It was like he saw the turmoil in my eyes.

I must admit, I really wanted to trust him. His face was kind, and he had been very compassionate and patient with me when he didn't have to be.

I nod once to him as I step out of the car and head inside the decrepit office building.

CHAPTER 32

Callon

The phone rings one too many times as I stand in the chilly evening air at a gas station pay phone. "Come on, Bo, pick up," I say out loud. I am just about to hang up when I hear him on the other end of the line. "Bo, what do you have for me?"

"He's clean. This detective is the real deal. He's actually a local hero of sorts in the community. He saved a child who was kidnapped about ten years ago and took down a few child predators at the same time who were working together."

I breathe a sigh of relief. "Man, that's great to hear. Do you think, based on his past, he can be trusted with the truth?"

"Yeah, not only that, but I had a tracker placed on his car over the last week. He is a simple man. He does his job and then heads home to his family. Nothing looks sketchy."

I roll my eyes and scoff, "I don't even want to know how you managed to get a tracker or how you placed it on his car."

Bo laughs. "No…you don't need to know that."

I blow into my cupped hands, trying to ward off the cold. I have been staying in the very same hotel as Maisy for a week now under a different name to keep tabs on her and to make sure she stays safe. I left long enough to follow a lead that Bo passed along regarding Jacob's possible whereabouts. Turns out, it was a dead end.

"So, where is the good detective today?"

Bo sounds confused on the other end of the line as he asks, "You aren't following them?"

"No, once I got back, Detective Sawyer's car was gone, and no other police officers were there."

"They were on the move over an hour ago and stopped a few towns over. I can give you the location."

"Okay, go ahead." I rip a page from the phone book hanging in the booth and jot down the location. Out of nowhere I have a sinking feeling in my gut. I know she should be fine. She's with a detective who can keep her safe, but something feels wrong.

"Bo, do you have everything in place for her?"

"She will be fine. I have it all worked out. Don't worry. This will all be a distant memory soon. We are getting her out of here this week and then you, my friend, are going to get your life back!"

"We will see." I mutter.

The problem is, I can't leave without knowing Jacob and Manny are dead and rotting in hell.

"Thank you for everything you've done for us. I have one more favor to ask you, Bo…take care of her for me, okay. Make sure she finds happiness. She deserves it."

"Don't talk like that, Cal. You won't be far behind us."

I had already informed Bo days ago about my plan. I had no intention of leaving with her. I hated lying to her that day in the kitchen. I would finish this, and then, God willing, I would hold her in my arms again one day. Her piercing green eyes come to mind and give me comfort and strength.

"I hope you are right brother," I say as I hang the phone up.

I climb into my truck and haul ass toward the location Bo gave me.

CHAPTER 33

Maisy

Back to the Present...

I steady myself on the desk as my eyes bore a hole through Mrs. Everly. My whole world seems to have just shifted on its axis. I look again to my coffee and know, without a doubt, she has drugged me.

"Who the hell are you!" I yell.

The fake Southern Belle disappears as she squints her eyes at me, and her face turns sinister. She slips off the glasses, tossing them across the room. "You really don't remember me, do you? Well, that's not surprising considering the number of 'special' drinks that you were subjected to." She air quotes the special drinks and laughs. "Look harder...we *have* met before, long before you were *privileged* to live under the roof of Jacob Rainer."

I push off the desk, stumbling a bit.

I look hard into her eyes and a memory does surface. Her hair is different, her clothes too, but her face was there the day I first came to the mansion. She had been the one to examine me, like a physical. And again, I remember her eyes the night I was taken from the cabin. The image is blurry, but bits and pieces remain.

"You bitch! You are more of a monster than Jacob. How? As. A. Woman! Can you work for him? Why are you doing this?" Something Jacob said the day I was given to Emil comes to mind.

"Oh my god…you were my nurse at the women's clinic. I remember you now. You are the one who orchestrates which girls are suitable for the taking!"

I feel bile rise in my throat.

The corner of her mouth turns up as she smirks at me. "Bravo, little bird."

My hands begin shaking with rage. "Don't you *EVER* call me that, you wretched piece of shit!"

"Simmer down, sweetheart. I don't think I like the new you. And to answer at least one of the questions plaguing your little mind, I do this for money. Lots and lots of money."

I take a step toward her, still wobbling.

She subtly shakes her head. "No, no…I wouldn't do anything rash. Let me explain how this is going to go. *You* are going to be a good girl and cooperate or else."

"Or else what?" I spat back at her.

"We know Callon is alive and well. We know he will follow you anywhere. Therefore, *cooperate*, or he dies. It is that simple."

My heart slams into my chest at her words. "I have Detective Sawyer waiting outside, right this second…I could scream."

She laughs under her breath. "You could, but I don't think you will. You seem way too fond of the bastard Callon. You know, he caused a lot of problems for us. Plus, I may have offered a hot cup of joe to the sweet detective."

She's drugged him too. I scan the room, eyes darting everywhere.

This can't be happening again.

I look at her dead into her soul. "You don't know the hell that awaits you when Cal finds you."

"We shall be long gone by then. Oh, didn't I mention…Jacob is down the hall, dear. By the way, you are not as…desirable as before, therefore Jacob has found a special buyer for you."

My blood runs cold, knowing Jacob is that close. "Why not just kill me?" I ask, still shifting my eyes around the room.

"That would be too easy. He wants you to suffer for a long…long time."

I slowly back up a little more, creating distance between us. I let her words sink in.

She's using Callon to keep me in check, but I know the truth. They will kill him no matter what I do from this moment on. He would want me to fight. She takes a step toward me, and I take another one back, placing me against the wall. I lean there for balance, grateful that I only sipped the coffee.

I shake my head to clear it. I have to keep my wits.

She creeps forward again, and I see her pull a syringe from her pocket. "Did you know that your mommy dearest didn't die instantly?" I feel the blood drain from my face as she continues. "She pleaded for your life, begged Manny to let you go."

I bare my teeth at her as I feel my hands shaking. I angle my body so that she can't see my hand inching toward my pistol.

"At least she is in a better place…better than the one you are going to." I say. My words are laced with venom.

Her calm demeanor evaporates, and the devil beneath comes to the surface. "Oh really…we shall see little bird."

All of a sudden, she launches herself toward me.

I dash to the left, barely missing her outstretched arm, holding the needle while simultaneously pulling out the pistol and aiming for her head.

She attempts to regain composure as she stares down the barrel. Her eyes widen.

"You think you have the balls to shoot me, girl!" Her face reddens as she yells.

I keep my finger on the trigger and take a deep breath, blowing out slowly as she eases toward me again.

"Today you get everything you deserve…I hope the money was worth it."

Just as she rushes me one last time, I squeeze the trigger.

CHAPTER 34

Callon

Just as I park the truck in an alley near the location, I hear it.

A gunshot.

My heart seems to stop. Panic and adrenaline have my feet moving. I rush toward the direction it came from. I first see the detective's car parked out front, and as I pass it, I slam to a stop. There, in the front seat, he is hunched over the steering wheel. I reach in and check for a pulse.

He's alive!

"What the hell is going on?" I whisper as I sprint to the building. I see a Mercedes out front but hidden behind is a black SUV. Both are empty. I decide to sneak into the back. All the windows are locked up or barred.

"The door it is, then," I say as I press my back against the block wall and gently open the door.

As it swings inward, I grip my pistol and clear the left and right hallway before slinking inside. I can hear a struggle coming from upstairs. The voices are muffled, and all I can make out are feet shuffling. It feels like I have ice in my veins as I make my way toward a set of stairs.

I hear the slightest scrap of a boot before I am tackled from behind.

My pistol slides across the floor as we hit the ground. I slam my elbow backward into the face of whoever has a hold of me and feel a satisfying crunch. Rolling away, I come face to face with Manny Tillman, with blood seeping from his nose.

"We figured you would show your face eventually. You made a big mistake coming here today!" He spits blood at my feet.

I look at the gun on his side. "You should have shot me, Manny," I taunt him.

"Boss wanted you tortured, but beggars can't be choosers, huh?" He cocks his head to the side and rests his hand on his gun. "All this trouble for a piece of ass." He grins, showing his blood-stained teeth.

"I suggest you don't even speak of her." My voice is ragged with unspent rage about to boil over.

"You know…I think when this is all over, I will have a few rounds with the whore and see what the fuss is about," he says as he slowly pulls a gun equipped with a silencer, aiming it for my chest.

He takes a step forward, grinning like a fool.

I wait for one more step and then slam one hand into his wrist and at the same time, the other into the gun.

One second, he has it aimed at my chest, and the next, it's pointed at Manny's head.

"Wait…you wait a damn second!" he pleads. "I can stop this! I can get her for you. Think about it, man, come on!" He pleads to me like a little child.

"You really should have shot me, Manny," I say, watching his eyes widen.

I smile as I squeeze the trigger and watch his body fall. Before it can hit the ground, I am bounding up the stairs toward the commotion I still hear.

"Maisy…just hold on a bit longer," I whisper.

CHAPTER 35

I stand over her body with trembling hands. I just killed someone. Panic is seizing my breath, and I can feel myself hyperventilating.

I have to get out of here.

I bolt for the door, and as soon as I reach for the handle, the door bursts open, slamming me to the ground. My gun is tossed from my grip, sliding across the floor. I shuffle backward, looking up into the eyes of the Satan himself.

Jacob strides in with a murderous scowl on his face as he surveys the room. His gaze lingers on Mrs. Everly…or whoever she really was.

Hello, Maisy," he growls.

My eyes dart to my gun, but before I can scramble to it, he rushes over, kicking it out of reach. My head is still fuzzy from whatever was in that coffee.

I pick myself up on shaky legs and back away from him.

He tsks at me, clicking his tongue, and then he cocks his head to the side as he looks me up and down. He is dressed in a grey three-piece suit and looks every bit the politician.

No one would ever suspect the skeletons he has in his closet.

"You are remarkably good at fucking up my plans."

"Go to HELL!" I say as I spit at his feet.

"You really have changed…the meek, mild, little bird has developed some talons, I see. No worries…I can fix that." I see his hand move to his side as he pulls out a pistol. Chills run down my spine.

"Come now, I have a car waiting. Do not make this any harder than you already have."

Somewhere inside, I hear Cal's voice telling me how I am not a victim…I am a survivor.

I am a phoenix.

"Why don't you just end this now, Jacob? Huh? Why not shoot me?"

"I can't leave a trail of your blood here. It wouldn't look too good, now, would it? I already have to dispose of Martha, thanks to you. No, the detective won't find a body here today and especially not yours. I can make a few calls, and the world will know that Callon Wolfe lives and that he is responsible for everything…including you going missing a second time."

I can see it in my head playing out like a movie. The media would eat it up, and once again, Callon would carry the blame. Jacob would wash his hands of us, and no one would ever be the wiser as to what really transpired.

I try to keep him talking for as long as possible. "What about the detective? Won't he be suspicious?"

"He won't remember a thing. He will most likely think he just nodded off while waiting. His coffee had a little extra spice today, too. He may assume what transpired, but the evidence will say otherwise."

At least, now I know Sawyer is an honest man—not one of them. He will hold so much guilt if he wakes to me missing again.

He will blame himself for sure.

Jacob takes a step closer. My heart begins racing frantically. I can't let this happen. I begin backing toward the windows on the other side of the room.

I have to try to get him clear of that door.

He continues stalking me with a sly smile on his face. He always did like the chase. Lifting the gun, he taps his head with it, the way he used to at the mansion when he wanted me to behave.

"Maisy don't do anything stupid. You can never be rid of me."

Suddenly, on groggy legs, I bolt for the door, but he is quick. He closes the gap between us, grasping my hair at the base of my neck and yanking my back against him.

I feel the cool metal of the barrel at my temple.

"Don't fucking move another muscle!" he spats in my ear. Keeping his hand wrapped tightly in my hair, he forces me to move toward the door as I refuse to go docile and struggle against him. He lets my hair go and wraps one arm around me as he keeps the other pressing the gun to my head.

I no longer care for my safety…I will not leave this place with him alive.

I feel a smack on my head as he bashes me with the butt of his gun. Stars blur my vision, and I feel blood trickle down the side of my head. Somehow, I manage to stay on my feet.

My mind drifts for a second to the sweltering summer day in the woods training with Callon. The sweat dripping from us as we fought and laughed. I see him so clearly.

I instantly drop my weight like I did with Emil, faking weakness from the blow to the head. When I feel his gun lower instinctively so that he can grasp me more firmly, I slam my head backward into his face.

I hear his cry and feel his grip loosen completely.

As Jacob stumbles back a step, holding a hand over his nose, my hand slips into my jacket pocket, and I pull out the Old Timer and slam the blade into his neck and then shuffle away quickly.

His eyes widen in shock as he gargles. Blood spurts from the artery I struck with precision.

Everything seems to move in slow motion after that. I run toward my gun on the other side of the room just as the door bursts open. I reach my Glock, Debbie, grasping the cool metal as I spin and aim toward the door. Cal looks at me from the doorway and then back to Jacob.

Just as I am lowering my pistol, Callon is running to me, and as he slams into me, I hear a gunshot.

But it wasn't my gun.

Callon is on top of me, holding me down beneath him. I feel something wet and sticky as I wrap my arms around him. From the corner of my eye, I see Jacob holding his gun toward us, but it falls limp to the floor as the light dies in his eyes.

Callon grasps my face into his hands and kisses me gently. "You did good, Maisy. I always knew you had it in you. You never needed me…I needed you all along." His voice was cracking.

Realization hits me like a ton of bricks.

I pull my hand away from his back slowly and see the blood that coats it. Tears pour from my eyes as I try to form words to match my horror, but nothing comes out.

Jacob was aiming for me. Cal saved my life…again.

I pull him tighter against me and then roll hard until I have him on his back.

"Callon, stay with me! Stay with me!" I scream as I hold his face in my hands. "I'll get help! You'll be okay!" Sobs racked my body as I kiss him fiercely and try to move away.

Cal shakes his head at me. "No, stay with me, please…" He pauses, squeezing his eyes shut with agony. "I had to find you."

"You always find me, Cal. It's what you do."

"I love you, Maisy."

So many words left to say, but I settle for the ones he needs most. "I love you too, Callon. I should have said it sooner."

My tears fall constantly onto his chest as I lay my head against his heart. I can hear how faint it is. "I have to get help, Cal, I'll be back."

As I raise my head to move, Cal's weak grip squeezes my hand, and I squeeze his back. His ocean eyes hold mine as his breathing becomes a struggle. "I would do it all over again if it meant…I could hold you just once." Cal's hand goes slack against mine, and his eyes drift closed.

My screams echo throughout the building.

CHAPTER 36

I am curled up in the passenger side of Cal's Silverado he calls Blue. A tiny whisp of a girl is barreling down the road, slinging us left and right, creating as much distance as she can between us and the town.

Her name is Maria. Cal told me a little about her, and one thing is for sure, she's too young to drive. Not that it matters at this point whether we are pulled over and hauled off to jail or smashed into a tree. My thoughts take a deep, dark dive into insanity as I wrap my arms around my abdomen to try to stop the ache inside. The drugs are finally out of my system, and all that is left is the pain, physical and mental.

Everything comes back to me in a blurry rush of memories and emotions. I remember feeling the tug of being pulled from Callon. I found myself in Bo's arms as he carried me out of the building, kicking, and screaming. I was *begging* him to leave me there—*pleading*.

Once he deposited me in the truck, I caught a glimpse of him placing something in Sawyer's police car before Maria spun out of the alley.

A few miles away now, I hear sirens blaring as we pass several ambulances and police cars.

I wonder if Bo stayed behind and called them.

"My name is Maria, and I know you do not know me, but I'm here to help you, okay?" The teen getaway driver finally talks, bringing me out of my downward spiral. "I've heard a lot about you, Maisy."

I ignore her and lean my head against the cold window.

"I know you are hurting, but you must listen to me," she says in her heavy Spanish accent. "Bo has set us up a place to live in a small town inside Yucatán called El Cuyo. We have documents behind the seat, IDs, and things like that. Tomorrow, we will cross the border, and you will have to drive us in. Do you understand?"

I nod without looking at her.

"Bo will travel separately bringing the rest of your belongings that you had placed in that storage unit."

I listen, but don't care. This wasn't the plan. I was supposed to be with Callon. He should be by my side.

Maria continues as if I am an active part of this conversation. "We will have to get jobs down there, of course, so that we can pay the bills and such."

I glance over at her, scowling. She's a bossy little thing who seems to have it all figured out.

"Don't look at me like that. I am not the enemy here. *We* will be great friends one day…you'll see. It will all work out in the end, Maisy."

I roll my eyes. I've heard that a time or two.

Maria's eyes soften a touch, and she reaches into her bag and passes me a bottle of water. "Take this, and I have snacks, too. We will stop at a hotel Bo has already paid for, but we will have to slip in without anyone seeing you." She glances over at me, and I catch her meaning.

I am covered in blood, Cal's blood. I lean my weary head against the window again, catching a glimpse of my reflection in the side mirror. Dried blood coats my head where Jacob clocked me with the gun, and my eyes are red and puffy. Try as I might, I can't ward off the images that keep replaying inside my head. Cal's last words are also on repeat.

"I would do it all over again if it meant…I could hold you just once."

I curl into myself, wishing I could disappear altogether. Silent tears stream down my cheeks.

After an hour or so the day finally catches up to me as I drift off into a fitful sleep.

My hands swish through the stalks of lavender flowers as I run through the rows that weave between them. My mother's laughter is gaining on me as she gets closer and closer to catching me. Suddenly, I am lifted off the ground as she spins me in a circle. My legs float through the air. The weightless feeling has me beaming.

One second, I am small and spinning in that field, and the next, we are sitting next to an ocean. I look down at my hands and body, and I am a woman…no longer a child.

My mother looks at me with her beautiful blue eyes glittering in the sunlight. "When did you grow up? You've changed so much," she says, placing her arm across my shoulders.

My face contorts with sadness, "I don't think I can ever go back to who I was before."

"Hard times can make you feel that way, dear. You have to remember who you are and don't let the bad days win."

"How do I move on. I have no one left."

"We are always beside you, walking through life. Look around you...look harder. There will be signs. It will all work out in the end."

"Why does everyone keep saying that." My voice hardens.

"Because it's true...you need to believe in yourself and have faith. A blazing bird riding a horse off into the sunset...with a wolf at her side."

I am about to ask her what she's talking about when I lean into Mom and smell nothing but lavender. It's the most calming scent. The smell is gone instantly, and I stand, turning in circles to scan the beach, but she is nowhere to be seen.

I am alone.

CHAPTER 37

Yucatan

New Year's Eve 1999

It has been two weeks and four days since we fled the United States and started a new life in Mexico. Turns out, getting through the border was a piece of cake. Bo had thought of literally everything. We had passports, licenses, and even birth certificates with our new identities. Bags of supplies were stashed in the toolbox, and we stopped only for a quick shower and nap at a hotel before driving into Mexico as Alexandria Marie Scott and Elena Rose Santiago. Maria had chosen her new name after relatives just like I did.

In that small way, we can honor them.

Cal's friend, Declan Carter, was prepared for us when we arrived. He had negotiated with a local realtor and helped secure the sale of a small house near the beach. His wife, Gloria, was very gracious and had boxes of toiletries, canned foods, and cold items for the fridge so that we wouldn't have to go to a store right away.

I was a basket case and, therefore, put everything off on Maria and Bo.

Bo arrived one day behind us. I was grateful that they handled things without complaint. Being around people was hard. I became socially distant. I attributed it to being in captivity for so long and then secluded with Callon at the cabin, but the truth was…I was just lifeless and didn't want to dampen everyone else's mood around me.

Bo called Jack for me, telling him everything that transpired. I couldn't bear to go over the events. He even told him how this all began. I could hear Jack crying on the line as I stood beside Bo. It broke my heart into pieces.

Soon after that, I had a check in the mail for the sale of my parents' estate. Jack managed to settle most of my affairs within the first week.

All except for the life insurance policy that I was the beneficiary of. I never knew how much money they had set aside for me in case something happened, but it didn't matter anyways. Jack explained that since I *am* a missing person again, he couldn't file for that insurance money on my behalf.

At least the house sold fast.

That was not surprising, considering the weirdos out there who love to buy tragedy houses.

I used the estate money to pay for the beach house and land. I gave Bo and Maria plenty to get them started here in this new place. Jack promised to keep in touch with me and visit soon. He also promised to keep my secrets safe.

The first few days being in this house were strange. I was numb inside. I didn't speak to anyone unless it was absolutely necessary. Most days, I would go sit on the beach wrapped in a blanket and stare out into the ocean. I often wondered if Bo and Maria would be better off without me here.

She got a job as a concierge at a local resort, and Bo dabbles in technology. I don't ask if it's legal. They both seemed to be moving forward while I was standing still.

Today is New Year's Eve, and not just any New Year's Eve. It's Y2K. People have convinced themselves that the world will come to an end, and all based on a computer's inability to distinguish dates correctly. Parties are popping up at every bar and restaurant along the beaches, which is why I'm glad that our stretch of beach is secluded. Bo and Maria, however, plan on making a night of it. They left a few hours ago, dressed to the nines, to bar hop. Her fake ID states that she's twenty-one…I am not sure who is buying that rubbish.

The sun is dipping lower in the sky, and soon, the beach will have a blanket of stars.

I have been standing in front of the mirror in my bedroom for a few minutes now, attempting to detangle my mass of waves. Finally, I give up, tossing the brush aside. I decided to wear my light-wash Levi jeans, a plain long-sleeved white T-shirt, and brown sandals. I grab my large fuzzy Aztec blanket and a sheet from the end of the bed, folding them into an extra-large canvas beach bag. I cut up some cheese and meat and add some crackers to a container. I plan on ringing in the year 2000 under the stars on the beach…alone. Before I go, I grab my bottle of moonshine from the freezer and a small glass.

"It's you and me tonight…white devil," I mutter as I pack a few more necessities into my beach bag.

I take a moment to look around our home. I am still wrapping my head around the fact that I own a house in Mexico. It's one-level with three bedrooms and two bathrooms. The exterior is stucco with tiled shingles, giving it that beachy vibe. My favorite part is that the walls are a different, vibrant color in each room. I swore off beige and white after my time in Jacob's house and the dark, dreary colors from his basement poker room.

I shudder at the thought.

The day we arrived; I immediately chose the bedroom with the ocean blue walls. It reminded me of Callon's eyes. Above my bed hangs my mother's painting of the two lovers in the rain. I imagine it's me and Callon when I look at it. I kiss my two fingers and touch the man in the painting. It has become my ritual before I leave my bedroom.

I grab my bag and head outside, making my way down to the beach. We have a walkway from our house that ends at the tree line, where a path through the woods leads to the ocean. Palm trees surround our property, and we have a small garden out back. Flower beds are along the walkway, and although it is December…flowers bloom in the Mexico sun. I didn't pay much attention to the flowers or the house in general over the last two weeks. I have been in my own world, trying to shake that numb feeling.

Today, I take notice of the flowers. They are beautiful, but it's the fragrant breeze that catches my attention the most. I recognize a few blooms. There are black-eyed Susans, foxgloves, Dahlias, and even one area full of creeping succulents. As I near the end of the walkway that leads to the wooded path, a familiar scent envelopes me, stopping me dead in my tracks.

It's lavender.

I hadn't thought about that dream of my mother since the day I lost Callon. She smelled like lavender in it. I have had a mixture of nightmares and dreams of Mom and Dad over the last two weeks. I always wake up wondering the same thing…why don't I dream of Callon. I go to bed every night picturing him—hoping that I see his face when I close my eyes. I'm so afraid that one day it will fade, or the feel of his kiss will disappear from my lips.

Cell memory is a real thing. It is said that even organs taken from a donor and placed inside the recipient cause changes in personality. I wonder if someone had my heart…would they feel the void and pain. The wind whips my hair, and the smell of lavender becomes stronger. Mom's words come back to me now…

"We are always beside you, walking through life. Look around you…look harder. There will be signs. It will all work out in the end."

My lip tugs up in the corner. I haven't smiled in weeks. I bend down at the last flower bed and inhale deeply as I pluck a few lavender sprigs. I admire the tiny purple blooms before tucking them behind my ear.

Once on the beach, I spread my sheet onto the sand and place my things along the ends. I kick off my sandals and sit cross-legged in the center while dragging the cheese and white devil from the inner pouch of my bag.

It's warm here in the winter, but it can still get cold at night. Right now, the cool breeze is just kicking up as the sun is sinking low. I wrap the fuzzy blanket around my shoulders and take a big swig of the liquor, letting it burn away my throat and my cares.

The sky looks as if it was painted just for me in all the brilliant colors that I love so much.

An hour later, the sun is gone, and my part of the world is blanketed in darkness. The moon and stars are so bright here that I barely need the lamp I brought along. I light it anyway and carry it to the ocean's edge, watching the light dance on the water as the waves creep near my toes. In a few hours, the ball will drop in cities all over the world. People will laugh, some will cry, and some will kiss. Far off in the distance I can see fireworks ignite the sky. It really is magical.

Setting the lamp down, I rustle around in my bag until I feel my Walkman and pull it out. Maria gave it to me three days after we arrived. She said music has the power to heal the soul if you just let it in. I place the headphones over my ears and press play on my Metallica CD. Hero of the day kicks off its rhythmic beginning and I nod my head along to the beat.

If music heals, then Metallica must be surgeons. I take another, much larger, gulp of moonshine and sway softly, side to side.

"You know…I never got to have that dance with you."

A low deep voice from behind me stops me dead in my tracks. My heart hammers in my chest as I pull the headphones off. I am facing the ocean and terrified of moving a muscle in fear that I'm hearing things or losing my mind completely.

I fight the nerves and slowly turn. My heart skips a beat.

"Hey, Maisy." Cal stands a few feet away, and even in the darkness, his eyes are shimmering.

"Hey, Callon," I choke out.

CHAPTER 38

I feel frozen in place as he comes closer, still in disbelief at what my eyes are seeing.

He is wearing distressed jeans low on his hips with a black Levi's jacket. His beard is a bit longer than when I last saw him, and his hair is pushed back in a wrangler cap.

He looks real. Surely, he's not a ghost.

Maybe I am going mad.

When Cal stands a few inches from me, he brings up his hand and gently wipes away the tears that I didn't know were cascading down my cheeks. Warmth spreads throughout my body at the touch that I was sure I would never feel again. I close my eyes and savor it.

When I open them, he is still there.

I throw myself into him, wrapping my arms around his neck, sobbing. He doesn't say anything for a while. He just holds me. As I squeeze a little tighter, I hear him grunt, and I release him instantly, seeing his hand move to his chest.

"Callon, you're hurt." I croak out. The memory of him dying comes back to me, and the blood drains from my face. I tip my head back, analyzing him.

"How are you here? You stopped breathing." I whisper.

"It's okay, I am going to be fine." He lifts my chin with his fingers and kisses me softly, then says against my lips, "It's a long story." Callon looks around at my makeshift camp for the night and smiles when his eyes land on the bottle of moonshine. "You mind if I share a drink with you…ring in the new year?"

I close my eyes for a brief moment and send a silent thank you towards the heavens. My whole world stands before me in the shape of this man I love so dearly. "I think I like that idea." I smile up at him.

We sit on the sheet, and I see the care Cal takes when he eases himself down. My eyebrows knit together with worry. He keeps his eyes on me. It's as if we are both making sure the other doesn't vanish.

Callon takes a swig and then looks out at the ocean. "Where do I begin…"

"Maybe begin with your ending," I say.

Callon wraps us both in the blanket and then me in his arms as we look out at the reflection of the moon on the water. He kisses my head before he begins his story. His lips leave warmth in their wake.

"I remember the worst feeling I had ever felt in my life. It was the moment I saw Jacob's gun aimed at you. I don't remember the pain of the bullet…just the terror when I saw where that gun was pointed." He squeezes me closer to him before he continues, "I remember hearing you call to me and your screams. I felt your screams deep in my soul. I felt relief that you were not hurt, even when I felt myself dying. I was relieved."

He pauses to take another sip, then continues, "The next events I can only retell from those who were there. I blacked out; I was dying. Detective Sawyer said he woke up in his car and immediately knew something bad had happened. He said he had never fallen asleep on a job before and remembered the way the coffee had tasted funny. By the time he ran into the building and saw the bodies, he could already hear ambulances in the distance. He said he checked my pulse and could barely feel it. He did CPR until the ambulances arrived. Someone else had called 911.

"Once EMS workers got there, they had to insert a chest tube to drain the blood out. I went straight into surgery at the hospital. Next thing that I remember was waking up in the ICU with police outside the door."

So many questions ramble around in my head. I settle on the first one that I have. "How are you not in prison right now?"

"That is something I had planned for a while…well, not the dying part, but the ending. A way to clear my name and make sure people knew the truth. I stole every bit of paperwork and all the electronics I could find at Jacob's mansion the day I burned it to the ground. I left them with Bo and Maria when I went after you. They found a ton of incriminating documents, receipts for payouts to police officers, and so much worse on his personal computer. I told Bo that if anything ever happened to me, to make sure the detective received that box. I wrote a letter to him and tucked it inside for good measure. It told the whole harrowing story. Once I knew we could trust Sawyer, I had hoped that he would be the one to clear my name.

"How did Bo know where we were that day?"

"That was pure luck, or maybe it was just Bo's intuition. I called him from a payphone to get your location. He had placed a tracker on Sawyer's police car."

My mouth drops open, "How did he manage to get a tracking device, let alone place it on a lead detective's car?"

Cal grins. "He told me I didn't need to know. He is resourceful if nothing else."

That triggers a memory. Right before Maria pealed out of that parking lot, when I believed Callon to be dead, I saw Bo put something in Sawyers car. "I saw Bo place a box inside his cop car after he put me into your truck."

"That was the box of evidence." Cal moves until he sits facing me and takes my hands into his. "That is not even the best part. After I was hauled away in the ambulance, Sawyer turned that place upside down collecting evidence…and found a hidden camera."

I shake my head. "I found it when the therapist, or Martha rather, left the room."

Cal nods. "He saw everything. Every single thing that was said and transpired was recorded."

My brows furrow as I replay everything that went down in that room. "Does this mean you are free?"

"No, Maisy…it means *we* are free."

My heart soars. "Are you sure?"

Cal's thumbs make small soothing circles on my knuckles as he talks. "Sawyer and I had a lengthy conversation. He has everything he needs to take down part of the Southeastern sex traders, thanks to the stuff I collected. He knows what happened to you. I told him everything. Right now, Jacob's face is on every news channel across the US, and he's all over national news outlets.

Sawyer took it upon himself to place me and you under witness protection."

"I don't understand…"

"He forged some documents, and as far as anyone will ever know, we are in witness protection. No one can come looking for you or your story. You are free, Maisy."

I am free, and so is Callon.

He is no longer a wanted man. The monsters are all either dead or being rounded up by the police. I breathe a huge sigh of relief as I tilt my head back to look up at the stars. A single solitary tear slides down my cheek. The breeze picks up, and my hair blows all around Cal and me.

Suddenly his eyes narrow in on my hair, and I can see his brows furrow. "What is it? Is something wrong?" I ask.

Cal plucks the flowers from behind my ear and closes his eyes as he smells them. "What are these?"

"Sprigs of lavender…why?"

"The day I almost died; this is what I remember smelling."

Fresh tears fill my eyes. Silently I wonder…was mom there with me that day? Is that why he recalls the smell, or was it all just a coincidence?

I would like to think not.

"I love you, Callon. I should have said it a long time ago. It shouldn't have taken me losing you…*twice* to say it. I was scared and not sure that I could ever trust let alone love again.

I'm not scared anymore. You are my hero, my soulmate. You are my everything."

"And you are mine, Maisy Murray."

We talked for hours that night, not just about what we had each gone through but about our lives before we met. Because, in reality, we were getting to know each other for the first time; getting to know who we were and who we wanted to be now that a future was possible.

We made love under the stars as 1999 turned into 2000. The world did not come to an end that night; but rather, it was just the beginning.

EPILOGUE

Seven Months Later...

I stop typing for a moment and rub the ache from my blurry eyes. I never knew how emotional writing could be. It's not just the recollections of a life but the actual way that putting pen to paper can bring you back to those moments—make them feel as if they are happening all over again.

I am a few chapters away from being finished, and it's bittersweet. I always wanted to be an author, but never imagined one day writing about myself. My book is lined up to be published with the launch date sometime this fall. I'm ecstatic to be a voice for other women who have gone through similar circumstances and for their families, but it is also terrifying. It is like opening your brain for everyone to pick it apart like vultures.

The rustle of the palms and birdsongs make the background noise magical through my open windows, and I breathe in the fresh air.

It is so quiet here these days. I no longer have Maria bossing everyone around in Spanish or Bo here cooking anything and everything he can get his hands on. To tell the truth, I kind of miss the ruckus they brought to the house, but not as much as I love my days alone with my husband.

I smile and gently touch my lips.

My husband.

That is so strange to the ears, but here we are making a life together. We got married on the beach six weeks after Callon returned to me. There was nothing to wait for and nothing to consider; we loved each other more than life itself and would spend the rest of it making up for lost time.

I simply can't stop kissing this man.

Maria, Bo, Declan, and his wife Gloria were there. It was simple and perfect. I wore my mother's wedding dress that I had packed away in storage before we fled to Mexico. It was in pristine condition even though it was twenty-four years old. The dress was a mermaid style fitting in white silk with a train in the back. The long sleeves were made of a delicate lace. The veil was my favorite part. It was handmade by a local seamstress who dabbled in the exotic. I wanted a sheer veil trailing behind me as long as the dress with a delicate phoenix bird shimmering through in the back followed by the moon phases. It was stunning to say the least.

My hair was curled half up and half down, thanks to Maria's help. She intertwined tiny pearls throughout. For traditional purposes, tucked away in my garter was the Old Timer…for the something old. For the blue and the new item, Callon gave me an exquisite aquamarine engagement ring.

Every time I look at the stone, I see his eyes.

For my something borrowed, Maria lent me a hairpin of hers made from moonstone. Lavender flowers were intertwined around an arch for us to stand under, and the breeze brought the fragrance spinning around us during the ceremony. Callon dressed in all black except for his deep gray vest. The suit hugged every muscle and fit him like a glove. He was truly breathtaking.

A few months after the wedding, we received the insurance money from Jack. He had it delivered to me.

When it came, I was flabbergasted. It was in the millions. I never knew my parents had set so much aside for me.

I decided, from day one, to split the money evenly and make sure everyone was taken care of.

Maria used her share to purchase the resort where she worked as a concierge. She's probably the youngest person to *ever* own an entire resort *and* run it, but no one needs to know that. Her attitude makes up for her lack in actual years on this planet.

She was right about what she said to me all those months ago…we are great friends. I love her dearly. Bo has his own techy business called Bowen Innovations. He bought a house directly on the beach not far from us and has been dating a woman named Molly, whom we really like.

Our hearts began to heal even more when we heard that the case involving Bo's sister was reopened. We all shed tears the day we found out. Sawyer got his hands on that incriminating box of evidence and went wild. He really was a good detective.

I keep in contact with Jack and his family. We have plans to meet up this fall and I finally reached out to Anna and told her the truth. Pouring my heart out to her. We are slowly making our way back to each other as friends should.

Everyone was doing well and moving on in life.

We heard that Sawyer received The Medal of Valor. I was so proud to have had someone like him on our side. Callon and I sent him a thank you card/congratulations card for everything he did for us.

I heard later from Jack that our favorite good detective almost had a heart attack the day Jack hand-delivered a check to him from us. He deserves more than we could ever give him, but I hope he is somewhere enjoying life.

Nurse Tammy also received a letter from Jack with a check inside. He said she wept and wept.

I close my laptop and stretch to get the blood flowing. It's hot as hades today, so I quickly change into my cut-off Levi shorts, flip flops, and Jimmy Buffet tank top. The beach life has drastically affected my clothing choices. I put the Old Timer in my pocket for luck and Debbie in the back of my shorts.

I still have trust issues.

I braid my hair down my back and grab some lemonade as I head into the flower garden.

Just as I am about to start pulling weeds, I hear the rumble of a loud engine.

Not many people travel this far out, and I would know Callon's truck anywhere. This is different and familiar all at once. I set down my glass and half walk, half jog to the end of our long driveway that curves through the trees.

A car comes into view, and I gawk in disbelief.

My mouth hangs open as I let it sink in what I'm seeing before me. As it gets closer, there is no mistaking it. It's Jovi…my mom's 1970 Mustang Fastback. The sharp lines of the muscle car shine in the sunlight. Callon is behind the wheel, grinning from ear to ear as he pulls up beside me.

Before he is fully out of the car, I launch myself into his arms, squeezing his neck.

"How did you get it back?!" I yell as I finally let him breathe.

"It has been in the works for a while now. Jack talked to me about it a few months ago. He got it out of impound for yo—"

"He's had it a few months, and you are just now telling me!" I interrupted him.

"Yes, *but* it had set for a while and needed some work done. I thought, why not surprise you with it closer to your birthday." He gives a self-satisfied smirk.

I clasp my hands over my mouth and squeal like a child while jumping up and down.

"Thank you so much. I never thought I would see it again!" I had completely forgotten my upcoming birthday. "This is the best birthday ever." I jump into his arms again, and he grabs me as my legs wrap around his waist. I place kisses all over his face, making him laugh out loud.

Through my kisses, he mumbles, "Wait a damn minute…best birthday ever? I remember a wild night of tacos and bar fights."

This has me hoarse, laughing at him. "I am soooo sorry, you are right. I am going to need you to headbutt someone to make the day perfect."

"I can make that happen, Mrs. Wolfe." He playfully bites my neck as I giggle. "You wanna go for a ride…Debbie."

I give him my most devious grin, "Sure do Billy Bob.

Soon we are flying down the highway headed toward Valladolid. I shifted down gears as we hit a long stretch of open road and hit the gas, throwing us back in our seats.

I am biting my lower lip in concentration when I look over and see Callon watching me.

Time slows down, and a memory comes to the forefront of my mind. Not a memory, a piece of a dream long forgotten.

A blazing bird riding a horse off into the sunset…with a wolf at her side."

I look out the window toward the setting sun, then to the Mustang horse symbol on my dash, and finally to the wolf at my side. A serene feeling washes over me.

It really did all work out in the end.

The End…

Acknowledgments

I want to give a huge thanks to my editor Maryssa Gordon with Pocket Editing for being patient with my endless questions whilst I navigated self-publishing for the first time. She was so kind and thoughtful. Her input on my book was priceless. She helped my ideas go from seeds to blossoms and I will be forever grateful.

I want to thank my graphic designer Rica Cabrex for bringing my visions to life. She formatted and designed the exterior of my novel. People tend to read a book by its cover and that is what makes your work so special.

I want to thank my family and friends for supporting me along the way. Especially my mother-in-law Mary and father-in-law Keith Elledge, for babysitting anytime I needed a break. You both have helped me in more ways than you can imagine. My mother Judy in heaven, who would have wanted to be the first to read my book! My father Kenny for giving me his stubborn attitude… it is the reason I never give up. My brother Jason and his wife April for being my downtime when I just wanted to hangout and have shop beers. To all my other friends who stopped by and listened to me rant and rave over the last several months… thank you, you deserve an award.

My biggest thanks must go to my husband and children. My daughter Megan, who is an avid reader like me, has always been an ear for my stories, and has become my best friend. My daughter Cameron, who is my biggest cheerleader. She never fails to stop everything and wrap me in a hug when she sees that I am stressing. My twins Emily and Ameila are wild and eccentric five-year-olds that give me inspiration daily with their free spirits.

Lastly, I want to thank the man that has stood by me through everything in life… the Callon to my Maisy. My husband Mitchell goes far beyond the normal dad roles and takes on most of mine as well when I'm working long shifts. He is a car and gun enthusiast, which was an enormous help to me during certain scenes in the book. In the beginning stages of writing this novel, we began sitting in our bathroom to have quiet moments to talk about my characters. This turned into something we did at least once a week and became known as our bathroom nights. Drinks were shared and laughs were abundant. I don't know where I would be in life without you. Thank you for being you.